The Cracked Chessboard

Elizabeth Emberton

 New Generation Publishing

Chapter 1

Sir Dennis Deane wiped the marmalade from his tie, fidgeted uncomfortably in his wheelchair in front of the breakfast table and scowled at the remains of his meal. As usual the porridge was lumpy and the toast pale and dufty. He liked it crisp and brown. Now he was obliged to sit and stare at Bob. Bob was a noisy eater and his false teeth clicked. He ate his food as if he had not been fed for weeks and continually reached across the table so that the sleeve of his tweed jacket dragged through the butter and frequently knocked over the sugar bowl.

Having to wait to be wheeled away from the table infuriated Dennis. His arms were too weak to move the wheelchair by himself, and when he did try he collided with the wooden column beside the table. He sighed loudly and impatiently and looked around for the girl in the green uniform.

 She came into the dining room through the double doors, turning away from him, ignoring his signals. A year ago he could, and would, have sacked her. Now there was nothing he could do. When he was Chairman he expected his staff to attend to his every demand, but these weren't his staff. After what seemed an age the girl in green flounced over and without a word released the brake on his chair and propelled him out of the room down the corridor where the pungent odour of urine grew in intensity as they neared the residents lounge. The room was small and hot. Oh God - first lesson of the day, Reality Orientation - the same every bloody morning.

They sat in rows around the room; next to him Margery had already began her morning ritual, listing

3

her complaints. "The sun is on my head. I'm too hot. Will someone move my chair?"

Any minute now she'd demand to be taken to the toilet, and then they'd all start calling out and pressing their buzzers. Across the room, Fred still wearing his tea stained breakfast bib, cried out querulously for his daughter. "Joan, Joan, Joan"

."Dennis needed to go to the gents but he wouldn't ask the girl. She pushed a bedside table above his knees and placed a cup of tea of tea in front of him. He fumbled in his jacket pockets for his glasses. The carer snatched them from his hands and as she set them on his nose and adjusted them behind his ears, her long finger nails scratched the side of his cheek. The plastic badge on her flat chest told him that her name was Pat. Her chestnut hair was a tangled mess, as if it hadn't been combed for weeks. He stared at her with distaste and wondered why beautiful girls never became carers? The thought of beautiful girls made him smile. He remembered them all, all the beautiful girls who been his secretaries and P.As. He'd picked a few good ones in his time.

The memory of his office transported him back to his room on the seventh floor in the Regional Office where Hilary, the blonde with sexy legs, sat beside him producing facts and figures on demand. In hospitals and clinics beautiful girls in starched caps and blue capes stalked the corridors. They rustled and bustled through outpatient departments and wards, swishing curtains around beds, checking the blood pressure and pulse of each patient. Beautiful girls became physiotherapists; they were the 'Slap and tickle' girls, the real 'hands-on girls' who provided the ultimate in enjoyment in an otherwise dull day, unless, of course

4

your particular physio happened to be male.

The rattle of a trolley cut into his thoughts as the tea cups were collected. He picked up his cup with his good hand. The tea that was left in the cup was tepid, stewed, and short of sugar. He grimaced and let the cup drop back onto the saucer. The tea slopped from the cup on to the table.

"So what day is it today?" asked Audrey, the therapist.

Who cares what day it is? It could be his last if he didn't get out of here. If he'd been sent to prison like the other two then at least he'd have a date for release. Could prison really be any worse? They all smelled equally bad.

Audrey stood in the middle of the room in front of the budgerigar cage holding a copy of the *Daily Express* peering through rimless bifocals, body shapeless as a sack of flour in a formless, loose fitting grey dress, her cropped ginger-grey hair was mannish.

"Monday the thirty-first." Her voice hardened. "The thirty-first of August. And who can tell me what happened a year ago today?"

He knew what had happened a year ago. The peroxide-blonde care-assistant with dark roots in her parting who'd dressed him and wheeled him into breakfast had reminded him; but he wasn't going to play any of her silly games.

"Dennis? Dennis will tell us. I'm sure he remembers."

He twisted around in his chair. Ignoring her, he turned his head to stare through the open window at the distant figure of the gardener mowing the bowling-green. The sound of the mower invaded the room.

Audrey moved quickly and shut the window. No chance of smelling the freshly mown grass, only the mottled green, urine stained carpet, pungent in the stuffy room The occupational therapist's stentorian voice demanded attention, demanded an answer.

"Dennis, I'm sure you can tell us what day it is?" She crossed the room and thrust a copy of the *Daily Express* into his hands. On the front page a picture of the Prince of Wales staring grimly as he strode up the path to Crathie church, with his sons beside him left the readers in no doubt. He remembered the day well. The day the news broke was a Sunday. He was shaving when his wife had called him. She'd gone into the kitchen to make breakfast and turned on the radio. Everyone remembered that day.

He tried to answer, tried to tell her that his name was Sir Dennis - tried to force out the words. He took hold of her sleeve. "I want...want..."

"Yes?"

The remainder of the sentence tailed off into garbled burbling. Audrey turned away impatiently. "Who can tell me?"

A year ago he would have sacked her. Everyone knew what she got up to with her dim-witted assistant Martin. Anyone who found the Therapist attractive must be dim-witted. Bill, in the room next to his, told him the news. He'd heard Matron and the night sister talking. Bill knew everything, or claimed he did. One evening after supper, he'd wandered into the Therapy Suite and switched on the light, searching for playing cards - or so he said - and almost fell over the two of them on the floor, hidden behind the desk, she with her skirt up to her waist. The Care Staff talked of nothing else, but no one dared to tell the director.

Emma, the plump, dark-haired staff nurse, wheeled in the drugs trolley and stopped in the middle of the room. She flicked through the flat packs of tablets, dispensing pills and medicine in small plastic glasses as if dispensing bread and wine.

"This is my body that is given for you..."Audrey scowled at the interruption. That pleased him. Such a domineering young woman, with her wheel-chair bowling for the disabled, armchair yoga and her sing-songs. Sometimes she wheeled him out into what she liked to call her 'therapeutic garden' to smell and touch the scented flowers. He wished he could have uprooted every one.

He should never be here. He wasn't mental, even now at seventy-eight, he wasn't old. When he was Chairman he'd always kept away from homes for the mentally ill - always sent his wife to perform the opening ceremonies. Edith was good with old people; they loved her expensive perfume, smart suits and understanding, gentle conversation. She would come home radiant with bouquets of flowers. He had no time for geriatrics - he would never end up like that - even now they couldn't understand. He refused to accept it - couldn't explain to them that he should be sent for tests. At his age he could recover. He'd make Edith get him into the Stroke Unit at the City General. Even the speech therapist had only been to see him once. After that they said she'd gone off sick. Nobody cared, not even Edith. She could have organised a private nurse, but the ambulance brought him here and no one even bothered to ask him.

When his wife came to visit it was always, "Lady Edith this and Lady Edith that." They never called him "Sir Dennis." Last week a care-assistant came on duty

7

and called out "Hi Den." A year ago he would have sacked her. Staff in the Regional office had always treated him with respect – Malcolm saw to that - as Chief Executive Malcolm demanded respect. Together they made a formidable team. Two rulers in their seven-storey tower block overlooking the city centre, controlling an empire of hospitals, surgeries and clinics.

He smiled as he remembered Malcolm's visit. Malcolm Yates had done well since he left the region. Eighteen months after taking over as Chief Executive at the new London Health Authority he'd been invited to move into Tory Central Office, as right-hand man to Jeffrey Archer, the Deputy Chairman, who'd tried his luck as the Party's nominee for Lord Mayor of London - but his name was neither Dick Whittington nor Ken Livingstone and look where he'd ended up, sent down for four years for perjury. But that hadn't stopped Malcolm. Now he was inside Number 10, managing Cabinet Committees. Everyone said that he was in line for the job of Cabinet Secretary.

Malcolm had accompanied Paul Vere-Rugglestone, Minister for the Environment, on a visit to the Midlands. Whilst they were there they took the opportunity to visit Dennis in Queenswood Care Village, the new Government backed Private Finance Initiative and last years' winner of the Department of Health's competition for architect-designed Care Villages.

Dennis had angrily dismissed the suggestion in the editorial of the *Morning Gazette* newspaper, that as a director of Vehicle Spares and Transplants, the company who had sold the land to the local health authority, that he had personally benefited from the deal. Although the editorial had been published several days ago, the attack still annoyed him. It angered him to be criticised for taking what was, after all, his due; and it infuriated him that someone should have discovered it. Nothing was safe from the prying eyes of the press, and when he was wheeled into the architect's celebration party and introduced to Henry Pye, the journalist who worked for the *Morning Gazette*, Dennis was unable to control his rage. "Get…rid…of …him!" he'd barked.

The rest of the media were there in full force. TV, local and national newspapers, the *Health Service Journal*, and the *Nursing Times* all covered the visit. But he, Sir Dennis Deane, should have been the one who was the central figure, running the show, making the welcome speech and setting out his future plans for the region. Instead they photographed him in his wheelchair with Paul Vere-Rugglestone and his wife Erica, and Malcolm, and the Matron and the Operations Manager, as well as the architect and someone from the builder. They drank champagne and ate smoked-salmon sandwiches, chicken in aspic, lobster vol-au-vents and strawberries and cream, but as he watched Henry Pye enjoy the expensive lunch, paid for by the Health Service, Dennis became increasingly angry.

It was just at that very time that he saw the cards laid out on the side table amongst the dishes. The script was in gold lettering, "Catering by Harry Furnell and Co." It reminded him that Harry had once again got away with it. It was typical of Harry. Dennis remembered him walking into the farm office, so confident that no one could ever pin anything on him; and then he recalled the quotation that he'd read years ago. "The law is like a spider's web. The big ones break through; the little ones get caught." He had no doubt that several little flies had been caught in the cobweb and taken the rap for Harry. He groaned noisily and choked on the crumbs of the last vol-au-vent that he had managed to reach from the side table. Once again the vice-like pain around his chest gripped him.

At a nod from Matron, the care assistant beside him released the brake on his wheelchair, swivelled it around, and wheeled him back to his room.

"You need a rest after all that excitement."

He tried to explain that he didn't need a rest.

Chapter 2

The dark blue Rover, RHA1, swung off the motorway, up the rise and into the car park of the northbound Westmorland services. Dennis cruised past a line of coaches, swerving to avoid a mob of noisy children stuffing burgers into their mouths, and a group of shaven-headed youths in black leather motor-cycle gear, lobbing empty lager cans into an over-flowing litter-bin under siege by wasps. Two plump women, wedged into matching tight pink trousers and weighed down with bulky white and gold handbags, teetered unsteadily on high heels across his path, heading in the direction of a Shearings coach.

"If I had my way they'd be confined to one vast holiday camp in Blackpool." he grumbled.

He heard Edith sigh and turned to glance at her. She sat beside him, impassive, wearing her martyred look. Lined face, salt and pepper hair. In her twenties when they were both members of the Young Conservatives, she'd been attractive. She drove a sporty two-seater M.G. to the tennis club, white shorts and nice legs. Her family were in shipping, cattle to the Argentine, banana boats and freight. Within a day of meeting them he decided to marry her. Her father made it clear that he didn't consider a small time turkey farmer good enough to marry his daughter but the offer, from a close friend, of a job as a retread tyre salesman which he could run alongside his turkey business offered lucrative potential. Within six months he had extended the business into a spares and transplants operation inside the agricultural buildings that had once housed the turkeys.

"Five minutes, that's all," he warned as he pushed his way through the crowd that milled around the coffee shop.

She raised her voice above the blare of the machines that offered to 'Test Your Driving Skill.'

"Coffee?"

He shook his head "We've got a flask. Wait 'til we're over the border." He hesitated. "Get some bread rolls, butter and cheese."

She looked surprised.

"Wrap them in paper napkins woman."

Unprepared for the sudden heavy rain a group of women had gathered, blocking the swing doors. He elbowed his way through them and took Edith's arm, hurrying her across the tarmac, through the glistening blue petrol-streaked pools of water, then backed the Rover and followed the exit signs to the M6.

"Why the rolls and butter?" she asked.

"Supper."

"I made sandwiches for lunch. I thought we could eat at the Burnside tonight."

The wipers squeaked against the windscreen as the rain ceased. He turned them off.

"Too expensive."

"You liked the place when the Thornes took us there for dinner." Edith persisted.

"They were paying."

"Shall we buy some tinned Haggis with Drambuie?" she suggested. "You always enjoy that."

It irritated him when she tried to humour him.

"Remember last time? There wasn't a tin to be had between Carlisle and Coldstream."

"We could try Gretna."

He gave a snort. "It's out of our way and you'd be

in there all day buying tartans and God knows what. I wouldn't take you within a mile of Gretna."

Over the border they hit road works. He spent ten minutes adjusting the wing mirrors on the Rover. Checking the visibility he caught sight of himself in the rear-view mirror. Steel-grey hair, lined face, and hooded grey eyes, forever alert. He never suffered fools; he prided himself on that.

In the outside lane the driver of a Mercedes shouted orders into his mobile phone. He could do with one of those things to keep in touch with his broker. He reached across into the glove pocket for his memo pad and wrote "check market prices" and "phone broker."

Edith turned her attention away from the distant view of the Solway Firth highlighted beneath a rainbow in the pale afternoon sunshine. "What's the problem?"

"No problem. Just a reminder to make some phone calls when we get there."

She sighed and shook her head in exasperation. "If you're going to use their phone you must keep a note of your calls and settle-up with them."

He cleared his throat. "Don't fuss. The Thornes can afford it."

"Last year you spent the whole two weeks on the phone. I don't know why you bother to go on holiday. You must pay for your calls." She saw the stubborn look on his face that he always wore when he knew he was in the wrong.

"I don't know why they invite us to stay every year," she persisted.

"They know which side their bread's buttered," he rumbled. "It's in their own interest. He's in the motor trade. That's how business works."

Edith stared out of the car window at the familiar

13

scenery of the Borders Each year she looked forward to returning and walking the tracks that she had come to know so well, especially whilst Dennis occupied himself on the phone with unending political discussions. She enjoyed the peace of being by herself, away from the farm where there was a new crisis every day; machinery failures, sick animals, EU restrictions, accountants, form filling, and herdsmen leaving for better jobs. She could understand why so many left; Dennis paid low wages to his farm staff and was short tempered. Day after day she suffered his cursing as he slammed doors and shouted down the phone. The only time she had any peace was when he had a day off to go shooting. Nowadays that didn't happen often as his back bothered him and when he returned home he was in a worse temper than when he'd left.

When their daughter Annabel suddenly announced that she was going to leave home and live with Sandy Stott, a roads protester, Edith was distressed, but she didn't blame her, not one bit. There was always trouble between Dennis and Annabel, but for Edith it was a relief to have someone to talk to. Now she missed her terribly. Annabel seemed to understand, although she usually ended her conversations with Edith saying that she just didn't know how anyone could put up with him; that you needed the patience of a saint and that she never intended to marry and end up being a doormat like her mother.

Dennis had stubbornly refused to discuss Annabel's departure. It was as though his daughter had never existed. Edith never did tell him where Annabel had gone and he never asked, although she had a feeling that he knew. Annabel kept in touch. From time to time they phoned each other when Dennis was not about and sometimes they arranged to meet for lunch. Edith usually chose a pub, out of town, where no one would be likely to recognise Annabel with her spiky red hair, faded black T shirt and heavy mascara.

She glanced at Dennis, trying to bring to mind the man she fell in love with on whose arm she walked down the aisle after the ceremony. There was little that she could even remember in this gloomy face and heavy jowls. He had been proud when Annabel was born and mapped out her future immediately after the birth. No turkeys or car transplants for his daughter. "The Law and then maybe politics," he declared. They took her on holiday to the Isle of Wight when she was three and built sandcastles on the beach at Sandown and visited Osborne. Amongst Dennis' new found theories on how to bring up children was the importance of impressing English attributes on young minds and that included history and the fine arts. It was the happiest time of Edith's life and she'd mounted the photographs in the new family photograph album that she bought in Shackling.

Ahead of them a Stobart lorry began to move. Its dark green tarpaulin glistened in the sun and Dennis, glad to find an opportunity to distract his attention from Edith's complaints, eased forward.

This year he found the journey to Scotland tiring. His back ached, but he had no patience with disabilities, relying instead on painkillers and drink to deaden the dull ache that constantly nagged him. He wondered whether Eric Thorne had left any whisky in the drinks cabinet. In the past he had always done so, but last year the cupboard was empty – no gin, whisky, Martini – not so much as a bottle of tonic. This year Dennis had put half a bottle of Bells in the car. Tomorrow he would send Edith into Kelso.

On the outskirts to the town familiar names and signs brought to mind the August holidays they spent in the Thorne's stone cottage above Coldstream. Bloodybush Edge, Coldsmouth Hill and the impressive picture postcard sight of Floors Castle across the Tweed with Highland cattle drinking from the river had welcomed him for the past three years. He drove across the bridge, turned north, and caught sight of the tall chimneys of the cottage through the trees.

The Rover bumped and splashed through the potholes in the drive and Dennis swore as he tried to avoid them.

The answer phone was winking as he stumbled across the flagged floor into the living room nursing the whisky, the *Telegraph* and *the F.T*. Behind him, through the open door, Edith hauled the cases from the boot. Surgery to his back years ago had prevented him from lifting. He inspected the drinks cabinet. A half-empty plastic bottle of Highland Spring mineral water and a can of Coke confronted him.

"Damn them," he grumbled as he went to the kitchen for a glass.

Settled by the phone with a Bells and Highland Spring he felt calmer and punched the "play" button on the answer phone. For a few seconds there was silence, and then the caller cleared his throat.

"Tom 'ere. Tom 'olcroft."

Dennis groaned.

"I rang you at 'ome an' they gave me your number - nice to 'ave your own pad in Scotland. Did you know that James Alton, the Chairman, died last night." Tom sounded excited. "Last night in hospital. I need to talk to you. Ring me back - it's urgent. You know my number, 2153."

Dennis replaced the receiver and stared out of the window across the fields towards the river. His whisky and Highland Spring water was warm and flat.

Tom never phoned anyone unless he wanted something and this time it was easy to guess what he was after - but he must surely have known that Dennis had the Chairmanship of Mercia Constituency in his own sights. They needed a man like him who'd have time to sort out the wets and the trouble makers in the party, who had time enough to raise money to fight elections; time to win the support of anti-europeans and those in favour of corporal punishment. Most of all, someone with time to campaign for traditional country sports, hunting, coursing and cross country – and especially time to select the right sort of chap as MP. Then they'd all know that they'd got a chairman.

The rattle of a suitcase being wheeled across the stone-flagged floor behind him interrupted his thoughts and he turned around. "We'll dine at the Burnside tonight if that's what you'd like."

Pleasure and surprise transformed Edith's face, and her eyes sparkled. "Oh, that will be -

"- but don't unpack – I'm going home tomorrow. You can stay if you like, but I've got to get back."

Edith sat down heavily on the arm of the Chesterfield, the pleasure draining away from her pale face."But we've only just got here."

I know, I know, but there was a message waiting for me – James Alton's died."

"But -"

"They'll want me to take over."

"I can't stay here alone, besides I wouldn't have a car."He waited until she went upstairs to the bathroom then rang the number.

Tom Holcroft's voice sounded confident. "They've asked me to stand as Chairman, and I'd like your support."

Did Tom really expect him to believe that?

"You mean you?"

"Who else? Unless you want a woman Chairman." He'd wrong footed him. It was easy to do. Tom always put his name in for anything that was going. Always got kicked in the teeth. Never gave up. You'd think he'd have learned by Dennis cleared his throat loudly "You're too late – The agent has already been in touch with me. I've just this minute put the phone down," he lied –" begged me to stand - and I've agreed to be nominated."

"Oh." The note of disappointment was clear."I am Vice-Chairman." Dennis reminded him. "Who else would you expect?"

"Erica's put her name in."

"That's no surprise. She is after all the other Vice-Chairman and Chairman of the Women's Advisory Committee. The women will support her. You'd be better supporting a strong candidate instead of splitting the vote."

"You mean you?".

As Edith came down stairs he replaced the receiver. "I need you to come back with me. I'm planning a dinner party next weekend for Sir Percy Dorrington, the Area Chairman and the Agent, Tony Gibbons - oh and pre-lunch drinks a week on Sunday for all Branch Chairmen."

The receptionist at The Burnside insisted the restaurant was fully booked. At Dennis's demand the manager was summoned to the phone and hastily assured him that he would always be able to find a table for a friend of Mr.Thorne. Not that Dennis had ever put his hand in his pocket at the Burnside, but a promise to see the restaurant manager "all right" resulted in a quiet table for two under the Head Waiter's personal direction.

Patterned curtains, checked tablecloths and smiling waitresses in green and brown tartan kilts welcomed them. In the dimly lit bar "Mull of Kintyre" played softly from hidden speakers. Coloured scatter-cushions covered the seats of wooden pews salvaged from a redundant chapel.

Edith gazed around the room. "Chapel Oak."

Her description of limed oak always amused him. Brought up in a Methodist family he knew what she meant. The altar and the large pulpit in the Weslyan chapel his family attended were of limed oak. Now they worshipped at Saint Marys, the octagonal Norman church where Colonel Sir Robert Grant, Patron of the Living and President of the Conservative Association occupied the front pew. They sat in the pew behind.

Having overheard Sir Robert express the opinion that Chapel was "strictly for trades people" and that "Gentry and the Professions attend Church" Dennis wasted no time and promptly switched from Methodism to the Church of England. They worshipped at ten-o-clock most Sundays for Solemn Mass instead of going to the later Family Service. Dennis disliked the Family Service where he was obliged to shake hands and mutter "Peace be with you" to those in the pew behind; besides he found the children annoying. Parents these days had no control over their off-spring who stood up on the pew, and ran through the aisles squealing and distracting the worshippers.

He enjoyed the High Church rituals from the moment when the priest, clergy and choir processed down the aisle following the stout Church Warden in his white robe who swung the censer with such importance that smoke billowed through the church and set the congregation coughing. Mass was conducted behind a fog of incense with tinkling bells, and the censer was swung with even greater determination whenever the fog threatened to clear. The choristers always came in for particular attention when the censer was flourished belligerently in their direction. The Priest mounted the pulpit and waved the censer on high above the lectern and over the notes he had made for his morning homily, as if he were ridding the documents of a malevolent infestation or infectious disease brought into church by an unwashed congregation. Nowadays it would more than likely be flu, or as a protection from measles and chicken-pox which raged widespread amongst the school children who would later be attending the Family Service.

Within weeks of adopting the Anglican Communion Denis pressurised local Tories to propose him as a Freemason and applied to join the County Palatine Lodge where both the Lord Lieutenant and the High Sheriff were members.

Waiting for the Venison terrine Dennis reached across the table and took Edith's hand. "Tom Holcroft hasn't got a snowballs hope of the Chairmanship."

"So that's all you're going back for." She looked at him accusingly. "Why do you want it so badly?" She pulled her hand away and reached for her glass.

Most other wives were supportive, enthusiastically backing their husband's plans, suggesting, advising, and even scheming - but not Edith. She seemed totally unable to understand his ambition.

"Don't you see that if I'm Chairman I'll choose the next MP?"

"We've got an MP." She stared at him stubbornly. "And in any case it's the selection committees that choose MPs."

She lectured him as if he was an idiot child, but he needed her on his side, backing him, accompanying him to Constituency dinners and branch events.

"Marcus Ward won't be standing at the next election. As Deputy Speaker he'll go to the Lords. Everyone knows that. As for the selection committee, they always work on lists supplied by Central Office and are briefed on the candidates. Regional Office organise that."

"But you personally can't -"

"Of course I can. Short-listed candidates and their wives are invited to dine with the Chairman and Branch Chairmen. You know the score Edith, a damning word about one, a hint of a worrying doubt about another, tailor-made references that leave questions unanswered so that the committee are able to read between the lines. Finally, glowing praise from the grandees of the party for the right sort of chap - a safe pair of hands."

"But why do you want to get involved? You've got Oldfield Hall, the biggest acreage in the county. The farm takes up all your time, as well as all the committees you go to and I've often heard you criticize other men when they became councillors or magistrates and neglected their farms."

"I've got a farm-manager and time to do other things. When I'm Chairman, with a decent MP, there'll be visits to the Commons, the party conference, and bun-fights at Number 10, not to mention other jobs that might come my way. Don't tell me that you wouldn't enjoy all that."

"If the party gets back in."

"It'll get back in. People are too well-off to want a change."

An auburn-haired waitress hovered beside the table and placed their starter in front of them, turning the plates carefully so that the initials BS in blue and gold on the surrounding lip of the plate were central. Edith gazed down at the terrine, it lay on a bed of rocket and red oak-leaf lettuce. She frowned and looked up at Dennis. "Why are you so keen to do this?"

Halfway through his starter he began to pour himself a second glass of wine and had no time to reply.

"Whatever it is it'll never satisfy you," she continued. "Anyone else at your age with an estate in the country would be glad to take it easy, but not you." She glanced around the room in case she had been overheard, but the music and conversation had drowned the sound. "You took a risk to get your knighthood," she hissed. " Exporting spare parts and retread tyres to Banana Republics and military juntas was a dodgy business. You were lucky – and you made sure that you got into the Birthday Honours for services to export."

Dennis banged his glass on the table, slopping wine onto the white cloth. The stain spread and conversation at neighbouring tables halted briefly. "I knew what I was doing. Anyway they need men like me – men with drive who don't allow people to get in their way when things need to be done. The trouble with you is that you are always trying to interfere in matters that you don't understand."

In the farm office Dennis unlocked the drawer containing the cheque-books and wrote out a cheque on Number 2 a/c (Building maintenance) for £500, payable to Dennis Deane, then pulling his personal cheque-book from his inside pocket he made out a cheque to Mercia Area Office for exactly £500, sliding it carefully into an envelope addressed to Sir Percy Dorrington. His subscription being long overdue he decided that the time had now come to be especially generous. Hearing the sound of the outer door being opened he hurriedly pushed the envelope into his inside pocket.

The farm manager David Crofton stood in the doorway; short and freckled, just six months out of Cirencester, with tweed cap and a Barbour in need of oiling. "I heard you were back Sir Dennis; nothing wrong I hope?"

"Business." Dennis grunted.

"I needed to have a word with you about the milk tank. You said to replace it; I've placed the order. "

"How much did you get knocked off?"

The manager hesitated, "I didn't ask - "

"Didn't ask? Didn't ask? If you work for me you always ask. I started as a tyre salesman and I'm proud of it. If you want to sell you've got to learn how to deal. Tell them you expect a discount."

"How much?"

"As much as you can get, demand twenty percent, never less than ten. If they want to sell they'll talk."

"And if they won't?"

"Then we won't buy and you'll be looking for another job."

James Alton's funeral was not a sad affair. Apart from close family mourners the occasion was more of a reunion of families and friends after a long hot summer spent harvesting in British fields or holidaying in Tuscany and the Dordogne. Dennis drove away from Saint Chads, through the narrow lanes with John Brown, the Constituency Agent, beside him, leaving others in the White Hart, opposite the church, before they too made their way to the funeral tea, allowing time for the family to return from the interment.

"A pity Marcus had to hurry away so soon after the service," Dennis grumbled. "It looked bad."

John nodded his head and smiled. "Well, you know how it is," he murmured placidly. "Apparently the Speaker is holding a reception this evening. The P.M. will be there, ambassadors, ministers, BBC governors - Marcus just had to be there. When he retires the new chap will have to spend more time in the constituency."

Dennis couldn't argue. He never could with John no matter how hard he tried. He habitually marched into the agent's office, ignoring the secretary in the outer office, demanding John's immediate attention, then departed within minutes apologising for the intrusion. No one ever ruffled the agent; he was unflappable. Tall, with white hair and perfect manners he appeared to run the constituency with the minimum of effort.

The oak panelled dining room at the Alton residence was packed with the family's friends. Dennis wandered around with a glass of whisky and a ham sandwich making sympathetic noises to all he met but there was no one there worth spending time with. They were still in the pub. Erica Barrington appeared from the kitchen with a plate of sausage rolls, sensibly ingratiating herself with any of the mourners who might be likely to attend the meeting to appoint the chairman.

'Sycophant,' he thought.

She caught his eye and made her way through the crowd whose voices were reaching an ever-higher pitch.

"So you and I will be fighting it out; I hope there'll be no hard feelings on your part when I'm the Chairman. I shall expect your loyal support." She tossed her head back and neighed with laughter.

"The party has always had my loyal support - you should know that."

He smelled her perfume but couldn't place it. Edith used eau-de-cologne. This was deep and heady. He noticed that the light ginger hairs on her pale arms matched the shade of her hair. Her grey eyes challenged him.

"Why don't you pull out Den? It'll be a blow to your pride to be beaten by a woman."

He wondered at her choice of words and suddenly felt the urge to assert his authority over her, to grab her silly warm body roughly - against her will.

Leaning forward so that no one could overhear he spoke tersely, hoping to shock her. "No man pulls out until the action is finished."

Disturbed by his inner turmoil he gulped down the remainder of his whisky. As he turned to leave her soft laughter followed him.

Chablis and Saint Emilion contributed to the genial

25

atmosphere of the dinner party.   Dennis doubted whether any of the wives could match Edith's cooking. Although she had been to a Cordon Bleu cookery course in Edinburgh before they were married he prided himself that he had taught her how to shop, often sending her back to the City when she came home with poor quality goods.

The meal was impressive - game consommé, moist pink gravadlax in a dill sauce, a thick standing-rib of beef reared on his own land, still red in the centre as he carved it, followed by a creamy peach brulee, raspberry pavlova, coffee and home-made Petit Fours.

The two most influential Tory bigwigs in Mercia Region were obviously impressed and Dennis felt in control, playing his cards with skill. Sir Percy Orrington, remembering the £500 cheque which Dennis had contributed to party funds, was effusive. "You will, of course, be standing for the Chairmanship of Mercia?"

Dennis appeared hesitant. "Well I wasn't sure - but if you think I should?"

Edith stared at him over her half-moons as she poured out his coffee, then quite deliberately neglected to pass him the sugar.

"My dear chap, we're counting on it; aren't we Tony?" Sir Percy turned to Tony Gibbons, the party agent, who nodded dutifully.

"Well if you want me to - "

"Absolutely" He lowered his voice, " In any case we can't have that damn woman running the show, never have a moments peace, seen too many women chairmen – don't want any more."

He hesitated and almost choked on his beef, " the P.M. excluded of course - she is exceptional. Leave it to us, eh Tony? Word in the ear of all Branch officers eh ? No problem. Tony'll sort it - won't you Tony?"

The Area agent nodded dutifully once more. Dennis had heard that he was in line for a Central Office job and would keep in step.

The party walked out into the warm September night to their Jags and BMWs carrying small presentation Cheshire cheeses made by Dennis' cheese maker.

Chapter 3

The following Sunday the pre-lunch drinks party got into the swing with Bucks Fizz, Asti Spumante, Whisky and Beer. Caterers circulated amongst the eighty Branch Officers, handing out sausages, canapés, grilled prawns and dips. At half-past two everyone was still there and the noise carried through the open French windows and across the gardens.

Tom Holcroft swore that his vote was secure. For whom Dennis wondered? Everyone knew that Tom promised his vote on any subject to anybody who offered him patronage. Dennis remembered the day, ten years ago, when Tom had sold his vote for the Chairmanship of the 'hung' Mercia County Council to the Labour party in return for the position of Vice Chairman. Although the LibDems had voted with the Conservatives, Tom's votes against his own party and for himself had swung the decision. When the vote was taken and the result declared Erica Barrington tossed a handful of silver onto the floor of the Council chamber to cries of "Judas." Totally untrustworthy, no one had relied on Tom's word ever since.

It was common knowledge that whenever Tom travelled to and from council meetings Derek the chauffeur parked the Rolls, well hidden, behind the lorry park of the town centre supermarket. Whilst the Rolls Royce waited Tom pushed his bike into the stand, chained it up and removed his cycle clips from his pin-striped trouser legs and Derek held open the rear door for him to step aboard. No voter would ever be given the opportunity to catch sight of him, chauffeur driven, lording it in the council's Rolls-Royce.

Across the room by the bay window Erica was holding court, collecting around her the manipulative hen party members of the Women's Advisory Committee. Blue rinses and Basler suits prevailed and heavily ringed fingers clutched Waterford glasses as their owners downed Bucks Fizz. Branch subscriptions and income from the Women's Advisory events meant that the Constituency could pay an agent and rent an office in the City centre; but there was always trouble amongst the women and more than one chairman had resigned in tears. Erica had so far lasted two years, spending hours on the phone cajoling, praising and smoothing ruffled feathers. Her gracious approach would carry a lot of support. He'd be reliant on the men, if he could get them to the meeting and that would mean lengthy phone calls and a fleet of mini-coaches picking up in the rural areas as well as rounds of drinks in the club after. Dennis reached for his stick and stepped out through the French windows. Small groups of members strolled on the gravelled paths between the herbaceous borders peering with interest at the alstroemerias and hemerocallis.

Beyond, through the small iron gate leading into the rose garden he heard the murmur of female voices. One voice rose hard and sharp above the others. He paused to talk to the strollers, hiding his impatience, agreeing that of course alstroemerias were invasive and that before too long he would need to deal with them. After ten minutes he excused himself and helping himself to a Bucks Fizz from a passing waiter strolled casually through the gate into the rose garden. As he expected the female Mafia were cushioned together on white painted garden seats, holding an impromptu meeting. He turned around and beckoned to the waiter. "Ladies,

29

your glasses are empty."

Della Morton eased herself to her feet. The stout, white-haired, eighty year old leader of the female "awkward squad" wore an expression of pleasure that was more of a leer than a smile. Dennis considered that the description "blue rinse brigade" was inaccurate.These senior members of the Women's Advisory Committee were all members of the 'silver rinse junta' and no women's committee in the country was complete without them. The agent, who always made it his business to know everything, had told him that Della was feuding with Erica over her Conference ticket. Della had never missed a conference since she first joined the party. This year tickets were in short supply and Erica had been given one for her son, so depriving Della of the only spare one.

"I knew there would be a rumpus," admitted John Brown. "But she has been to every party conference since the last war. No one else stood a chance; there've been rows every single year." He sighed heavily. "I suppose I'll have to start ringing round other constituencies for tickets."

Dennis watched with amusement as the women held out their glasses and fell upon the last plate of canapés. Where food and drink were concerned party members never missed a trick. He recalled numerous 'Two-hundred Club' parties he'd been obliged to attend where all the food and free drinks disappeared in the first twenty minutes.

They settled themselves back into their places like nesting hens. He leaned over the back of a garden seat and placed a hand on Della's well padded shoulder.

"I've told John Brown to do everything he can to get you a ticket. He might even get you in as a steward.

Don't worry, he'll sort something out. After all, someone like you, the backbone of the party -"

She got to her feet once again and bustled around the seat towards him. "Oh Dennis, I knew you'd help. I was just saying to them ..." She waved a hand towards her small group. "Of course I can understand Erica wanting to take her son with her, she takes him everywhere since her husband died, but he isn't even a Branch Officer." Dennis backed away as a shower of spittle hit his face. Della had always had that unfortunate affliction. She moved closer as he went into reverse and together, she leading with her glass in her hand, they slowly foxtrotted along the gravel path, between the roses and around the fountain.

"Of course you'll have our support - she's not popular you know. The constituency needs a political animal like you." She swallowed her last mouthful of wine and carefully examined the empty glass. He took the hint and beckoning a passing waiter, he moved off in the direction of three panama-hatted farmers leaning heavily on their sticks.

The dark brick building across the town square, opposite the churchyard and next to the bank, had been the headquarters of the local Conservative and Unionist Party for as long as anyone could remember. From the high pitched roof the Union flag fluttered proudly above the shoppers hurrying between Boots, W H Smiths, Ocean Breezes Fish Shop, the Post Office and Woolworths At street level the Club with its small exclusive car park (members only) offered a bar and billiards. Those who were not able to display their car-park pass found a typed reprimand stuck firmly to their windscreens in front of the driver and were obliged to

31

spend an embarrassing ten minutes scraping off the offending notice before they could drive away.

On the first floor, the committee room and kitchen smelled of gas that leaked from the perished rubber tube of an ancient burner, presided over by Mrs. Hassall, who, wearing a floral 'pinny', spent most of her day dispensing tea and coffee for meetings, whist drives and the agent and his secretary, Mrs Gunn.

Up the heavy dark oak stairs next to the agent's office a conference room hosted meetings of the party faithful, whist drives (Fur and Feather at Christmas) and jumble sales. Around the walls posters of Margaret Thatcher had been pasted over those of Edward Heath (*Man of Principle*), Alec Douglas Hulme and Harold Macmillan (*You've Never Had It So Good*). Dusty portraits of the Queen and Prince Phillip relieved the bareness of the faded distant wall.

Half an hour before the Extraordinary General Meeting called to elect the new Chairman the paid up members of the Conservative Party, or party activists as the media referred to them, jostled for position on the stairs that lead to the conference room, clutching their membership cards, waiting for their names to be checked against the agent's register.

At half past seven the bell ringers in Saint Mary's octagonal tower, that dominated the main square, began their Thursday evening practice with a touch of Bob Doubles, whilst in the conference hall Sir Robert Grant opened the meeting, explained the procedure and quoted the relevant extracts from the Rules of the Association. Beside him sat Tony Gibbons ready to answer questions and fend off challenges from dissident factions who, fearing that their candidate might not be elected, had already plotted their points of order challenging the legitimacy of the proceedings.

Dennis and Erica had only five minutes each to address the meeting.

"Ladies first." Sir Robert Grant smiled at Erica and stood aside as she took her place at the table.

Dennis smiled benignly, his old pussy-cat smile as a colleague had once described it, and noticed that she wore the same old blue dress he'd seen so often on formal occasions. She began gently and persuasively; her voice, nervously high, settled to its normal pitch after the first minute. He was forced to admit that her speech was well thought out - all about unity, money raising, branch activity and the importance of being able to afford a qualified full-time agent. Amongst the members of the Women's Advisory Committee expensively coiffeured heads nodded approvingly.

"You have always supported me in my work as Chairman of the Women's Advisory Committee, now I hope that I shall receive your vote of confidence to move on and undertake the work of Chairman of this Association."

Erica received enthusiastic applause from the women seated in the front four rows. They turned to each other smiling and whispering. From the seats behind there came polite but cautious support as Branch committee members waited to judge the next speech.

It was a satisfactory address, no more, no less, thought Dennis who had planned a rallying call to the troops. Tony Gibbons watched as Dennis moved to the speaker's table exuding self-confidence, his silver-grey hair shining beneath the lights, his portly figure filling out his navy pinstriped suit. A trickle of applause died away as Dennis poured himself a glass of water and waited for absolute attention. He began confidently, sticking to the script which he had rehearsed in the bath before he dressed for the meeting, listing the objectives set by Margaret Thatcher…"the only Prime Minister since Churchill who has lead our country with determination and conviction, liberating it from the dead hand of the unions and the crippling recession that threatened to engulf us. She and she alone," he asserted " has untied the apron strings of the 'nanny state.'"

He called for renewed conviction and effort throughout the constituency and vowed that under his leadership members would find fresh enthusiasm to follow the Prime Minister's lead. In his final minute he referred to 'Law and Order', family values and the strength of the pound and ended his speech vigorously predicting "…a great future for Great Britain." The reaction was as predictable as the questions that followed.

"If you don't win will you support Erica ?"

Dennis turned to face her, smiling, grasping her hand firmly between his two hands. "Erica would have my full support."

"What about fox hunting?" called a voice from the back of the room.

Erica reached for the microphone. "That all depends if you believe in freedom of choice."

When the voting slips were collected and counted Dennis triumphed, with a majority of thirty-two votes. As he reached the end of his speech of thanks he was pleasantly surprised to see Edith at the back of the hall clapping enthusiastically, then watched as Erica stepped down from the platform, surrounded by her supporters. For a moment he felt sorry for her. She had taken her defeat well, on the chin, as he expected she would and she would have made a good chairman. She had the time and the ability. He brushed the thought aside. This was politics and the party needed tough men like him.

Tom Holcroft pushed his way through the crowd. "Wonderful result - must be one of the first to congratulate you. I told everyone that you were the right man for the job."

In the Club tweed jackets and blazers crowded the bar. Pints of Speckled Hen and Uncle Tom, dripping creamy froth, and tin trays laden with whisky and soda were passed back to friends. Members, anxious to be seen congratulating the new Chairman, pushed their way into the crowd surrounding him. Erica and the members of the Women's Committee engulfed Edith and pressed a glass of gin and tonic into her hand.

Across the room John Brown, the agent, waving his arms, tick-tacked and tried to shout above the noise. Eventually despairing of attracting Dennis' attention he dived into the throng and grabbed his Chairman. "Marcus on the phone."

In the booth, insulated from the cacophony outside, Dennis received the congratulations of the Deputy Speaker direct from his office in the House of Commons. "Your first job will be to select a candidate. I spoke to the PM today and told her that I don't intend to stand at the next election. It'll all be in the press tomorrow; you may not have much time. There's talk of a snap election."

The Area Chairman wasted no time in phoning. "We've got a good list. They've all been through the interview and training sessions and there are some strong contenders. Of course you're bound to get a few hopefuls who have not contacted us - you may need to short-list one or two to pacify your locals." Sir Percy sounded excited. "We've an ex-Minister who lost his seat last time round - you'll want to avoid him, people still talk about the scandal. There's Chris Ferris who writes a weekly column for the Gazette, criticising the PM's policies. He's an avid Ted Heath supporter – very pro-Europe, wouldn't go down well at all. As for the others - well I do have one or two special favourites, Vere-Rugglestone for example - he's the right sort of chap for you - good safe family - sister's a lady-in-waiting to the Queen Mother. But don't waste time. The PM could go to the Queen any day if the opinion polls stay in our favour. I'll send you our list in tomorrow's post."

Six weeks later with applications closed, Mercia office began photocopying three hundred and forty letters and CVs from hopeful candidates and the selection committee of Chairmen from every branch in the constituency dedicated the whole weekend to reading through the applications. They sat at frayed green-baize card tables in the conference room, warmed by a noisy gas fire, under the critical gaze of Margaret Thatcher whose picture hung over the mantelpiece and the supervision of Tony Gibbons, passing the papers around the room, from one to the other, until by Sunday afternoon the long-list had been reduced to twenty-four. Amongst them was Paul Vere-Rugglestone and three local candidates who had failed to make the Conservative Central Office candidate's list. Interviews were programmed to take place two weeks later. At that stage three candidates would be chosen to go before the General Purposes Committee for the final decision.

Although the selection committee had been sworn to secrecy over their choice of candidates, news still leaked out and Dennis was angered to read the headline "Carpet-bagger for MP?" in the weekly '*Mercia Echo*,' which was already running a strong campaign in favour of Bryan Stilwell, leader of the Conservative Group on the Danebridge Borough Council. The *Echo* had always been fiercely critical of consideration being given to anyone who had not got family roots or business connections in the Constituency.

"I expected it." John Brown spoke soothingly as Dennis stormed around the office. "He's ruined his chance." He held up the newspaper. "This'll annoy the selection committee. They'll never allow themselves to be browbeaten into selecting Stilwell."

"If I knew who'd been talking out of school I'd make them resign."

John laughed. "Well, I've a good idea who it is, but I'm not telling you. It would only make matters worse if you were seen to be interfering in branch affairs. For the selection committee this is their moment of glory and their opportunity to influence the future fate and face of the parliamentary party."

On a damp Saturday morning a fortnight later the committee met again. They had only twenty-one candidates to interview; other constituencies had already met and chosen two and one had withdrawn. Nevertheless the quality of the applicants was impressive, several had already fought unwinnable seats and spectacularly reduced Labour majorities and one forthright young woman from Yorkshire had forced a recount in a Labour stronghold.

Paul Vere-Rugglestone was tall and dark and had the wiry athletic figure that would attract women

37

thought Dennis. Unfortunately he had never fought a seat before, but he spoke with conviction and said all the things that Tory activists who live in a semi-rural constituency wanted to hear; closely following the Prime Minister's line, deploring the bureaucracy of what he called the Euro-Gravy Train. As the younger son of a Berkshire landowner, who had studied estate management, he clearly understood farming issues and also argued the case for business and industrial reforms with assurance, tossing in quotes from CBI Directors, the President of the Board of Trade and the Chancellor of the Exchequer. He couldn't be faulted and Dennis soon realised that he really need not have bothered to lobby on his behalf. By tea-time on Sunday the selection committee had reached a decision and chose Vere-Rugglestone, the Yorkshire woman, and a barrister from Manchester to go forward to the General Purposes Committee.

Two weeks later the General Purposes Committee met for a buffet supper with the short-listed candidates. The small, dark, outspoken young woman from Yorkshire and her equally forthright husband, who was in textiles, quickly antagonised every one by their outspoken criticism of the workings of Westminster, Whitehall, the Monarchy and the British establishment in general. It didn't take long for Dennis to realise why she had appealed to the electorate in a socialist mining area. The barrister and his elegant wife from Manchester were more worrying; an expert in Trades Union law, he was a smooth, self-confident, successful character who had already made a name for himself in the Courts. Dennis recognised a man who would eventually rise swiftly through the ranks to become Home Secretary, Attorney General and eventually Lord

Chancellor. In fact he would be so respected in the House that he would have little time to spare for constituency work.

The three candidates moved steadily around the room interrupting the enjoyment of those who were scavenging from the buffet, causing them to listen with full mouths and polite attention to their individual political views and impressive qualifications which would ensure their selection as Mercia's prospective MP.

Dennis followed them around quietly murmuring into the ears of the Branch Chairmen. "Brilliant - absolutely brilliant, but not the type to make a good constituency MP... The woman could be a troublemaker... What we want is a good constituency man, a safe pair of hands that we can trust... Vere-Rugglestone is the only one."

Several times he raised his hand to wave away half-doubts that hung in the air. "Yes, I know he's not married." His tone became impatient. "I'm sure he's got a nice girl tucked away somewhere. There's plenty of time for that sort of thing once he's settled down and bought a house in the constituency."

He turned to Erica who was standing beside him.

" I bet that's already crossed your mind, eh?" He roared with laughter as she glared at him and quite deliberately turned her attention to the scanty remains of a dish of hors d'oeuvre that only twenty minutes earlier had graced the centre of the buffet table.

At ten o'clock the following evening the General Purposes Committee enthusiastically approved the selection of Paul Vere-Rugglestone as Prospective Parliamentary Candidate for the Mercia Constituency by a large majority. His official adoption as

Parliamentary Candidate at a meeting of members of the Association, would automatically take place as soon as the date of the next election was announced. It would be a *'fait accompli'* despite the fact that the *Mercia Echo* had begun an immediate campaign to persuade its readers to call for a re-selection procedure in favour of a local candidate.

Three weeks later, during supper, Dennis told Edith that Paul had signed a contract to lease an apartment in a converted barn in the village of Hatley. "They're moving in next month."

"They?"

"He and a friend."

"Girlfriend?"

"No." He shook his head. "James something-or-other."

His wife placed the pheasant casserole carefully in front of him. "You don't think that, in these days, it might appear ?" She paused, waiting for his reaction.

He tucked his serviette into his waistband. "You're as bad as some of the Selection Committee. They said something like that. No, no; the fellow is his Research Assistant. He'll only stay till the election's over. It's not what you're hinting at, at all."

A week later the Prime Minister drove to the palace to seek the Queen's permission to call an election. Feverish preparations got underway and the *Echo's* campaign for a local candidate ran out of steam as Paul Vere-Rugglestone was quickly and unanimously adopted as the Parliamentary Candidate.

Chapter 4

Amidst resounding cheers in the main conference hall of the city's leisure centre, crammed with flag waving supporters, Paul Vere-Rugglestone took his place, beside the Prime Minister and Leader of the Conservative Party, the Rt.Honourable Margaret Thatcher. Surrounding them, highlighted by laser beams, and in front of a mega-sized Union Jack that dominated the platform stood the Area Chairman Sir Percy Dorrington; Dennis and Edith, John Brown the Conservative Party Constituency agent and Tony Gibbons, the Area Agent. The reverberating sound of the Willis organ, rescued from a demolished stately home and restored by a theatre organ trust, filled the hall with the swelling resonance of "Land of Hope and Glory" and the Prime Minister enthusiastically endorsed the newest and most recently adopted candidate for the Mercia Region.

Edith and Erica Barrington devoted every minute in the run-up to the election working with John Brown organising teams of canvassers, collating the returns and phoning branch chairmen to make even greater efforts to compile lists of tellers and hire rooms in schools and village halls for election meetings. The agent decided to drop the "Vere" in his poster campaign - so the cobalt blue posters bore the diagonal words 'Rugglestone Conservative.' Every minute of every day was accounted for as John Brown filled the candidate's diary with engagements, directing him to distant towns and villages with his party 'minder.' In the agent's office wall maps became smothered in blue flags that tracked the progress of the Range Rover -

decorated with blue balloons and posters and carrying a loud-speaker on the roof. Touring science parks, housing estates and shopping centres Paul fought off his initial nervousness and developed new interests and greater confidence as he walked through factory workshops and into boardrooms.

At half past eight each evening the team of canvassers collapsed into armchairs in Paul's flat. At that time of night no one wanted to answer the door to strangers. Interruptions to the evening's activities and favourite TV programmes only annoyed the voters. The elderly kept their front doors on a chain and peered suspiciously at visitors.

Paul valued his team of dedicated activists, local councillors and committee members who had been knocking on doors and filling envelopes for years and were proud to tell him how long they had been working for the party. They were experienced canvassers who knew every house in every street and provided a running commentary..

"A waste of time calling at number four," Erica Barrington ignored the rough garden of a semi and hurried past the rickety gate. "You'd be lucky to find her sober..."

"He lost his wife last month. Be careful what you say, he gets very upset – but you'll get his vote. He always votes Tory."

In front of number fifteen Erica pulled a piece of paper from her pocket and consulted it. "They live together and take *The Guardian*. Lib Dems I should think. I wouldn't bother to call – just stick a leaflet through the letter-box."

Paul glanced at the list. "What's that?"

"Paper boy's list. *Four Times, Six Telegraphs and*

five Guardians. It's a fairly accurate picture of the political views of every house in the street."

"How on earth?"

"The boys throw their lists away when they finish the delivery. I look out for them."

Paul shook his head admiringly. "You don't miss a trick."

In the evenings when the supply of beer ran out Erica always offered to stay behind to wash up the glasses. Paul found her a source of useful information and was glad of her company.

"I get the feeling that the Chairman is not all that popular." He said quietly as he began to place the glasses inside the cupboard.

For a moment she was silent.

"Well he's one of the old brigade and he does tend to ride rough shod..."

She picked up a glass and began to polish it. "But he gets things done."

"Seems full of prejudices to me."

"What's he said now?"

In the short time I've known him he's criticised the French, the Germans -" He held up his hands and began to count off the names on his fingers. "The Italians, the blacks, Chinese, Japanese, gays, Catholics ..." He paused. "You think of any section of society, excluding white Church of England Conservatives, and they're all the subject of his scathing comments."

Erica laughed. "Even white Church of England Tories get a tongue lashing at times. They're definitely not immune."

"Hardly the ideal Constituency Chairman?"

"I suppose you'd call it tactless, but those who know him tend to ignore it. We're used to it. Eventually

43

you'll laugh it off too." She hung up the tea towel on the rail beneath the cooker, folding it neatly.

It was a diplomatic answer he thought. The gold ring on her wedding finger shone under the kitchen lights and Paul experienced a brief stab of disappointment.

"I mustn't keep you from your family." he said.

She smiled. "There's no family to keep me from. I was widowed two years ago. My daughter nurses in London and my son, Tom, is an accountant,"

He regretted his obvious curiosity. "I'm sorry."

"I'm getting used to it already. They say that you do get used to it after two or three years."

He nodded, feeling awkward.

"M.N.D." she said.

He nodded again, unsure of the initials.

"Motor Neurone Disease," she explained.

"Oh yes. I've heard of it."

"I nursed him for two years, but both Jim and I knew that he would never recover."

"You must have gone through hell," he said automatically and put an arm around her shoulders, more in sympathy than affection.

He felt the warmth and firmness of her body, and the pin of his blue rosette caught against her sweat shirt. She leaned forward, her head against his jacket as she carefully disentangled the ribbon from the material. He felt a wild desire to kiss the top of her head, but resisted it and moved away. "If you want someone to talk to – company you know – but then I'm sure you've got lots of friends."

"You can never have too many friends." Erica took his hands in hers, "but I'm always here if you need some help. Well that's it for tonight." She moved close towards him and gave him a swift peck on the cheek. "So, what's the programme for tomorrow? Oh, I know, ten a.m. at the cattle market. I hope you know your Friesians from your Limousins? After that you're lunching with Julian Morrisey at Brockley Hall."

"Remind me," begged Paul.

"President of the Country Landowners Association," she said, "and Dennis will be there."

The sounds and smells of the cattle market relaxed him, and transported him back to the days when he helped with the milking in the lime-washed shippon at home.

Tethered in their stalls in the market the animals stamped uneasily and turned their heads to watch the strange men who slapped a number on their haunches, washed their tails, cleaned their hooves and brushed the caked mud from their coats. Paul felt at home and chatted easily with the stockmen and farmers, discussing the price of milk, EU regulations, paperwork and the records that had taken over their lives. Nowadays any spare room in a farmhouse was turned into an office with a computer, printer and files bursting with ever increasing regulations and forms from the Department of Agriculture.

At mid-morning James was waiting with the Landrover and a clean pair of shoes to take him to Brockley.

"You can call at the office for a wash." he suggested, "although it won't do you any harm to arrive there smelling of the cattle market – it's more acceptable than after-shave."

Erica was waiting in the office car park. "I've been trying to phone you."

45

Paul pulled his mobile from his jacket pocket and stared at it.

"You never had it on," she scolded. " I thought you ought to know that Sybil Morrisey disappeared to London with the chauffeur last week - to have her hair done, and neither them, or the car, have been seen since,"

"So the lunch is off?" asked Paul hopefully.

"Oh no. Julian's got a new chauffeur and a new car – just don't ask about Sybil, that's all."

Dennis met them on the steps at Brockley. "You're late," he barked.

Within days Paul became hardened to the cat-calls and the heckling and learned to keep smiling when Labour voters told him that "Thatcher had done more damage to this country than Hitler." Most evenings he jogged along roads, knocking on doors, introducing himself and asking for support, avoiding those with a "Vote Labour" or " Lib-Dem." poster in the front window and shrugged his shoulders as doors were slammed in his face. He spoke at public meetings in village primary schools, sometimes finding himself talking to only a handful of people that committee members had brought with them. In town it was different, school halls were usually packed, often with trouble makers from the BNP looking for excitement.

Police in the hall drew shouts of "Wha'cher scared of ?" and James' presence beside him drew yells of " 'oose yer fancy man then ?"

As the campaign entered its last week the press and television turned up the heat alleging cash shortages in the NHS, long waiting lists and sick children in need of surgery being refused hospital beds, whilst the PM proudly announced that all NHS Trusts had balanced their budgets. Ministers and Shadow Ministers slogged it out in front of the cameras and studio audiences.Presenters and editors analysed and dissected the day's political points until the exhausted viewers and readers turned off their television sets, threw down their newspapers and retired to bed.

As the nation waited for the first result from Billericay, in what was to be a long evening, exit polls predicted a narrow majority for the Conservative party, and as the arrow of the BBC Swingometer began its inexorable move into the blue, another defeat for Labour looked certain.

The Marton constituency count began late as boxes from distant country schools and village halls were brought in to the Civic Hall. Groups of party members wearing outsized blue, red and yellow and green rosettes stood around in anxious groups, or stared fixedly over the shoulders of those counting the votes, occasionally leaning forward to stab with an index finger at a spoiled ballot paper. At midnight Paul welcomed Dennis and Edith to the Civic Hall; Dennis slapped him on the back, muttered good wishes and promptly retired to the bar whilst Edith set off with Paul to tour the hall, to shake hands and chat with supporters. As the night wore on the atmosphere became tense.

By one-thirty in the morning the bundles of papers on the top table, each bearing a cross for Rugglestone, stretched at least two feet ahead of the opposition who, becoming increasingly gloomy, appeared to concede the contest. They stood disconsolately in small groups whilst their candidate, wearing a brave smile patted Paul on the shoulder and shook him by the hand. On the opposite side of the hall Erica and her team, not wishing to gloat, were quietly jubilant. At two o'clock the Returning Officer gathered the candidates together and the losers, with fixed smiles, reluctantly accepted that as Paul had a majority of over twelve thousand there was no need for a re-count.

"I Frank Ashcroft, being the Returning Officer..." Paul Rugglestone, stunned and exhausted did not take in the detailed figures. It was sufficient that he had won and won well. Before the cacophony had totally subsided he felt in his inside pocket for his speech, the speech that Erica had helped him draft some days before. On the platform, grasping the microphone he stared down at the crowd, at first seeing no one, then he focused on Erica, laughing and waving. Soon he would celebrate and drink with these people who had invaded his life and worked alongside him for three months, passing him around the constituency from one to another following the dictates of the calendar, the clock, and John Brown's campaign diary. He wished his father could have been here to witness his success, but he was a widower confined to a wheelchair following a motorway accident, and his only brother ran a G.P. practice single-handedly in Cornwall.

Paul stepped down from the platform, engulfed by the cheering throng, banging him on the back, pumping his hand and pushing and sweeping him through the hall as reporter's cameras flashed. He longed for the opportunity to savour the events of the evening over a quiet whisky with James - and then the peaceful comfort of his bed. Instead he was obliged to attend the traditional victory party that would continue until breakfast followed by a quick wash and shave before a celebratory tour of the constituency. There would be no time to rest and relax and relish the reality that he, Paul Vere-Rugglestone, was MP for the Marton constituency.

Chapter 5

Dennis never settled down to the business of the day until he had watched BBC television news, eaten his egg and bacon, scanned the Daily Telegraph, and opened his post, most of which he aimed in the direction of the wastepaper basket. It was normally junk mail that lay scattered on the dining-room carpet awaiting collection. The waste paper basket was large, but his aim was poor; every morning Edith, sighing with annoyance, gathered up the torn envelopes and their crumpled contents. Occasionally, hidden amongst the catalogues and requests for support, there were letters from Central Office or Mercia Area. These he opened first, ahead of any bills which he ignored until they re-appeared as a 'Reminder' or as a red 'Final Demand.'

On this particular morning he re-read the letter from Sir Percy Dorrington with a feeling akin to excitement. It informed him that Sir Percy had regretfully accepted the resignation of Sir Graham Whalley as Area Treasurer due to health reasons. Dorrington was now seeking a suitable person, able to devote time and energy to raising funds for the party in the Area.

"Mrs. Thatcher considers that the post of Area Treasurer is of vital importance to the future success of our party. The last election campaign left Conservative funds at an all time low and Lord Maclelland, the Party Treasurer, had written to all Chairmen, members of the CBI and party members. This nationwide appeal for party funds is to be launched at a gathering of Area Treasurers at 10 Downing Street in the next month."

Dennis wasted no time. Hurriedly brushing the

crumbs from his tweed jacket he gulped down the last mouthful of tea and tossed aside his serviette which slid across the table to join the discarded mail on the floor, awaiting rescue by Edith. The shining star of ennoblement 'for political services,' twinkled on the horizon and he limped off heavily in the direction of the farm office to compose his letter to Sir Percy and offer his services as Area Treasurer.

It was fortunate, Dennis decided, as he left home to stay with the new MP, that young Rugglestone had gone himself a decent apartment in Cromwell Court, W1.

"Mind you, he can afford it..." he told Edith as he left for New Street station "unlike me, still fighting for every penny from the Lloyds mess up."

He looked forward with a feeling, almost amounting to childish excitement at the prospect of talking with Margaret Thatcher. There was a woman he admired - knew exactly where she was going and swept aside anything that got in her way - tough as old boots.

On the journey to Euston Dennis settled himself in the dining-coach.Travelling by train with Edith always meant a day-return and sandwiches from the buffet.Now, on party business, as Area Treasurer, it was a first class Pullman and a British Rail dinner. He had heard that the meal was quite passable. He ordered a dry martini, browsed through the menu and wine list, and allowed his thoughts to run ahead. Of course he wouldn't always stay with Rugglestone - mustn't appear too greedy with his expenses – but he needed to keep an eye on that young fellow who shared the flat, just in case Edith was right. If she was, he'd soon put a stop to that kind of nonsense pretty damn quick. The sooner Rugglestone got himself a nice girl the better.

On the other hand a stay in a decent London hotel would have been pleasant. He'd need to find out where the others stayed when they met at Central Office. They'd obviously want to discuss business, and where better, than over a meal in a good hotel. Then of course there would be dinners at the House with the MPs. He smiled contentedly to himself at the thought - picking up bits of inside gossip, being in the know, meeting Ministers. Through the pate, the grilled salmon in watercress sauce, stilton and celery he allowed himself the luxury of anticipation of the benefits that his new sphere of influence might bring. By the time he had finished lunch Dennis felt able to put right the whole of the Tory cabinet and deal with any unusual traits that the new M.P. might present them with.

Yellow-ochre brick and soot-stained windows backed on to the railway line giving way to blackened walls and a faded sign that announced 'Euston half a mile.' Dennis settled his luncheon account, tucking the receipt into his wallet to provide evidence for his next expenses claim.

The train was on time, which was an improvement on past inter-city travel. Stewards waited on the platform by the open doors to assist passengers. In the concourse a West Indian cleaner swept up litter around 'Sock Shop.' A crowd of back-packers stood staring upwards, scowling as they digested the information that the clattering departure boards spelled out. Through the background noise a loudspeaker apologised for delays to trains from Glasgow due to a landslip. Dennis followed the sign that indicated 'Taxis' and joined the queue.

The porter behind his desk at Cromwell Court

handed Dennis a key. "You're to let yourself in Sir. Mr. Rugglestone is still in The House. He expects to be back in time to join you for dinner."

With time to spare, Dennis dropped his overnight Samsonite in the hall and pushed open the door into the lounge. Comfortable cream leather armchairs, eastern rugs and a mock Adam fireplace accompanied Audubon prints and silk flower arrangements.

Beside the television stood a drinks cabinet its doors open in welcome. He examined the bottles, selected a Famous Grouse, picked up the remote control, collapsed heavily into a comfortable chair and switched on the six-o-clock news. Satisfying himself that there was nothing new since breakfast he heaved himself from his chair, replenished his glass and began a tour of inspection.

The bow windows of a large en-suite double bedroom looked down the busy road, lined with barrows and crowded with taxis and buses, towards Knightsbridge. Furtively he prowled around the room, noting the feminine floral duvet, the King size bed and matching furnishings. He ran his hands along the edge of the curtains, felt the thickness and crossed the room towards the built-in wardrobes, turning the key to open the mahogany doors. He inspected the clothes with curiosity, fingering the lapels of a dinner-jacket, touching the cloth, then pulling out the drawers he read the labels on the shirts - Armani and Versace. From the shoe rack he picked out a pair of patent-leather evening shoes bearing the signature Ferragamo.

He moved across to the bathroom and stood in the doorway and sniffed. It stank like a whore's boudoir. What did the fellow want with two marble hand basins and gold plated taps? Bottles of after-shave and boxes of talc covered the window ledge. He lifted the electric razor from its cradle and it sprang into life as he gazed at himself in the mirror and thoughtfully stroked his chin. Hurriedly he replaced it and turned his attention to the contents of the bathroom cabinet. It was years since he had opened a packet of Durex. There was one left inside the packet.

Built-in bookcases lined the walls of the dining room. Dennis glanced at the titles, 'The Philosophy of the Guru', 'Sex and the Single Man', 'The Art of Zen', 'Hinduism'. He gave a snort, and turned away and circled the mahogany pedestal dining-table and Chippendale- style chairs to reach the window. Lifting a muslin curtain he frowned in disapproval at the grimy backs of other apartments that encircled the area. The odour of curry mingled unappetisingly from kitchen ventilators with fish and cabbage. From an open window opposite a woman shook a duster and waved to him. Hastily he let the curtain fall and moved away.

The last room down the corridor appeared to be a guest room. Bottles of after-shave, a new tin of Imperial Leather talcum powder and a box of Kleenex Man-size tissues were set out on the dressing-table. He turned back the duvet. The sheets were clean, and the wardrobe was empty. It was obviously the guest room.

The idea of the two men sharing the bed in the other room was bad enough - but whilst he was there - in the flat. The very idea sickened him.

He retraced his steps to the lounge in time to hear the whine of the lift. It stopped outside the apartment and Vere-Rugglestone let himself in.

"How d'you like it?" Paul, dressed in a pin-striped dark suit and waistcoat stood in the doorway. "Good you've got a drink - pour me a G and T – plenty of ice and lemon - while I change."

The electric razor buzzed in the bathroom and Dennis surprised himself by easing himself from his chair and complying meekly with the request. He was equally surprised with the re-appearance of the MP in twills and a sweatshirt bearing the embroidered logo of Yves Saint Laurent. He recognised the initials. On special occasions Edith wore Yves Saint Laurent perfume - 'Left Bank' - heavy, sickly - and clinging. He preferred her usual eau-de-cologne.

"Had a good look round ?" It was more of a statement than a question and Dennis felt caught-out and uncomfortable.

"D'you think it's suitable for an up-and-coming MP ?"

"Very suitable," mumbled Dennis, embarrassed that he had been forced to admit to snooping. "Nicely furnished ..."

"That's the advantage of having a sister in town. She's got all the right contacts - I left it to her. By the way we're eating Italian tonight - a little place Madeline recommended. Hope you like Italian food ?"

Dennis couldn't ever remember eating anything Italian. He had looked forward to dining with his MP in the House. Now that they were going to eat out he'd have to pay - well at least offer. He couldn't let Rugglestone treat him, even though he could well afford to do so. If they'd dined in the House the MP would have paid. The meals would be subsidised anyway and he'd surely be able to claim an allowance for entertaining. These MPs did themselves well - they all had their snouts in the trough.

"You like Italian food ?" Dennis heard the question repeated anxiously. "It's not all pasta and pizzas you know." Dennis nodded, accepting the situation.

The very act of being admitted and walking over the threshold into Number 10 gave him a buzz of excitement and self-importance, although he tried to behave as if he'd done it a hundred times before, and it was no big deal. In the hall, beneath portraits of ex-Prime Ministers who looked down from the stairway, he joined the queue to present his card and select a glass of wine. Percy Dorrington walked ahead of him into the reception room. Thankful to find someone he knew Dennis tried to elbow his way through the gathering, but found his path blocked as Lord Maclelland and party officials made way for the PM. There was no mistaking her voice, demanding and strident, as she emphasised a point. He skirted around the group and waited impatiently for Percy to end his conversation and introduce him to others.

Unexpectedly Sir Percy reached out, grabbing him by the arm, bringing him into his circle, including him in the discussion. " We need to talk." His tone was terse. "If you've got time we'll go back to Smith Square when the meeting is over."

Behind him Dennis heard the unmistakable voice of Kenneth Clarke which puzzled him as he'd heard that the PM and Ken had little respect for each other. Over a pint of beer, the Secretary of State for Health, brown suit and Hush Puppy shoes, mixed joviality with earnest conversation "...we're always looking for good people ...successful business men and women to carry forward our reforms...of course they get useful salaries...just write to me..."

Dennis turned to Sir Percy "Will you introduce me ?"

"To the PM ? As our new Treasurer ? Of course."

"To Kenneth Clarke ."

Margaret Thatcher scurried around the room, her head pushed forward, symbolic blue dress with regulation blue bow beneath her chin, persuading, encouraging, demanding - leaving her guests overwhelmed by her presence. Due back in the House in an hour, she moved swiftly from group to group.

Sir Percy Dorrington smiled and shook hands. "Dennis Deane. Our new Regional Treasurer."

She scrutinised his face as if filing his image in her memory. "Get into the boardrooms. Write to the business men and industrialists. Get to know them... business breakfasts, lunches and dinners... Never take 'no' for an answer - they may squeal now but in the end they'll be the ones to thank us... Point out to them how we've handled the unions... we'll send ministers to talk with them if you want." She moved on, leaving him speechless with admiration. He turned to see Kenneth Clarke chortling with amusement.

"I heard you were looking for Chairmen," began Dennis.

Clarke put down his beer glass on a polished table beside him. The glass was wet and the Secretary of State wiped his hands on his jacket. Dennis winced.

"I've got to get back to the House. Write to me."

As the PM departed for the Commons leaving a flurry of instructions in her wake Lord Maclelland began his appeal; urging party officers to renew their efforts to persuade business, commerce and industry to increase their financial contributions. Letters would be sent out signed by Margaret Thatcher and regional offices would follow up the contacts. Dennis knew that outstanding results would achieve quick recognition.

When the reception had ended Sir Percy phoned for a taxi. "Central Office, Smith Square," he told the driver.

"It's the best place to talk," he said quietly.

A small interview room, sparsely furnished with a desk and two chairs, had already been made available for them. It smelled of cigarette smoke and stubs remained in the tin ashtray.

"I think I should tell you, if you don't know already - " Sir Percy leaned forward on the table and stared at Dennis, as if awaiting confirmation that he might already know that there was a problem. "Well I've only just learned, from the Chairman of North Downs Region - that your chap - Vere-Rugglestone - was in a spot of bother some years ago."

"A spot of bother ?" Dennis' tone was brusque. "What does that mean ?"

"It appears that Rugglestone ran a scout camp -"

"Oh no." Dennis closed his eyes and clamped a hand over his face. "You mean?"

"Yes - one of those cases. It never came to court. The boy's mother who made the complaint was known to the police." Sir Percy's tone was reassuring.

"So how old was the boy ?"

"Twelve or thirteen. Apparently the family bore some sort of grudge against the Rugglestone family. They were trouble-makers - went straight to the police after the alleged incident - but because of their reputation and in consideration for Paul's father who had just been widowed the police decided to take no action."

"Did he admit it ?"

Sir Percy shook his head. "No. Denied it, absolutely."

"Then perhaps they made it up?"

"Could be - but the police weren't too happy. Rugglestone was very frightened - left the scouts and left home too."

Dennis scowled. "Why weren't we warned.?"

"There was no case - nothing was proved."Sir Percy shrugged his shoulders. "You can't go round telling tales like that."

"But surely, if the police knew – it would be down on some sort of record. Aren't these people vetted?"

Sir Percy shook his head sorrowfully. "apparently not."

"So what do we do now?" Dennis asked. "What can we do?"

"Not much." Sir Percy's reply was matter-of-fact. "Keep an eye on him. Warn the agent, perhaps he should decline invitations to scout camps, school visits and youth clubs - pressure of work, other commitments, that sort of thing. He's not the first – there's quite a few on both sides of the House - oh, and make sure he always has a minder - just in case." He stood up, walked around the table and patted Dennis on the shoulder. "Cheer up there's probably nothing in it, and if there was it may never happen again – unless of course someone local remembers him, puts two and two together and tries blackmail; then it's a real problem."

"Bloody young fool," growled Dennis. "How did it happen, do you have any details?"

"No more than I've told you. But not to worry, I'll get Tony Gibbons to talk to your agent – they need to be warned." He paused and rubbed his hands over his face. "How the party whips sleep at night, I don't know. We've a Minister who's being blackmailed because he meets call girls; and most of the members have affairs with their secretaries – what can you expect when they are away from home five days out of seven?"

Dennis hailed a taxi, relieved to be returning home and not having to spend another night in the company of Paul Vere-Rugglestone. The party had let him down and no mistake. If this got out he'd be a laughing-stock for selecting a chap like that. The sooner he got rid of the fellow the better. The gossip would spread like a forest fire, from Regional to Central office, to the party hierarchy. None of them would take the blame for it, not even Percy Dorrington. He of all people should have had the fellow checked out, but who would have suspected it in the Rugglestone family?

The Chairman of the Mercia Conservative and Unionist Association sat with his head in his hands staring into his gin and dry martini, not bothering to study the British Rail dinner menu.

Chapter 6

Dennis gulped down his coffee and stared impatiently through the grimy windows of the agent's office. Constituency coffee, made in mugs bought at jumble sales - for party funds - was invariably tasteless.

In the town square below, John Brown the Constituency Agent, strolled back to the office threading his way between the market-stalls in the early spring sunshine carrying a blue and gold cake box. He slalomed through the crowds, past the great oak door of the church and took the cobbled path alongside the old cemetery where thick green moss covered the inscriptions on the head stones and yellow daffodils sheltered beneath silver birch trees. Pausing briefly to chat with shoppers who habitually took the short cut between the market stalls and the square he crossed the road towards the Conservative Club car park.

The smile on his face vanished when he saw the Chairman's Rover in its designated parking space. He had always enjoyed his job as Constituency Party agent, that is... until Dennis took over as Chairman. Now he began to wish that he had sought promotion when he was younger. By now he could have been Area Agent, or even in a job at Central Office. There was a rumour going around that Tony Gibbons was in line for promotion to Central Office. Maybe it was not too late to apply for his job...

Every morning at eleven-thirty John Brown left his desk, poured the tepid contents of his coffee cup into the wash-basin, clattered down the bare oak stairs and crossed the square to Bratts, Bakers and Confectioners, where he enjoyed a Cappucino and chose his lunchtime snack from the hot dishes, displayed in the glass-fronted cabinet. Today, inside the blue and gold cake box were two mushroom vol-au-vents, a Florentine and two chocolate eclairs to take home for supper.

In the outer office his Secretary, Mrs.Gunn, pointed towards the door of his room, rolled her big brown eyes and silently mouthed the word "Chairman." John Brown nodded, accepting the news with resignation.

The flavorless coffee had done nothing to improve Dennis' humour. "We've been conned. The party's misled us," he barked.

The agent gently placed his lunch box on top of the filing cabinet, pulled back his chair and positioned himself behind his desk. He leaned back, hands clasped behind his head and waited, adopting a tolerant smile.

"Vere-Rugglestone - the MP - he's a paedophile - or a poufter. I don't know which - in any case he's a criminal."

"Oh, I wouldn't think so." John Brown spoke calmly. He intentionally assumed an air of practiced composure, which infuriated Dennis, who had witnessed it many times in the past when he or others had stormed into the office.

"Why d'you say that ?"

As Dennis related the events of the past two days the Agent listened patiently. "It sounds like a put-up-job."

"Whatever he's done or not done, he's a liability and the sooner he's gone the better."

"You've no proof, and you can't do anything about it - and I certainly don't intend to do anything." There was a warning note in John Brown's voice.

"What if this gets out ?"

"Then we'll consult Area Office and handle it appropriately. But I don't suppose it'll get out - Central Office is not likely to broadcast it around." He shrugged his shoulders. "In any case it's libellous."

"What about this fellow James?"

"What about him?"

"Well, he lives with Rugglestone."

"Does he? I don't know where he lives - I've never asked him. I know his parents live somewhere in London. I understand that he's Rugglestone's research assistant."

Dennis tried another approach. "Sir Percy thinks that Rugglestone should have a minder."

The Agent pursed his lips. "Well, that could be arranged - when he's here - but in London... well, that's out of the question." He leaned forward and smiled. "You know, this may prove to be a storm in a tea-cup, we mustn't make too much of it. You need to keep things in perspective."

Dennis studied his watch and pushed back his chair. He was wasting his time. "I need to get back for lunch."

In the Rover he sat for a moment before turning on the ignition. The morning hadn't been entirely wasted. He knew the agent well enough to expect that John Brown was unlikely to leave matters unresolved - and he smiled at the thought that probably at that very moment Brown would be on the phone to Tony Gibbons. But as far as he was concerned - one way or another - Rugglestone had to go.

One month after he had written to the Secretary of State for Health Dennis was invited to Richmond

House to discuss the possibility of him taking on the Chairmanship of Mercia Region. Although Mercia was the smallest NHS region in the country it controlled a dozen Area Health Authorities, each one containing several Hospital and Primary Care Trusts, and more than a hundred G.P. practices, medical centres and specialist clinics that were dedicated to providing health services to the community.

It was widely reported by those who had attended last year's health service conference in Brighton that the previous Regional Chairman, Nicholas Bell, hosting a social 'get-together' in the conference hotel, had encouraged rebellion amongst his colleagues by referring to the previous Secretary of State as "Simple Simon." As a result several non-executive directors who had already spent some time propping up the bar had unwisely joined in the fun singing. "Put your hands you know where, Simple Simon says... Do it in double time." Their contracts were terminated within days and Nicholas Bell retired as Regional Chairman 'for family reasons.'

The only sure way of keeping your job and the twenty-five thousand that went with it, reflected Dennis, was to do whatever the Department asked - without question - no matter how lecherous the Secretary of State might seem. And that meant succeeding at the almost impossible task of cutting waiting lists at the same time as managing a woefully inadequate budget. It was normal procedure amongst surgical staff in many Hospital Trusts, to take the opportunity of having a chat with patients and asking whether they had plans to go on holiday. If by chance they had already booked a holiday they would receive an appointment for their non-urgent surgery on that date and their inability to keep the appointment ensured that they were then put back to the bottom of the waiting list.

"I intend to create a new post of Director of Waiting Lists - performance related, and directly responsible to me. I've picked the man already." he assured the junior Minister and Alan Greenspan, the Chief Executive of the NHS.

Dennis' arrival at Argyll House, a concrete seven-story office block in the city centre, headquarters of Mercia Regional Health Authority caused alarm. Dennis set aside three full days to interview the senior managers of every Hospital and Primary Care Trust from Chief Executive to Director of Public Relations. Those who were not on time, or were on holiday, later discovered that they had been replaced.

Next in line were Health Authorities. Weeks of intensive analysis, between the Regional Treasurer and the Chief Executive identified those who in the last three years had been unable to balance their budgets. Letters were sent out demanding the attendance of Chairmen and Chief Executives of every Area Health Authority in the Region to discuss their year-end figures. No excuses were accepted and none were offered. NHS phone lines had relayed Dennis's reputation into every office in Mercia Region. Every meeting was followed up by a personally dictated account of the proceedings that had taken place and the letter ended with a stern threat to the Area Health Authority Chairman in the final paragraph. "You assured me that you are now taking measures to balance your accounts by the end of this financial year. I must ask you to let me have details of your proposed savings within the next four weeks otherwise it will be necessary for the Regional Treasurer to critically examine your Health Authority's staffing levels."

Chapter 7

From its position on Medbury Hill, overlooking Marton, Queenswood Hall dominated the countryside. The Edwardian mansion had for many years provided a home for the elderly mentally infirm in the west wing. Newfields, a small private preparatory school leased the east wing. The building was owned by Marton Health Authority; and John Tyler, headmaster of Newfields , was in debt to the Health Authority for more than forty-thousand pounds in rent, and the shared costs of the water and electricity supply to the whole building.

When John Tyler opened the letter from Tom Anstey, the Chief Executive of Marton Health Authority, telling him that his lease would not be renewed unless he paid off the debt in full, he immediately set about arranging a meeting with Dennis Deane. Years earlier they had attended the same school and from time to time had met at Old Boys reunions and social functions.

"Renew the lease." Dennis had thundered down the phone to Barbara Millar, the slim, brunett Chairman of Marton Health Authority, recently appointed to her post by Dennis Deane on the recommendation of Conservative Central Office. Barbara was known to be obstinate when confronted. He owes us forty thousand pounds and the lease is due for renewal in June." Barbara's voice hardened. "If he doesn't pay up you would hardly expect us to renew the lease."

"Renew that lease." Denis bellowed, unused to having anyone argue with him.

"John Tyler will be bankrupt within weeks."

"Renew the lease. Our solicitors say that you are obliged to do so."

"Alright, but if he goes bust I'll look to you to bail us out; otherwise we'll end the year in the red. Just get it in writing from your legal department."

"Do as I tell you. Renew the lease." Dennis shouted, slamming down the phone.

By the time that the Marton Health Authority had been called to account to Region for its anticipated budget deficit of over forty thousand pounds at the end of the financial year, John Tyler had not only been declared bankrupt but had died suddenly of a stroke.

"What plans have you made to recover the money?" demanded Dennis. "You can't end the year in deficit."

"There's no chance of recovering anything unless we can sell the hall and grounds. The building is listed and the whole estate is in the Green Belt. There are twenty acres of woods and gardens. If we could get planning permission we might be able to sell off some of the land for building. That should pay off the deficit with something to spare." Barbara paused, "Of course if you hadn't insisted ..."Dennis swivelled his chair around, stood up and turned his back on the attractive woman who had faced him calmly from the other side of his desk. "That's all. Just get that money. You had better talk to the Land Agent."

Outside, across the City, the bells of St. Mary the Virgin began their Thursday lunchtime carillon practice. "The Bells of St. Mary's." When he first arrived at Argyll House Dennis had found the bells enjoyable, but within days they became monotonous. This morning he found them annoying.

68

Chapter 8

"Political Scandals rock Westminister...MPs Expenses Scandal...Fraud and corruption revealed."

"Is this Government fit to govern ? Only the Morning Gazette is able to reveal the exclusive facts. Find the hidden secrets of life inside the House of Commons in the centre page."

The billboards propped outside kiosks and newsagents shops throughout the country caused rush hour commuters to pause, queue, and buy, then turn to the centre page where the leader article asked "How much do you know about your MP?"

The Morning Gazette, subject of a take-over only two months before by a European business consortium, devoted the first weeks of its re-birth to questioning the ability of the elected members of the House of Commons to govern; and set about disparaging the role of British MPs, in comparison with - as its Editor claimed - the superior qualities of the members of the European Parliament.

Every member of the Lords and Commons became the subject of its intrusive investigations. The series was planned to last for twelve weeks throughout the summer which led up to the Euro-referendum on the Lisbon Treaty. Each day, except Sundays, the faces of five MPs faced the readers on page three and each day their private lives were exposed in detail to public scrutiny. Both MPs and Lords expenses, fraud and business deals were probed, sex lives investigated and allegations and innuendos filled the centre pages. The readers of The Morning Gazette, their fingers blackened by printer's ink, were left in no doubt that the House of Commons was, as Sodom and Gomorrah, riddled with sleaze and deviancy. The Inland Revenue, and the Fraud Squad set up investigatory teams and as even more allegations were revealed the number of MPs who decided to resign from politics grew in proportion. Claims for overnight hotel expenses in London when MPs had actually travelled to their own homes; another claimed for the cost of building a mock Victorian garden folly whilst many compiled false claims for mortgages and rental charges which filled the columns of the daily papers with reports and photographs.

To the delight of the consortium and its backers, who had already received three summonses for libel and hoped for more, the circulation of the Gazette had tripled. Members of the Press Complaints Commission were in ferment, facing months if not years of discussion and argument, whilst the remainder of the British press and television raced, with cameras and recording equipment from one London address to the next, in a feeding frenzy.

In the tea room, in corridors and committee rooms, lined faces and whispered conversations reflected the anxieties of M.Ps. Voices raised in argument, noisy discussions and outbursts of laughter were replaced by confidential revelations in the Whips offices. Was there a single member able and confident to assert that there was absolutely nothing in his life that now and again did not return to haunt and remind him of acts or indiscretions, past or present? Such a paragon would surely never have become involved in politics. "How could anyone discover such secrets? How do they come to light?" Some tried to laugh it off, but they too eventually joined the rush through the streets of the

Capital to consult their accountants and lawyers.

Those who had not so far featured in the series set about preparing detailed statements of their business interests and their blameless family lives in an effort to reassure their electorate. Hurried meetings in constituency offices with Area agents and MPs resulted in press statements that members had "nothing to hide," and "all allegations would be strongly contested."

Arguments became even more heated when The Daily Examiner, a right-wing Euro-sceptic broadsheet countered the allegations, and began its own investigation into the private lives of Euro MPs under the headline "The Eurocrat's Gravy Train."

From Docklands to Fleet Street the whole of the British press became drawn into the row. Reputable broadsheets, having sat on the fence, sniffily deriding this 'intrusion into public life,' were eventually obliged to report on the forthcoming libel actions as they too began to lose readers in the circulation battle.

Paul Vere-Rugglestone was in no doubt that the embarrassing episode at the scout camp, twenty years ago, would feature in the Morning Gazette. With growing public concern about child abuse, it would be seen as a serious matter.

"The trouble is..." began John Brown, "that the very hint of a libel action, or an application for an injunction, will make the Gazette quite sure that you have got something to hide."

"Even if it wasn't true ?"

"Do you really think that all the other tales in the Gazette are true?"

Paul shook his head.

"So we'd better go along with the solicitor's advice, or we could be in deeper trouble."

Two days later a half page picture on page three of the Morning Gazette featured Paul Vere-Rugglestone outside a well-known Regent Street store, holding the hand of his ten year old great-nephew,the boy's parents who had accompanied them had been air-brushed from the scene. The caption read, "Would you let your son hold his hand?" Beneath it were details of the alleged incident at the scout camp, and an interview with the boy's mother, his accuser.

"It's obscene that that man should now be an MP. It shouldn't be allowed. There ought to be an enquiry. We drove him out of town twenty years ago, and we haven't seen him since - and good riddance I say!"

Dennis Deane sat in the leather armchair in front of the popping gas fire in the agent's office and stared down at the photograph. Central Office hadn't done their homework on Paul Vere-Rugglestone, and now it was left to him to pull their chestnuts out of the fire. Six years spent at a Welsh boarding school, waking each day to ice-cold showers, rugger, and Outward Bound courses left most boys derisive of Gays, and Dennis dreaded the thought of being sneered at by his colleagues for appointing a 'queer' as MP. The seat was rural and middle-class. Unless the voters believed in their MP and were prepared to turn out and support him at the next election, the party would certainly lose the seat to the Lib Dems.

John Brown read his thoughts. "He's suing the Gazette for libel. We can't do much until the case is heard, and that could be months - if not years. Until then, we have to support him - loudly and loyally." He passed Dennis a typewritten sheet of paper. "Press release, put together by our solicitors, for your approval."

Dennis glared down at the notepaper, headed "Fairman and Firbright" in copper-plate writing, and read the advice.

"The MP for the Mercia constituency, Paul Vere-Rugglestone, has instructed solicitors to serve a summons for libel on the Morning Gazette. The Conservative constituency chairman, Dennis Deane, today issued the following statement: "Every member of the Conservative party in the Marton constituency totally supports their MP. Paul Rugglestone. The behaviour of the Morning Gazette is disgraceful. I have contacted the Press Complaints Commission and urged them to take the strongest possible action against the newspaper. Paul Vere-Rugglestone has our full backing in his action against the Morning Gazette."

With the press camped on the pavement outside, Paul Vere-Rugglestone packed two Vuitton suitcases, and took the lift down from his apartment to the basement car-park. The navy Lancia coupe took the photographers by surprise as it roared up the slope from the basement garage, into the narrow street behind Cromwell Court, completing a tight slalom between the rows of green waste bins as it headed out of town towards the M40 and Erica Barrington's Old Rectory.

Chapter 9

Angry noises from the Executive suite delayed Bernard Lord, the Regional Land Agent, from seeking a meeting with the Chairman by at least thirty minutes. Dennis Deane's bellowing could be heard the length of the corridor that ran outside the outer office, past the lifts, the toilets and the canteen.

"Well, telephone! Telephone! Don't waste time. I told you this morning!"

Lisa, his secretary, clutching her dictation pad, scurried grim-faced into the safety of her office. Peace descended once again, broken only by the clatter of cups and saucers as the secretaries attempted to restore their shattered nerves with cups of Nescafe, and tossed up to decide which of them would take the Chairman his afternoon tea.

Bernard Lord meanwhile reached across his desk for the Queenswood Hall file. Clutching his mug of coffee he re-read the notes that he had made following his meeting with John Short, the Borough Council's Planning Officer. Twenty five years earlier the Health Authority had been granted permission to convert Queenswood Hall into a nursing home in the west wing and a preparatory school for boys in the east wing. Conditions were laid down that no planning permission would be granted for residential development in the grounds as the whole estate was protected as part of a designated Conservation Area.

The nursing home accommodation was Dickensian, with elderly residents sleeping in rows in long dormitories. There was no privacy and the toilets, along the corridor, had only half doors. In today's world it was surprising that the patients and their relatives continued to tolerate such conditions. Many residents, coming from the poorer areas of the city, knew no better or were so senile that they were oblivious to their surroundings It made Bernard shudder to think that he might end his days in a place like that. It would kill him. The home should have been closed years ago. It must have been beautiful in its heyday, the ornate plasterwork on the ceilings, the bow fronted windows and the large rooms, were clues to the fact that the house had enjoyed a period of gracious living, but flag-stoned floors and out of date plumbing made cold weather unbearable.

He ran his hands through his grey hair, gathered up his papers, and made his way, hesitantly, along the corridor towards the Chairman's room where Dennis Deane waited impatiently.

Every afternoon before he left the office Malcolm Yates, the Chief Executive, briefed the Chairman on all formal meetings and discussions and even the gossip that had taken place amongst regional staff that day. That way Dennis was rarely caught out by events. It gave him time to think out his strategy.

"If we can't get planning permission for development, then we'll sell it."

"Sell Queenswood Hall ? The whole place ?"

"Certainly." Dennis enjoyed seeing the look of astonishment on the Land Agent's face."

"But - the old people ?"

"Move them out!"

Bernard realised that, like so many others before him, he had become the butt of the Chairman's whimsy, and was now expected to ask the obvious question.

"Where to?"

"Parker's Paddock!"

Bernard Lord shook his head. "The Council will never allow it."

"What d'you bet?" Dennis leaned back in his chair and smiled. "It's totally in line with Government policy. Re-locating the elderly and people with learning difficulties out of old institutions into new purpose-built accommodation - that's what Community Care is all about! Parker's Paddock is the ideal site."

Parker's Paddock had changed ownership four times in the last twenty-five years. As the name suggested it had been owned by the Parker family as part of their farm, but when the County Council decided to build a by-pass around the town of Marton the land was compulsorily purchased. The new road separated the farmhouse from the land, and the house and land were sold in separate lots, forcing the County Council to purchase twenty five acres of poor Grade 3 land which was then earmarked as a suitable site for a hospital. A local committee, who were already raising money to provide the town with a cottage hospital, then bought the site.

Within months the re-elected Government reorganized the Health Service. District Health Authorities were given new powers to award contracts and purchase services and Regional Health Authorities became outposts of the Department of Health. Financial cut-backs resulted in the closure of small hospitals which were replaced by District General Hospitals with substantial resources close to large centres of population in towns and cities, and the Marton project was cancelled. The land lay idle and was eventually advertised for sale as 'surplus to requirements.' VS&T bought it, at the knock down price of five hundred pounds an acre. On the edge of the town, the company directors foresaw that one day it would be in demand. In spite of local efforts to raise money to buy it as playing fields for the town, the new owners applied for planning permission for an out-of-town shopping development. Their proposals angered the town-centre traders, and were quickly rejected by the District Council, despite everything that the large supermarket chain, who proposed to develop it, could do - short of bribery.

"You're quite serious about this, Chairman?" Bernard asked cautiously. "I mean, well, to others it might look - well - improper, to say the least."

"What on earth is improper about making money for the NHS, balancing your budget and benefiting patients ?

Dennis demanded.

Bernard Lord sat silently staring down at the table. He needed to talk to the Chief Executive.

Dennis looked smug. "The owners, VS&T, will sell it to the Marton Health Authorit at the District Valuer's recommended price. What could be fairer ?"

Only the Chief Executive and the Land Agent were aware that VS&T were the initials of Vehicle Spares and Transplants and that the two directors, Dennis Deane and Gareth Gilbert, started their business in the same sheds where Dennis once housed his turkeys.

The Marton Health Authority met two weeks later to discuss their Chief Executive's recommendations on the sale of Queenswood Hall.

"It's in an ideal situation." agreed Barbara Millar. She looked down along the two rows of polished tables on either side of the room where the members of the authority sat. "Ideal for a hotel - or even company offices."

Tom Anstey, the Chief Executive sitting beside her, nodded. Queenswood Hall, set high on the side of Medbury Hill, overlooked the river, and the distant Welsh Marches. "I've heard that Geoffrey Tate, the physician, has got his eye on it for a private clinic."

"How did he get to know? We haven't decided to sell yet," grumbled a member.

"Pillow-talk," suggested another. "His wife works at Region and she wants him to build her a private house in the gardens."

"How much could we ask for it?" Mick Sedley, the DHA Treasurer, was anxious to make progress. Aware of the board members' enjoyment of a good gossip, he had hoped to leave early to take his girl-friend out to choose a birthday present. "Will it clear the budget deficit ?"

"We'll need a bridging loan from Region - interest free," advised Anstey who had already arranged the matter with the Regional Treasurer. It was standard practice. Faced with the fact that the Regional Chairman had already decreed that Queenswood Hall should be sold to pay off the budget deficit, the discussion that followed amongst the members of the District Health Authority, took the form of a token debate, and by ten past three, the meeting having started at half-past two, the sale was agreed.

After some deliberation, the Marton District Council granted planning permission to re-house the patients from Queenswood Hall in a purpose-built Nursing Home at Parker's Paddock and a date was set by the Regional Health Authority for the closure of

Queenswood Hall.

The directors of the VS&T took no time at all to decide to sell Parker's Paddock to the Marton Health Authority at the District Valuer's valuation, for ten thousand pounds an acre, and the members of the DHA, whose only financial interests were to balance the books, gave no thought to who were the directors of VS&T.

Tony Bradshaw, Regional Treasurer, satisfied that Marton Health Authority would now balance their budget, felt confident that the Chairman's worries about budget deficits had been satisfactorily resolved; and Barbara Millar, dreaming of the projects she would recommend to the authority when the contract for the three hundred thousand pounds sale of Queenswood Hall was signed, slept soundly that night in the belief that her troubles were over.

Chapter 10

Charlie Bastow reversed his red Porsche into the yard behind the kitchen block and surveyed the car park, waiting for a vacant space. He had time to spare. He had been told that the Chairman never arrived before nine thirty. His Rolex Oyster showed nine fifteen. Charlie reached into the glove pocket for his comb, removed his aviator sunglasses and carefully inspected himself in the rear view mirror. He slicked back his black hair, paying especial attention to the side-burns which had been re-touched at the salon in the High Street the previous afternoon.

He watched as a member of the kitchen staff, white hat and coat flapping in the breeze around her thick stockings, came out of a back door and emptied a bucket of potato peelings into a bin. A District Nurse, in cobalt blue dress and burdened with files, hurried officiously from a side door. Car keys dangling from one finger she made her way to a small Rover and balancing the files against the car opened a rear door. Leaning forward she placed the files on the back seat revealing two perfectly proportioned creamy thighs beneath the hem of a white petticoat. Charlie whistled in appreciation, switched on the ignition and eased forward.

He parked the Porsche next to a notice that warned drivers that the space was reserved for 'Chairman's parking only.' On the passenger seat beside him lay a presentation box whose label bore the arms of the County of Shropshire and the words 'Floreat Salopia. The very best of Shropshire produce.' Beneath the - polythene a selection of cheeses and a half bottle of

Cockburn's Port were packed artistically.

Barbara Millar eased her Volvo into the Chairman's parking space, bumping into the wooden notice that proclaimed her sole right to use of the space and pushing the notice further into the rose hedge in front of the car. She saw Charlie Bastow leaning against the Porsche and wondered what business he had with the Health Authority. He joined her on her walk towards the front entrance, holding the presentation pack in front of him.

"Mrs Millar ? They said I should be able to talk to you at nine-thirty. It's about the school buildings at Queenswood. I understand they're empty. Mr. Deane said I should speak to you."

She turned to look at him. "Dennis Deane?"

He nodded. "Yeh, good friend of mine." At the entrance he went ahead and held open the door. She nodded good morning to the receptionist.

" You'd better follow me up to the office."

Charlie smiled. Dennis Deane's name always opened doors. He adjusted the presentation pack firmly under his arm.

In the Chairman's office he put the pack on the desk. "Nice set up you've got here." He walked around the room inspecting the photographs. An aerial view of Marton General; facing the Chairman's desk two large portraits of the Queen and Prince Phillip, and behind the desk a Mission Statement in green print.

She was on the phone ordering coffee as he examined the computer. "Bit out of date for the Chairman, isn't it ? You need a Pentium three at least."

"It's a throw out from the offices. I have to put up with what I'm given. I don't use it much."

"He peered down at the printer, and drew in his

81

breath. "Out of date.. Went out with King Tut. Now I could get you a good 'un...state of the art."

She frowned and shook her head, and pulled a chair away from the coffee table. "Perhaps you'd explain what your visit is about."

Charlie perched on the side of the desk, reached inside his jacket pocket and produced a card.

"Charles Fitzallen Bastow," she read. "Wholesalers and Suppliers. Est. 1946."

"I get whatever you need. I open doors." He grinned. "Whatever you want I have...just ask Charlie Bastow...leave it wiv me, and in a shake of a lamb's tail you've got it...delivered straight to your door -"

"But Mr Bastow I don't need anything - "

"Charlie's the name..Betcha' like Port and Stilton ?" He swivelled round on the desk and reached for the presentation pack.

"Mr. Bastow ..." the Chairman's voice rose in irritation. "I don't take presents."

He gave a chuckle. "Okay...gotcha." He tapped the side of his nose. "But if it were delivered to your home, like..."

She shook her head. "No Mr Bastow - I've told you."

"Fair enough. Okay, fair enough, I'll tell you what I'm really here for. We can do each other a favour."

Barbara sighed impatiently and pursed her lips.

"The Head Sirag -"

"Head Sirag ?"

"Yeah - Head Sirag. Big White Chief - Your boss man, Dennis Deane. Well he says that you got an empty building up at Queenswood. Half unused like...Says that fings are fin an' you're in need of the ready." He waved his hands in the air. "Well I'm lookin' for a bit of temp'rary storage 'till Christmas at least, maybe longer. I'll pay a years rent - wotcher say ?" He reached into his inside jacket pocket and withdrew a roll of notes. "Nothin' formal like...there's more where this comes from if I need it longer."

The coffee remained untouched. Barbara walked across the room, opened the door and held out her hand. "Mr Bastow, if you wish to rent some accommodation that is surplus to our requirements you must discuss the matter with our Estates Department. The office is down the corridor on the left. You'll see the notice on the door. I do assure you that all our business has to be formal."

Charlie looked down at her and smiled happily. "Gotcha Chairman - one word from you and the Head Sirag and it's as good as fixed. I'll tell them you sent me."

Chapter 11

Dennis glared at the papers on his desk, his red highlighter pen poised over the list of applications for regional funding.

"How long before Marton Health Authority accept that we are not going to fund an A&E unit at the General?"

"The MP is campaigning for it." Malcolm Yates reminded him.

"Bob Reath knows very well that there is a fully equipped A&E department at Charrington, only a few miles away. Anyhow, he's got a safe seat."

"Thirty-eight miles away, actually, "His Chief Executive corrected him, ignoring the politics "Last week the local press ran a front page report on the death of a motorcyclist who died before the ambulance could get to the A&E department at Charrington. The swing-bridge was closed and it took two hours to get there."

"Not much traffic on the ship-canal these days," stated Dennis tartly. "That's just one case, and he'd have probably died anyway."

Malcolm raised his eyebrows in horror.

From the Church of St. Nicholas and our Lady the carillon rang out above the city streets.

Dennis grimaced. "Wouldn't be so bad if they changed the tune from time to time."

"If there's a major accident on the motorway, this side of the bridge..." persisted Yates. "It's a bad place for accidents. There was a pile up in the fog last autumn - a young girl was killed...you remember that letter from her mother?"

"Can't afford it - and that's that." Dennis's

highlighter moved swiftly, scoring a bright red streak through the Marton application.

"Number twenty-seven." Although it was only noon, Malcolm Yates already felt weary as he read out the application. He could guess what the outcome of this one would be. "A four-bedded specialist M.E. research unit at the Royal Infirmary, part funded by the Medical School."

"M.E. unit? What's that? Never heard of it."

"We've only got three cases in this region, but there are several hundred altogether and it's on the increase. We could be the first research centre in the country."

"But what is it?" interrupted Dennis.

"Myalgic encephalomyelitis...It used to be known as Yuppie Flu - ."

"Oh - I've heard of that. We'd be the laughing stock, using taxpayers' money to carry out research on layabouts who prefer to stay in bed all day watching television, too idle to do a day's work!"

"They've now decided that it is a genuine illness, probably viral ..."

"Huh! And who are 'they' ?"

Dennis's red highlighter bit deep into the paper. "Next one?"

"Twenty-eight. The last one. Two dialysis machines for the City General."

Dennis reached for his pen. "The Dialysis Support Group has done a good job there. I promised we would match them pound for pound." He ticked the application.

"They'll need to fund a specialist nurse..."

"We're funding machines, not staff." Dennis eased himself out of the chair and stomped off out of the office towards his private lavatory which, just lately, he

85

had to visit more often and spend much longer there than he liked. "I'll see Burton next. Send him in."

Michael Burton settled himself in the black leather-padded swivel chair in front of the Chairman's desk, and gratefully accepted the cup of coffee that Lisa set in front of him. He had been Chairman of an Area Health Authority for more than seven years and when other Chairmen had so often fallen victims to Dennis Deane's irascible moods, he had always managed to achieve a degree of harmony and understanding, even though at times he had been driven to disagree with the Dennis's point of view. At sixty-six he was the most senior of all the Area Chairmen, and the only one who felt comfortable enough to call Dennis Deane by his Christian name.

Dennis lumbered through the door into his office, hitching up his trousers and adjusting his zip. Collapsing heavily into his chair, he swivelled it around to face his desk then reached for a file and flipped it open.

Ignoring the niceties of a greeting he plunged into the morning's business... "I've just come back from Kent. There's a young fellow there, brilliant chap, hospital manager. Big hospital, trauma-unit, Regional cardio-thoracic unit, MRI, you know the sort of thing. You name it, they've got it. He's looking for a Chief Executive's job. I want you to take him on..."

"Take him on? What as? We can't afford extra staff."

"To   replace   that   fellow   ...   what's   his name...Wheeler."

"Replace my Chief Exec?   But he's not leaving - is he ?"

"I'm sorry to come at you like this but you have to

admit that Wheeler's had his day. ...been with you far too long... I want you to talk to him. Get him to take early retirement."

Michael, unable to believe what was happening, saw Dennis's hard glittering eyes, lined face, RN tie, although he had never been in any of the services, and soft white manicured hands that lay on the desk in front of him. He'd heard of this happening to other Health Authority chairmen, men who relied on their Chief Execs, who looked on them as friends. The Management Executive in London never did tolerate cosy relationships and usually moved in to break them up. The message was clear but unspoken, either he goes or you go. It was always the closest and the best teams that got broken up. Sometimes if the Chief Exec. was outstanding he was head-hunted, picked out for promotion to a bigger hospital or authority. Now it was happening to him. They were vulnerable pawns on the NHS chess board under threat of perpetual check by the Management Executive in London and the Regional Chairman in his seven storey tower block

Black's move. Only a few games end in checkmate. Most end with the resignation of one player because his position is hopeless, or his forces have been reduced to decisive inferiority by captures.

"Graham Wheeler has been with us six years -"

Black Knight cannot be obstructed by intervening pieces

"Long enough!"

"We operate as a team. We're a good team. We've always balanced our budget   - provided all the services you asked for -"

"You need new blood."

"Carried out Government policies -"

87

Dennis watched him closely and saw a man past his prime, startled, unprepared for change. If he obstructed his plans he too would be overtaken

"You need a fresh approach, new ideas. Time for a change Michael!"

"Dennis - for goodness sake - this is change for changes sake. Don't break up the team! If Graham wants to retire ok, but I'll be sorry to lose him..."

"If he won't take early retirement we'll find him something –

White's move

"His contract's still got three years to run..."

"We'll find him a job at Region."

"Yes, I know the form, "Michael spoke wearily. "He'll be sent out on secondment, or as an acting Chief Exec. if someone is taken ill, or he'll be given a special project to work on. Eventually, who knows, if he proves valuable, he could be offered a permanent job. In the meantime you've taken away his self respect and turned him into a boot-licker, anxious to do anything just to keep himself in a job."

Dennis stared at him. He'd allowed Michael Burton to stay too long in the job. As Regional Chairman one thing he could never put up with was resistance to change. It was a dangerous attitude. He needed men around him who challenged complacency, men of ideas; men who never slept but used the midnight hours to produce papers that questioned the thinking of Whitehall and came up with the answers. Questions and answers that he as Regional Chairman would be able to make use of. Burton was the longest serving Chairman in the Region and he had run out of ideas and was living with a seven year old attitude to seven year old problems.

"Tell Wheeler that I'm offering him the choice - early retirement or a job at Region."

Check.

Michael stood up, his cup of coffee, cold and untouched. "I need to think it over." He paused and glared at the Regional Chairman. "I offered him the job and I signed his contract. I'll talk to him and the Board. Then I'll get back to you."

Michael put down his briefcase and searched in his pocket for the key to his office. In the past, the sign on the door 'Chairman' and his name in the slot beneath, had given him a feeling of satisfaction. How much longer would his name plate remain on the door? Although he was Chairman of the Health Authority he was no longer in control. The controller was Dennis Deane, a power crazed Mikado, in a seventh floor office in down-town Argyll House; carrying out the diktats of Whitehall mandarins, in the certain expectation of an even higher reward or, at the very least, another gong.

He remembered the late Richard Crossman saying that when he stood for election to a local authority he believed that that was where the power lay- but it was not there. Then when he stood for parliament he thought he would find it in the corridors of Westminster, but it was not there either.

Dennis was, after all, in a constant search for more power. Would he ever find it, and in the end, was the search really worth it? Maybe those MPs who unexpectedly announced their decision to retire, 'to spend more time with their families' had it right, although other motives were usually attributed to them - a secret that was likely to be revealed about their private lives, or a court case that was pending.

His secretary, Cathy, hurried down the corridor, one cup of tea and one cup of black coffee on a tray. "Have you time to see Mr Wheeler, Chairman?"

They sat down opposite each other on either side of the round, glass-topped NHS coffee table, in low wooden armchairs upholstered in green plastic, as supplied for all offices and waiting rooms.

Graham Wheeler leaned forward, his tall, thin frame resting on bony knees clad in navy pin-striped trousers. Freshly laundered white shirt, cuffs just showing beyond the sleeves of his jacket, colourful geometric M&S tie. The overhead light glinted on his spectacles and the highlights in his stylish close-cut hair.

"I had a call last night from Malcolm Yates."

Michael waited.

"Asked me if I had ever thought of taking early retirement..."

Michael, lips pursed, stared at the damp circle that his saucer had left on the table top.

"Chairman - was it your idea?"

Michael shook his head. "Not at all. It's Dennis Deane's idea.. He seems to think it's time you moved on. I told him that I didn't agree with him. I'm sure that everyone will be horrified when they hear."

"Move on? Where to - Region? Retirement? I've got three years of my contract left, and I'm only fifty-five. Why? Did he give any reason?"

Michael sat back and looked squarely at his Chief Exec. In the car, on his way back to the office he'd made his decision. If he opposed the wishes of the Regional Chairman he would almost certainly be replaced. If he went along with Dennis Deane's plan it would be the first of many times that he would be expected to continue to do so. He'd smiled to himself at the thought of the list that was lying in a drawer in his desk. In a rare and idle moment of introspection, when he reached the age of fifty, he had written out a list of all the things he still wanted to do during his lifetime. He'd accomplished none of them, and on that list were things that he was already too old to attempt.

"Graham, I'm not asking you to apply for early retirement - unless of course you want to … I know that all the Board members will agree with me. They won't want to see you go. I'll talk to them, and if they're of the same opinion I'll write to Dennis Deane and tell him that we intend to keep you. It is after all our decision, not his. I am the person who appointed you, and it's my duty as Chairman to appoint or dismiss the Chief Executive of the authority."

Michael saw a glimmer of relief cross Graham's face, only to be replaced by a worried, uncertain look.

"But you? You'll be replaced if you oppose the Regional Chairman. I suppose I could work at Region, although it is known to everyone as 'the dustbin.' Anyone who's sacked works out their time there...I've always pitied them...three years at Region...what a way to end. Where did it go wrong?"

"We didn't do anything wrong Graham... we just made the mistake of working too well together...there was no friction...friction's what they like. As far as I'm concerned, I've got a damned good Chief Exec. When I go to meetings and conferences I meet other Chief Execs - and I'll tell you this Graham - I wouldn't pay them in washers! There'll be no change as long as I'm Chairman. "

Less than half an hour after Malcolm Yates had left the Regional Chairman's room the phone in Bob

Reath's Westminster office rang. His secretary, Kathleen, took the call. She recognised the voice that called regularly from Mercia Regional Headquarters and put the caller on hold whilst she paged the M.P. who scribbled notes on his memo pad as he listened to his informant.

"Application for an A and E department at Marton General, Labour seat – refused. Application for a M.E. Unit at Royal Infirmary, Labour seat – refused. Dialysis unit for the City General, Tory seat – approved. Queenswood Hall to be closed and sold. Old people are to be given notice to quit - next week - just weeks before the election. They're moving them into a home that's to be built at a place called Parker's Paddock on the edge of town. "

"I'll get on to the Gazette."

Bob strode down the corridors and took the stairs two at a time. The office was empty. Kathleen had gone for lunch, which was lucky. He preferred to make these calls without being overheard. It was safer to use his mobile anyway. He punched in the number for the Morning Gazette and asked for Henry Pye. Good relationships with the press were always a protection from parliamentary man-hunts, drip feeding inside information, the first when it came to breaking news, who was for the chop in reshuffles. The stuff that sold papers to home-going commuters on the streets and in newspaper kiosks.

Following the takeover there had been staff changes at the Gazette. Henry had been lucky to keep his old job, dealing with day to day news and Obits. He'd worked for the tabloid for thirty years, almost as long as Bob had been an M.P. for his inner city constituency. Together they'd established a working relationship that

92

suited them both.

"I'll need photographs of those three hospitals." said Henry thoughtfully. "It's probably worth a visit...I could do with a few days off... take a look at Parker's Paddock - that name rings a bell."

Chapter 12

The navy Lancia turned off the lane and slowly negotiated its way along the rutted, pot-holed drive. For Paul the Old Rectory provided a welcome retreat, where Erica waged a constant battle against rain and wind, replacing broken roof tiles and replenishing log baskets in the stone-flagged corridors to feed the fires. Leather sofas and armchairs draped with throws lent an air of comfort, and back numbers of week-end papers, stacked on the living room floor, provided hours of reading, as well as beds for two liver and white Springer spaniels and a tortoiseshell cat. As well as all that, Erica was a marvellous cook.

Widowed, more than four years ago, Erica had flung herself, with enthusiasm into the social life of the Conservative party, helping to organise money-raising events and giving dinner-parties. It was all part of a plan to relieve the loneliness, and the aching sadness of her husband's death from Motor Neurone Disease. As the sharp edge of her sorrow dulled, and she reached her fortieth birthday she re-assessed her plans and decided that a new life should, as the song put it, 'begin at forty.'

Paul parked in front of the stone Georgian rectory, allowing himself to smile at the thought of all the papparazzi camped outside the apartment block in town. Word would have spread that he had left London. That would be the last they knew of his whereabouts.

When Erica had phoned him and invited him for the weekend, his only disappointment was that she had also invited someone else as well.

"Someone who I'm sure you will find useful." Paul detected a note of mystery in her voice.

A maroon Mercedes crunched onto the gravel. As it parked alongside the Lancia two springer spaniels appeared around the side of the house, barking a greeting.

Paul's heart sank as he saw the driver extract a case from the boot. He had hoped for a weekend alone with Erica.

The stranger smiled, patted both dogs and strode ahead towards the door with the assurance of a man who was a frequent visitor and knew that he was welcome.

"I didn't need to change, did I?"

Erica smiled warmly at Paul as she turned and presented them with their drinks. "Gin and dry, and Tom Collins. Got it right, have I?"

"But the long skirt?" questioned the new-comer.

"When you live in a draughty old rectory it's either trousers or long skirts. You folk who have centrally-heated luxury flats in town have no idea how the rest of us manage to survive... Paul..." To his surprise, she took his arm. "Meet Samuel Madrugada, barrister, who spends all his waking hours fighting injustice and serving libel actions"

Samuel put down his case and carefully arranged his suede coat over the back of a settee. He was tall and stout, with a solemn, round face, and gave the impression of a middle-aged man who seriously appreciated food. It crossed Paul's mind that here was someone who preferred the theatrical performance of a five course menu and an impressive wine list, presented by a maitre d'hotel in a splendid dining-room, surrounded by a team of waiters, and supported by an echelon of cooks with a batterie-de-cuisine, rather than a plate of pasta and a Chianti Classico Reserva in a small Italian restaurant.

Samuel stuck out his hand. "I've been looking forward to meeting you."

"I need to explain..." Erica quickly took charge of the situation. "Sam represents The Campaign for Personal Freedom, the CPF. I'm sure you heard of it?"

"The three freedoms," Paul thought quickly. "Freedom of Choice, Privacy, and..."

"Justice." Erica reminded him gently as she waved him towards a chair. She manoeuvred her armchair close beside him. "Now I have a confession to make and I wouldn't blame you one bit if you accused me of interfering and walked out right away."

Unsure of what was to follow Paul managed an apprehensive smile.

Sam collapsed heavily into his armchair in front of the fire, leaned forward to unlock his case and selected a file. He passed a letter across to Paul. "These are the aims of our campaign and you will see that if you wish we will work with you to take up your case against the Gazette. The Campaign has offered to fund the full costs if I decide to take up the case and bring a libel action against the paper..."

"Please don't think we're interfering. We'd like to help," Erica said.

Sam nodded gravely. "Erica's husband, James, and I were in the same chambers for years and she and I still keep in touch. In fact we see each other quite often. You've certainly impressed her..." He paused and looked at Erica for confirmation.

She spoke hesitantly. "When I saw the report in the press I phoned Sam immediately – perhaps I should

96

have asked you first?" She reached out and began to stroke one of her dogs as if seeking reassurance.

. "She said she had every faith in you, that the Gazette was wicked and that you weren't that sort of chap. I have to tell you...I have great faith in Erica's judgement."

Waiting for Paul's reaction, Erica hurriedly explained. "Sam's probably the only person that has! But there are an awful lot of people who are only too happy to believe the worst - even Constituency chairmen..."

"But his Press statement?" asked Paul.

"Oh that was the Agent's doing. Dennis Deane is blinkered and dogmatic... a dyed in the wool, traditional Tory...the Chairman of a traditional Tory constituency." she shrugged her shoulders, "and that's being kind."

Erica led the way down the draughty corridor into the oak panelled dining-room. Following behind her, enjoying the scent of her perfume that hung in her wake and following behind the confident, solid dark-suited shape of Samuel Magrugada Paul experienced the first small sense of comfort and reassurance that he was no longer on his own having to face the censure of the press and the public, and even his friends. Of course he already had plenty of advice from his Agent and the party's legal advisors, but there again; the Chairman hadn't even bothered to phone.

Paul stood and watched as Erica removed the fireguard and replenished the logs. Sparks fled skywards up the wide chimney as the fire crackled and his sense of comfort and reassurance slowly developed into a kind of happiness.

97

Throughout the meal the discussion became intense and even diverted Sam's attention from Erica's excellent roast partridge. Nevertheless, Paul reminded himself, he must remember to congratulate her later, when he hoped that they'd be alone.

"There'll be publicity, the CPF will see to that, television interviews, front-page headlines, but it's all necessary. You'll become a public figure. Can you handle it? More important, can you handle public disapproval and the inevitable link with Gay Rights?"

"That began a long time ago. I wish I had never joined the Scouts!"

"If you hadn't joined the Scouts they'd have found something else to pin on you. How did it all start?"

"Shall I go and wash up?" asked Erica tactfully.

"No, stay. I want you to hear." Paul sighed. "I was so naive – but in those days It was all so stupid!"

Erica sat with her eyes fixed on Paul, her elbows on the table, the empty coffee cups pushed aside, waiting...

"I enjoyed the Scouts, liked the company and the outdoor life. Most boys left after a few months - got interested in other things – football... girls... you know...anyway, I collected quite a lot of badges, got rather keen, and then became a Scout Leader. I was seventeen at the time and took a party of ten to a Jamboree camp at Tatton Park in Cheshire." He frowned and hesitated, studying Erica's face for her reaction.

"And - ?" urged Sam.

"I'm trying to remember!" protested Paul. "It's twenty years ago...It was a big site...parkland, with lakes. I had to keep a close eye on everyone. We had two boys who had never been away from home before. One was young and homesick... We cooked sausages over a camp fire and after the usual sing-song they turned in. There were some high jinks going on in the tents, and I had to go around quietening things down. The young boy, Tim, was crying...two others were mocking him, and he wanted to go home. Well of course it was too far and much too late - also very dark, so I helped him to move his clothes and his sleeping bag into my tent..." Again he hesitated.

"And so –" persisted Sam.

"So he did-"

"And?"

"Don't rush me," Paul began to smooth out the napkin that he had clutched during the interrogation.

"Give him time..." Erica spoke gently and nodded her head encouragingly.

"Well at first he settled down, then after a bit he began to shiver and started crying again - so I told him to get dressed properly."

"Did you help him?"

"Yes."

"How could you see?"

"I had a torch. It was moonlight and there were lights outside the tent. He was in his underpants and shirt. None of them had pyjamas..."

"Did you fasten-up his trousers?"

In the silence Paul could hear Erica breathing. Her eyes were fixed on him and he watched the expression on her face as he spoke.

"I can remember that the zip stuck, and the top buttons were stiff. His trousers were new - he'd only been in the troop four weeks."

"Did you do anything you shouldn't?" Sam's voice was harsh, "Like, put your hands anywhere you shouldn't?"

Paul stared at them both. "I did not."

"Answer me again. Did you do anything like that? I have to know."

"I did nothing at all like that. I never touched him... I did nothing wrong – nothing I would be ashamed of. Foolishly I helped him to dress – I never gave it a thought – after all it was twenty years ago."

"And after?" Samuel persisted. "What happened then?"

"He got back into his sleeping-bag, and I got into mine. Then, to keep him warm I covered him with a spare blanket."

"That's all? You're sure that he got into his own sleeping bag – not yours?"

Paul nodded. "Sure. You couldn't fit two into it. It would be impossible."

"And next day?"

"He was ok. It was only a one night camp - we went home. One week later the police called, and took me to the Station for questioning."

Erica let out a sigh of relief, "And that's all that happened?"

"That's all. No more than that."

Paul turned to Erica. "If you're both content with what I've told you then I'd be grateful for your help."

"Can we meet again next week, in town? I need to talk to the police – find out what they have on their records." Sam extracted a diary from his case. "Friday afternoon? I've heard you chaps shut up shop on Thursdays." He jotted down the arrangements, snapped the diary shut and closed the case. "I've got a long journey back - unless, of course you need a hand with the washing up."

"There's a dish-washer in the kitchen - anyway Paul

100

will give me a hand."

"Rather thought he would," said Sam, and bent to give Erica a lengthy kiss. "By the way - meant to tell you, you're wearing a ra-ther seductive perfume."

They stood side by side in the hallway. As Sam drove away Erica reached for Paul's hand. "I never doubted you for one minute," she said, lifting his hand to her lips.

As he drove through the lanes towards The Heath Agricultural College, Paul began to feel more cheerful. The college, under the control of West Mercia County Council, trained young farmers and horticulturalists as well as running courses for agricultural machinery engineers and the dairy industry. Just getting away from Westminster and London was a rest cure in itself. The sun was shining, and new bright green hawthorn leaves were showing on the hedges. Daffodils were in bud, their heads still pointing spear-like to the sky, and birds were singing. Spring had burst forth full of promises, and best of all, Erica had appeared on the scene, enthusiastic to solve his problems. The heavy weight of anxiety that had lain like a dark cloud, pressing down upon him, had lessened. Two big guns, the Law and public opinion were being primed for action, and last night, sitting by the fire, after that barrister with the funny name that he couldn't remember, had gone, Erica had kissed him - again - twice in one night. Of course it might have been in sympathy, like kissing a child better, but it certainly made him feel a lot better.

George Barnett, Principal of the college, had invited him to look around and have lunch. Paul had no illusions about the reason for the invitation - finance.

All colleges and universities were invariability short of money. 'Under resourced' was the usual description, and that meant that important courses planned for many years ahead by the Governing Body were in danger of being closed and hundreds of students turned away. He followed the signs to 'Visitors Car Parking'. Outside the redbrick administrative building, a student was on duty, waiting to lead him to the Principal's office.

"I propose we take a walk and look at the buildings and machinery workshop before lunch." suggested George Barnett.

The Principal was a short, stocky man, in his forties, prematurely balding, wearing a shapeless tweed jacket. With leather patches at the elbows and bulging pockets it had seen better days. Paul had seen smarter clothing on scarecrows. He wondered what was so special about Barnett that he had been chosen for the position of Principal rather than farm labourer.

Barnett glanced down at Paul's well-shined shoes. "It's clean concrete out there, hosed down every morning. You don't need boots."He led the way through the agricultural machinery workshops where students dismantled and repaired tractors and harvesters. Pasted on the breeze-block walls lurid posters depicted the hazards of operating farm machinery, and listed the safety regulations in garish colours. They paused for a while in the calf sheds and the lambing area then crossed the yard to the pig unit.

Two heavy wooden doors, rotten at the base, the ochre paint blistered and flaking, squealed as George Barnett hauled them apart on their iron wheels.The stench of months of accumulated pig manure hit them. Roof ventilators whirred and clattered noisily, making little impact on the heat and the intolerable stink. Paul's eyes watered and for a few seconds he managed to hold his breath. The Principal led the way and turning to one side lifted a rotten wooden flap so that they could peer beneath. Inside, fifty or sixty young pigs milled around in the dark in thick mud, pushing, squealing and blinking at the light that filtered through cobwebbed windows into the pen.

Paul wrinkled his nose at the rank smell. "Good God. Why on earth do you allow this?"

"Short of space." George Barnett dusted the dirt from his hands and rubbed them down the sides of his jacket.

"You mean there's nowhere else to keep them?"

The Principal nodded. "There's no other place. Let me tell you - three years ago we applied to build a new unit. It was approved at a cost of only sixty thousand pounds. Last year the scheme was axed - no money. Can you believe it? It's frightful, isn't it?"

"Then why keep pigs at all, in these conditions?"

"We have to - to teach young farmers."

"So you teach young farmers to keep pigs in these conditions?"

On the other side of the concrete path that ran through the building sows, heavily in-pig were confined to farrowing crates on slats, unable to turn round, grunting, and grinding their teeth in boredom on the metal rungs in front of them.

"I thought farrowing crates had been phased out ?" Paul shook his head in disbelief at the conditions.

"Same story Paul - no money." replied the Principal, as he closed the wooden flap that was caked with manure, confining the young pigs to darkness once again.

"It's like the Black Hole of Calcutta." said Paul as they walked out into the bright spring sunlight.

Opposite, the door of a brick building swung in the breeze. Paul glanced inside. On the concrete floor lay a dead pig, bloated and caked in mud.

"What happened to that?" Paul asked.

The Principal shook his head. "We're waiting for a post mortem."

"When you get the report send me a copy..." Paul hesitated. "You brought me here deliberately...what do you expect me to do? Go to the press?"

George Barnett shook his head. "Oh dear me no. Whatever you do, don't do that, there's a good fellow."

"Why not?"

"Animal Rights - they raided a battery unit the other day. They're quite frightful, worse than the hunt sabs. If they get to hear of it, they'll raid the place! No, no, just get on to your party colleagues on the County Education Committee. Get them to cut something else out of their budget. It's big enough in all conscience, six million pounds for education.... There must be something they can cut out."

"Have they seen the pig unit.?"

"I took them in - but they hurried out - said there was no money. They ate their lunch and left."

The lunch that awaited Paul in the staff dining-room, had already lost its appeal. He realised that it would be paid for out of the college budget, under the code 'hospitality'. After a meeting with the Heads of Departments, he drove back into town, back to his own home and was relieved to see that the house was not under siege by the press as he feared it might be. Had it been so he might have been tempted to have directed them to the college where a better story would be

104

waiting for them.

He sat at his desk leafing through the booklet that listed all the members of the West Mercia County Council, and marked a large cross by the name Harold Tuck, Chairman of The Heath Agricultural College and Chairman of the Education Buildings sub-Committee. Paul gazed out of the window at the velvet green lawn, bright under the afternoon sunshine, imagining it filled with happy little piglets.

Several days later Dennis was surprised to get a phone call from Harold Tuck. Dennis knew him well; they met at Party meetings and dinners. Both were farmers, with large acreages and well managed coverts for the Hunt, and both were members of the Country Landowners Association.

Harold, Chairman of the neighbouring constituency of West Allingham, short, stout and in his seventies, had a large, round red face with matching thick round glasses. His chubby fingers grasped the receiver tightly as he voiced his annoyance through fleshy lips.

"That young chap of yours - what's his name - you know...the M.P. fellow."

"You mean Rugglestone ?"

"Yes him... You'll have to bring him to heel... He's interfering in County business. Wants me to find money to build a new pig unit...Can't be done, you know."

Dennis gulped down his evening whisky, and lifted the heavy decanter to refill his glass. "Well I'm sure you told him. So, what's the problem?"

"The problem is..." blustered Harold, "He's threatened us with the Press, and the Animal Rights Movement...That's the trouble with these youngsters, they're anthro...what's the word...? Anthro...po...morphic." Harold sounded jubilant that he had remembered the word. "That's the word...they treat animals like humans. Well he's put me in a bit of a fix. I can't risk it getting to the press. Okay, we need a new pig unit - I've said so for years - after all I am Chairman of the Governors of the Heath College, and it's in our plans for the future, when we can afford it So, call him off. Talk some sense into him, there's a good chap."

Dennis sipped his whisky thoughtfully. He really didn't want to talk to Rugglestone. He didn't care for the fellow at all. But he wasn't going to admit to anyone else that he had a problem. He'd pass the word to the Agent - John Brown would sort out Rugglestone. With talk of a snap election next year they could do without publicity like this.

"I'll see what I can do." he promised

"Another thing," continued Harold, "he's asked George Barnett for a Vet's report on a dead pig he saw. Barnett fobbed him off...told him it would take some time, Post Mortem, Path Lab reports etcetera. Actually, we've got the report already and I've got a copy. Of course I suppose he could get a copy himself as an M.P. but at the moment we're playing for time."

The light was fading, and Dennis switched on the desk light, " Why? What's it say ?"

"That's the trouble...It says 'Death caused by viral pneumonia, due to overcrowding.' "

Dennis sucked in breath noisily. "If I were you old chap, I'd try to find something else to cut from your budget."

"I don't tell you how to manage the health service, and I don't expect you to tell me how to manage

106

County business." retorted Harold.

"And I don't phone you up for help." boomed Dennis, before replacing the receiver.

Chapter 13

The queue for platform 12 snaked the length of the Euston concourse, and back again. Dennis, annoyed at the delay, elbowed his way through the crowd towards the bookstall. By the time he had bought an Evening Standard the queue had started to shuffle forwards. He joined it, impatient to claim his seat.

He was annoyed to find that his reserved seat was one of four. The three other seats were also reserved and the table set for dinner. He wedged his briefcase beside him against the arm rest, and unfolded the evening paper.

"Waiting lists out of control" screamed the headline. Dennis read on. "Frank Fenwick, M.P. for Tottenham, yesterday claimed that the London Hospitals had lost control of their waiting lists, and their total budgets were ten million pounds overspent. In a debate in the Commons, he called on the Secretary of State for Health to make a statement to the House on NHS provision in the Capital."

As his dining companions took their seats and the waiter wrote down his order Dennis acknowledged their presence and chose from the menu.

He leaned back in his seat, watching the rivulets of rain racing each other across the window, blurring the view of Harrow and Wealdstone, and Watford. Playing-fields and gardens faded from view as amber street lights and fluorescent tubes in office blocks flickered and illuminated the blue-grey afternoon.

The morning's meeting at Richmond House had been entirely satisfactory. It was how he expected

Government business to be carried out. Now he was on the inside. He smiled with pleasure as he remembered the warm welcome from the Secretary of State "…Dennis, with his years of experience, his important contribution to our discussions…"

The rattle of the tea trolley; the Permanent Secretaries on the other side of the long table. he stuffy room, unrelieved by any ventilation, grimy windows closed to shut out the noise of Whitehall traffic.All his colleagues in shirt sleeves, including the Minister, chortling, confident.

"So, who's got any spare cash?"

They laughed, supposing it to be a joke, but it wasn't.

"Lend me every spare penny you've got, and I'll pay you twelve months interest on an overnight loan. Just for one night - you'll never get a better offer!"

Tea-cups clattered onto saucers as the twelve Regional Chairman listened carefully. Departmental secretaries flanking the Minister smiled at their astonished looks. It had all started off as a joke when they had met to draft a statement in reply to Frank Fenwick. Someone, no-one would now admit to it, had light-heartedly suggested that if every health authority in the country were to lend their spare cash overnight on the 31st March to the London Hospitals, they would balance their budgets at the end of the financial year, and the health authorities would be laughing all the way to the bank.

Then suddenly, to everyone's surprise, the idea was taken seriously. During the heated discussion that followed, one doubter dared to warn that the plan could be construed as money laundering, but he was hastily corrected by a lecture from the Permanent Secretary on the merits of creative accounting.

Now the Minister was actually instructing the Regional Chairmen to go back to their health authorities and offer them a deal. It might even mean that some may negotiate a bank loan at a cheaper rate, but was anyone going to question the means, just as long as the auditors were happy? All governments operated with their eyes firmly focused on the next election, and the next election was imminent. Obviously the department's Permanent Secretaries must have been given the green light by their colleagues at the Treasury, otherwise they would have advised the Minister against the course of action. Maybe they had even suggested the idea. The thought made Dennis smile and he began to tot up the amount he might extract from the thirteen health authorities in Mercia region. Mercia, one of the smaller regions, always managed to head the league when it came to performance on matters such as waiting-lists, efficiency savings, post-operative deaths, and cancelled operations. He was determined it would keep that position. Being top of the league meant that recognition was a dead cert. in the New Year or Birthday Honours.

The waiter leaned across and removed the empty soup bowl. Dennis hardly remembered drinking his mushroom soup, but supposed he must have enjoyed it. Around the table the others were silently engaged, reading documents, and correcting papers, as they dined. The air of concentration was abruptly interrupted by the ringing of a mobile phone. The three looked up accusingly, annoyed by the unwelcome disturbance, and irritated that they would be obliged to listen to another's conversation no matter how uninterested they were. Dennis wished he had phoned his Chief Executive before boarding the train, but as he had arrived on the platform the train was about to pull out. He unzipped his briefcase, extracted the phone, and stared down at the offending instrument, trying to remember which button to press. He'd owned the thing two weeks before he'd used it, calling Edith to say he would be late back. All of his colleagues and the staff in the office had mobiles. They left them lying on the table at meetings and hurried from the board room to take calls. A mobile seemed to go with the job, so they fixed him up with one. Yesterday he had told Malcolm Yates that he would phone him after the meeting.

Whilst Dennis was trying to decide which button to press, the man next to him sighed with annoyance, balanced his documents on his lap, reached across and impatiently pressed the 'O.K' button.

Dennis acknowledged the help and pressed the phone to his ear.

"Chairman?" Malcolm's voice sounded impatient, "Next week's agenda - will you give a report on your meeting with the Secretary of State? The Agendas must go out tonight."

Dennis cleared his throat in embarrassment. "Yes. Put an item on the agenda - something short - Chairman's report would do. I'll phone you later this evening with the news. You'll be interested - give you the weekend to think about it." He tried to speak quietly but was forced to shout above the noise of conversation in the carriage and the waiter, who serving mixed grill to all four diners, scraped the gravy from the serving dish with a metal spoon.

"Queenswood Hall, Chairman. Can you hear me?

111

It's been sold - three hundred and twenty-five thou....that'll put the Marton budget in the black."

"Who's bought it?"

"Geoffrey Tate - for a private nursing home. Thought you'd be interested."

"My dinner's getting cold. I'll phone you back later."

"O.K. Enjoy!"

Dennis stared at the silent phone, and this time managed to remember which button to press to end the call. 'Enjoy!' What sort of a goodbye was that?

A week later the Chairmen of the thirteen Mercia health authorities gathered in small groups around the Board Room. Sober men, in dark suits, most of them stout and wearing glasses. In their sixties they had taken early retirement as senior executives in one of the country's biggest petro-chemical industries. They had managed their departments from offices on the outskirts of the industrial zone where the smell of chemicals hung permanently in the air; and chimneys and cooling towers spewed acrid pollutants into the skies above housing estates where the workers and their families lived.

Sipping cheap NHS coffee and leaving half cups of the undrinkable liquid to go cold on the side table, they concentrated on the chocolate biscuits and pink wafers. Some had already reserved their seats at the horseshoe table, draping their jackets over the chair backs and leaving agendas, minutes and mobile phones on the blotters set out around the table.

Dennis limped into the Board Room. His back had kept him awake most of the night, and was still paining him, but it was not bad enough to distract his attention from the assembled chairmen. He made his way to his seat, glancing around at the small groups, noting who was talking to who.

With a brief nod he acknowledged the offer of a cup of coffee from Malcolm Yates, and taking a small brown bottle from his pocket extracted two pain-killers.

"Item one. Apologies?" he barked.

He steered the meeting through the agenda. Item two - minutes of the last meeting. "All agreed?"

Matters arising.

Item three. Gold paper 'D'. Waiting lists. The same inner city hospitals, with the same problems. The numbers on the waiting-list for surgery at the Royal Infirmary had increased.

Dennis scowled at Jim Fowler, Chairman of the Hospital Management Committee. "We're pouring money into a bottomless pit!"

He looked down the table at Mcgowan, the Waiting List Czar. "Get down there and sort things out."

He turned back to Fowler. "Sorry Jim, but if you can't organise the work, then we'll have to take over."

James Fowler bowed his head, accepting the criticism and the sympathetic looks from around the table.

"Green paper 'C'. Authority budgets." Dennis stared down through his half moon spectacles at the list. "Good thing we got you sorted out over Queenswood Hall, Barbara."

He glanced at the Director of Finance. "What about the others? There's a few running close to the wind?"

Tony Bradshaw smiled reassuringly. "As usual it's the wrong time of the month, Chairman. If we'd been meeting one week later, those figures would have looked a lot better. Salaries and wages have been paid

113

out and income is expected tomorrow. It's the usual end of the month cash flow problem."

"Are you suggesting that we should alter the dates of our meetings to accommodate the cash flow problems of three hospitals?" Dennis laughed at his own question, and every Chairman seated around the table joined in the laughter, showing their appreciation of his wit.

"Pink paper 'A'. Manpower." Dennis flicked over the pages. "Take a look at the appendix. The chairmen shuffled through the pages and stared obediently at the graphs and pi-charts.

The numbers are not falling fast enough. We set you a target of five percent per quarter." He stabbed at the graph with his forefinger. "This is nearer two percent!" He leaned back in his chair and searched the table. "Where's Hilary? Where's our H.R. Director?"

Hilary Mayer, tall, blonde, early thirties, stalked the length of the board-room on shapely legs to the distant flip-chart. Dennis smirked appreciatively. Who would have guessed that that long flaxen hair concealed a head for figures ? He'd stolen her from beneath the noses of two Marks & Spencer directors who were extolling her qualities during a director's business lunch at their auditors in the city.

Hilary flicked over several sheets, and with a pointer indicated figures she had prepared earlier. "Blue are early retirement figures; green - natural wastage, and red are disputed redundancies. As from today we have a two point five percent reduction in manpower. We're halfway there. By the end of the year it might reach four percent if we can agree a deal with the union over long-term sick."

Around the table heads swivelled to watch her

114

return.

"Bet he had the flip chart placed over there," whispered Michael to his neighbour, "so as he could watch her cross the room."

Her hips swung smoothly beneath the cream silk dress. Dennis beckoned, and she leaned over his shoulder, pushing her hair aside and nodding as he talked.

"Show off." sighed Michael.

Dennis grinned and rearranged his papers. "Item five. Meeting with the Secretary of State. I told him categorically that all authorities in this region will, without any doubt, balance their books at the year end; and not only that; every authority will also make a loan to the London Hospitals over night on the thirty first of March. In return, next day, you'll get back twelve months interest." He leaned back in his chair and grinned with satisfaction at the bewildered looks on the faces of those around the table.

Barbara Millar swallowed hard. The money from the Queenswood Hall sale should be safely in their bank account well before the end of March. It sounded too good to be true, but if it was, she'd forgive Dennis his moment of stupidity. Twelve months interest would go a long way to fund dialysis machines for the new kidney unit. She sat up and listened with near disbelief as Dennis continued.

"The loan would be transmitted by us at Region to the Department who would credit the accounts of the London Hospitals. They can then balance their books at the year end. Tell your Directors of Finance to arrange it with Tony."

Tony Bradshaw smiled reassuringly.

"If you play your cards right the money need not

115

even leave your account - but it would of course be shown as a debit on your statement."

"But if we went into deficit over night Chairman...?" Michael spoke slowly. "Surely it's not all that simple..."

"How you arrange it is up to you entirely." Dennis waved a hand dismissing further questions. "Talk to Tony here. He'll advise you."

Around the table the Chairmen appeared thoughtful, some frowned, puzzled, whilst others took careful notes.

Chapter 14

The Principal's house in the grounds of The Heath Agricultural College overlooked the playing fields. It seemed to George Barnett that ever since Easter it had rained non-stop. Now at the end of June the turf on the cricket pitch, despite the new land drainage scheme, was discoloured and marshy.

George tapped out the powdery stubble from his razor into the washbasin, and padded across the carpet to the bathroom cabinet for his aftershave. The glass door of the cabinet swung open at his touch reflecting the view through the bathroom window. For a moment George stood and stared, unable to understand the image that he saw in the mirror. A herd of cows were moving steadily in front of him. In disbelief he turned around. Through the window he saw the whole of the college's herd of sixty large, black and white Friesian cows advancing towards the cricket table as they plodded heavily away from the new milking parlour, through the stack yard, across the drive and on to the outfield, their empty bags swinging loosely. As he struggled to open the window George Barnett saw that the newly mown cricket table in the middle of the field was already pitted with deep hoof marks, its oozing turf wrinkled and corrugated.

Twelve bullocks, solid sturdy Herefords, their damp brown coats matted and steaming, milled around at deep square-leg, pushing and shoving against each other, turning the pitch into a muddy swamp. Wild-eyed, blowing noisily, they spotted the advancing dairy herd and set off excitably in a tumultuous charge across the field towards their cumbersome female cousins.

The flask of after-shave remained unopened as George grabbed his jacket and stumbled breathlessly from the house.

By the time the Principal arrived at the dairy unit the rain, which had fallen   steadily all night, had become torrential and staff and students in waxed jackets and wellingtons splashed across the yards towards the playing fields in ankle-deep water that bubbled from a blocked drain.

George parked the Land-Rover and reached for his boots. Remembering too late that they were in the back, he stepped down into the muddy water.

"They couldn't have chosen a better day to do it, Mr. Barnett." Giles Harvey, the Senior Lecturer, hurriedly helped him to extract the wellingtons and umbrella from the clutter in the back of the Land-Rover.

"They?" The Principal hopped on one foot as he removed a wet sock, and plunged his bare foot into a cold Wellington boot.

"Animal Rights Mr. Barnett. They've opened every gate, demolished fences, sawn through the lock of the pig unit, and released every animal we've got."

The Principal came to the conclusion that he was in the middle of one of his regular nightmares and prayed that he would wake up and find himself still in bed.

"So where are the pigs?" he asked slowly and carefully, doing his best to appear calm.

"Round the front of the Admin. Block, in the gardens."

The thought of sixty-five pigs rooting in the herbaceous borders that only last week had been planted up, in time for a visit by the Minister of Agriculture caused George to lean against the vehicle

118

for support, but forgetting that he had left open the driver's door he staggered backwards into the wet puddle that had formed on the seat and slid down on to the step in an ungainly heap.

"They're trying to round them up now, but Gracie -"

"Gracie?"

"Gracie, Mr. Barnett. The bad tempered sow has already bitten John Graham – made a nasty mess of his arm and knocked down a student. Don't worry, a doctor and vet have been called."

"Don't worry. Don't worry? What sort of advice is that?" The Principal got to his feet and slammed the door of the Land Rover in a fit of frustration.

"Phone the Chairman. Call a meeting of all Heads of Department and S.Ls this afternoon. I'll need a full report as quickly as possible from all departments, with costing for labour and materials."

"And the Press - will you make a statement?"

"How have they found out?"

"Tip-off Mr Barnett. They want a statement."

"They'll have to wait. Tell them I'll make a statement as soon as I know the full extent of the damage."

Raindrops dripping from the peak of his cap mingled with tears of fury as the Principal angrily stuck his wet hands into his pockets and marched off across the muddy fields to join the search for the escaped animals.

At the same time as George Barnett returned to his office Paul Rugglestone obeyed the disembodied voice that warned passengers at Westminster tube station to 'mind the gap' and joined the milling throng of tourists that charged en masse up the steps. He manoeuvred his way through the crowds that blocked the pavement, past stalls selling guide books to London, shiny silver heart-shaped balloons, Union Jacks, postcards and newspapers. The imposing sight of the Palace of Westminster and Big Ben glittering in the morning sunshine never failed to thrill him just as much as it did on his first day as an M.P. This morning was no different. It was one of the reasons why he liked to walk across to the House instead of using the underground passage when it was raining. The walk to and from the tube station was the only exercise he took during the week.

Japanese and American tourists swarmed in front of the black iron railings, their cameras clicking. The noise of traffic, screeching to a halt at the lights, and accelerating away, horns blaring, added to the frenzied scene. Paul enjoyed being recognized and greeted by the policeman as he walked through the gates into the Palace Yard. People stopped to stare and it gave him a feeling of importance. Once inside there were the usual reminders that he walked in the steps of great men who in the past trod the same corridors, sat in the same seats, argued in the same committee rooms and debated in the same chamber. Their statues and portraits stared down at him. To aspire to such greatness was foolhardy, but if - when he retired, or - heaven forbid lost his seat, he wanted to be able to point to something that he'd achieved as an M.P. - maybe making a memorable speech, taking part in a vital vote, or steering through a Private Member's Bill. Then he would feel that he'd made a contribution to the work of the House. Even better if one day he were able to say, just now and then, but not too often "When I was a Minister..." Despite the poor public opinion about politicians he was nevertheless proud to be an M.P. in the 'Mother of Parliaments.'

In his room, shared with two others, a pile of post awaited him. He began to sort it out, putting on one side constituency matters which he would need to discuss with John Brown. A sheet of A4, its letterhead decorated with drawings of animals, attracted his attention. The banner heading, in large green letters, bore the title 'Animal Rights - Mercia Branch.' He unfolded the paper and two colour photographs fell onto his desk. One was of a dead pig, lying exactly where he had seen it only a few days ago and the other was a flash photo taken inside the pig unit, showing the crush of small piglets, huddled together in the dark, in thick mud, snouts in the air - their bright eyes startled, gazing up at the camera. A piece of paper detached itself. Paul turned it over. It was a photocopy of a veterinary certificate, dated the day following his visit to the Heath Agricultural College. Carefully he began to read the Vet's report, muttering each word to himself under his breath. Impulsively he reached out a hand for the phone, then withdrew it. He needed time to think.

Paul studied the covering letter, and wished that the writer had made use of a word processor. The writing in green ink was almost indecipherable. "As students at The Heath Agricultural College we are aware that you visited the college last week and were able to see for yourself the dreadful conditions inside the pig unit. Many students are members of the Animal Rights Movement and we took the enclosed photographs. The vet's certificate is a photocopy of the one sent to the college Principal." The next part was heavily underlined three times in red ink. "Unless the County Council decides at its meeting next month to include a

121

replacement pig unit in its capital buildings programme we intend to send a copy of the photographs with the Vet's report to the local and national press, radio and television. Please e-mail your reply to the Branch Office."

The anonymity of the e-mail 'Batman@ animalrightsfreeline.com' held no clue to the author. The small print at the bottom of the page informed him that the writing paper, printed for the Animal Rights Movement, was produced from re-cycled paper. Paul looked at the postmark. It was posted two days ago. He smoothed out the copy of the vet's certificate and searched for the date alongside the scrawled signature. The postmortem had been carried out on the afternoon of his visit. Beneath the heading 'Cause of death' he re-read the words 'Viral pneumonia due to overcrowding.' He examined the rest of the unopened letters. There was nothing else from the The Heath Agricultural College. He sat and stared at the phone, then pulled it towards him and dialled George Barnett's number.

Harold Tuck, red-faced, breathing heavily, extracted himself from the driving seat of his Jaguar and stared in dismay at the sight of his brand new maroon Range Rover lying on its side in the ditch. Beside it, still upright, was his old pick-up truck. A lone policeman wearing a black and yellow flak jacket stood guard beside a police car. A maze of tyre tracks criss-crossed the muddy lane.

Until the police phoned Harold had not known that there had been a robbery.

"The break-down unit will be here soon," said the policeman, a note of sympathy in his voice. "It's a bad business...second robbery in the area...last week four sides of bacon and six hams disappeared from the farm shop down the road. What have you lost?"

Harold wiped his glasses. "Twenty Double Gloucester cheeses," he muttered sadly as he peered through the smashed window into the Range Rover. The radio was missing.

"CID are on their way. They'll want to get a statement from you... check out the tyre tracks and go over the vehicle for finger-prints."

"They can keep it." said Harold gloomily.

"Looks like a write-off," agreed the policeman. "Don't suppose you've got any idea who could have done it?"

"Salesmen, buyers?" Harold shrugged his shoulders. "There are always people coming and going. It's difficult to check them all Whoever it was knew where the cheese was stored, and that we were taking twenty down to London today."

"Cheeky to use your vehicles to move them." The constable stared at the Range Rover and sniffed. "It still smells of cheese inside."

The mobile in Harold's Barbour pocket trilled. His wife's voice was tense. "I've had George Barnett on the phone - wants you to phone him."

Harold Tuck tried to turn in the narrow lane, backed into a muddy gateway and bumped the gatepost. In his mud-spattered Jag he set off back to the Grange.

George sounded weary. "Thought I'd better let you know that Animal Rights have got photographs of the pig unit, the dead pig, and the vet's certificate..."

"How ?"

George Barnett sighed, "It was in my in-tray - someone must have seen it -   They've sent copies to the M.P."

Harold raised his eyes to heaven in exasperation. "Paul Rugglestone? I'll get on to him."

"Too late. He just rang to tell me that he's arranged to meet Sandy Stott at the weekend."

"Sandy who ?"

"Stott- Chairman of Animal Rights."

"Wasn't he that fellow...?"

"Yes...the chap who used to live in trees and build tunnels. Yes, he's a road protester as well. One of the great unwashed..." Barnett wrinkled his face in distaste at the thought.

"No, I mean...Wasn't there some tale about a girl he was living with?" Harold Tuck frowned as he tried to remember. "Someone told me recently..." His voice tailed off.

George Barnett listened to Henry's heavy breathing and heard the noise as Henry banged the desk. "By God - I remember - there was a tale going round that it was Dennis Deane's daughter - what's her name? Annabel...She left home and went to live with a chap who was an Animal Rights activist...His name was Stott...got some bee in her bonnet...No wonder Dennis was upset when I mentioned Animal Rights."

"Dennis?"

"Yes - you know him. Dennis Deane. He'll blow a fuse when he hears what's happened...He won't want the M.P. finding out. Someone's got to stop that fellow interfering...he'll make us all look fools."

It wasn't difficult for Paul Rugglestone to find Stott's house in Wordsworth Close on the new development known as 'The Poet's Estate.' All the streets were laid out in alphabetical order, Burns,

124

Coleridge, Keats, Longfellow, Tennyson and finally Wordsworth.

No one could be in any doubt who lived at thirty-eight. In the front garden, in place of flowers, placards of varying colours and messages sprouted from the overgrown herbaceous borders encouraging passers-by to "Say 'No' to the Bypass," "Stop terminal 5," "Ban Nuclear processing," and "Save the Seals," whilst the front door and windows were plastered with stickers that appeared to trace the history of political protest. He paused to read them. "Make love not War," "Save the Whale," "You are entering a Nuclear Free Zone," and "Ban the Bomb," were some he remembered from protest marches he had taken part in more than fifteen years ago. He pressed the bell and the tune "We shall overcome" played from a speaker above his head.

The appearance of the man who opened the door came as a surprise. Sandy Stott, even with a white bushy beard, looked less like a protester than a benevolent uncle. Thinning grey hair and twinkling brown eyes dispelled all Paul's expectations of an unwashed youth with long hair, sporting an offensive message on a faded tee-shirt. Stott didn't even wear a tee-shirt. His check viyella shirt and tweed jacket with leather patches on the elbows were years out of date.

If Paul's apprehension began to fade, it quickly returned when he was lead into what must have once been a living-room. It had already been difficult to negotiate the hallway as he was obliged to inch his way past documents piled high on every side, but once inside the living-room he could see that the walls were covered with maps and plans on which flags and push-pins identified sites and locations. Papers and documents were piled high on chairs or lay in

125

disordered heaps on the carpet. The dining-table served as a desk for a computer and printer and an untidy heap of discs, letters, pens, pencils and highlighters. In the midst of the conglomeration sat a young woman hunched over a keyboard, scowling at a monitor.

"Annabel - Paul Rugglestone, our M.P." Sandy Stott broke through her glowering concentration.

She stood up, young, immature, uncertain as to whether it would be appropriate to offer any form of greeting. The look on her face showed her intense embarrassment of finding herself in a situation where she was obliged to receive a member of the Tory party inside the house. Blonde hair that had never seen the inside of a hairdresser's salon for years, self-trimmed, standing on end, combined with the dark frames of large round spectacles gave her face an owlish effect. It crossed Paul's mind that to achieve such an appearance she must run her fingers through her hair rather than comb it. As she moved from the table he saw to his amusement the message on her black tee-shirt. Across her thin chest, in large white letters, were the words "Women need men..."

Obviously no feminist, he thought – until she turned away from him to gather up her papers – then the words on the back of her faded tee shirt dispelled his ideas "...like fishes need bicycles."

"Annabel organises all the activities," explained Sandy. Paul longed to ask how these two unlikely characters had ever got together.

She returned to her lair behind the computer. "You've had our demand - what will you do?"

Paul frowned. "Look I really do understand how you feel, and I'd like to help -"

Annabel cut him short. "It's the animals that need

126

help, not us..."

"Annie..." Sandy chided her softly. "We all have to work together.." He turned to Paul, grimaced, and shrugged his shoulders. "How about a pint ? We've a good local down the road."

Paul nodded. It might help.

"I'm coming." announced Annabel, diving frenziedly into a mound of paper lying on the floor. "Hold on a moment...." She returned to the table, triumphantly waving a sheaf of papers, "...something I wanted to show you."

"Do you think you really ought to come ?"

"I'm not going to be banned from my own local." Her words challenged Sandy to contradict her.

He turned to Paul "She was thrown out of the White Hart last week - "

"I wasn't thrown out - they asked me to leave." Annabel shouted.

"You would have been thrown out if you hadn't left there and then." Sandy sighed. "Another fox-hunting row, that's the second time. She's already been banned from The Swan."

The car park at The White Hart was already filling with cars driven by pensioners from Marton who week by week looked forward to a home cooked lunch in the cosy bar - specials on the blackboard - a glass of wine for her, a half for him and a reasonable bill that they had budgeted for in their weekly expenditure.

Behind the bar, John, the normally friendly landlord, wagged a cautionary finger. "Do you guarantee her behaviour Sandy?"

Sandy Stott put an arm around Annabel's shoulders and grinned. "Just one peep out of her..." The threat was left unsaid. "Do you know Paul Rugglestone, the

M.P.?"

The landlord reached across the bar top and shook his hand. "Can't say I voted for you, but your lot aren't doing a bad job - so far."

Over bangers and mash, sausages made by the local butcher, and onion gravy Annabel handed Paul a copy of a report which was due to be discussed by the County Council's Land and Buildings Committee the following week. It itemised the cost of refitting and refurbishment of the kitchen and dining-room, and new seating in the Council Chamber at County Hall. The total cost amounted to sixty-seven thousand pounds.

Sandy nodded as Annabel read out the Estates Department's proposals. "Just think what they could do at The Heath with that money!"

"Is it public knowledge?" asked Paul.

"Part two of the agenda - press and public excluded - not that anyone ever attends County committees unless there is something controversial on the agenda, like school closures."

"Then how did you get hold of this?"

Sandy smiled and shrugged his shoulders. "The County employs hundreds of people in its offices...we have contacts."

Annabel's voice rose. "If they refuse to build a new pig unit at The Heath we'll publish this - with the photographs."

Customers turned around to look. Sandy put his finger to his lips.

"Would it help if I set up a meeting with the Leader of the Council, plus Harold Tuck - and the Constituency Chairman." He saw Sandy and Annabel glance at each other. "It's got to be political," he explained. "The party won't want this sort of publicity with the election only weeks away. I'd like you both there."

Annabel shook her head. "Not me. Sandy O.K., but not me."

"But you're forceful...with all due respect to Sandy...you'd frighten them."

Sandy laughed. "You're right, but it's quite impossible." He shook his head. "Your Constituency Chairman, Dennis Deane, is in fact Annie's father."

Paul stared at Annabel. A less likely young woman as Dennis's daughter he would never have expected. He supposed she had been driven to rebellion by her domineering father. It sometimes happened.

Annabel nodded. "I left home last year and moved in with Sandy - "

Sandy reached across the table for Annabel's hand. "Make no mistake - I want her to marry me, but at the moment she won't. Despite what you may have heard, I'm really a very conventional chap."

"But why leave home?" asked Paul.

"Could you live in the same house as my father ?" She laughed. The laugh was hard and hollow. For the first time Paul heard the sound of bitterness and disappointment beneath her tough veneer.

"We met at Law School," explained Sandy. "I used to lecture there, part-time, on local government law. Annie feels strongly about animal rights - and human rights as well. I spend all my time trying to keep her on the straight and narrow and showing her how to channel her energies and stay within the law. She wanted to pack in her law studies but I managed to persuade her to finish the course..."

"But I wouldn't become articled."

"Well she sails too close to the wind. No firm

would want to take on an articled clerk who's a member of Animal Rights and spends all her time protesting...now I've lost my job too..."

How do you manage ?" asked Paul.

"Oh, writing books and lecturing."

"Mother helps," explained Annabel. "My Father doesn't know. I meet her for a pub lunch now and again, and she usually gives me some cash - if she can afford it, never cheques - she has a joint account, and he's very mean." She hesitated and sighed heavily. "They had terrible rows – I couldn't stand the rows – always at supper times. Every night he'd bellow at her and she'd threaten to leave him- she did once – then weakened. She came back hours later, and I left next day." Paul heard the note of distress in her voice.

"He hates me being in Animal Rights - blames everything on Sandy." She sighed, "Poor Sandy, he'll get the blame for our attack on The Heath. It was nothing to do with him - he advised against it."

"Then why?"

"They deserved it – besides - I feel I'm actually doing something." She paused for a moment and a smile lit up her face. In that instant Paul caught a glimpse of an attractive and mischievous young woman. "The pigs couldn't believe their luck; they made straight for the flower beds. The best part was letting the hens out of the battery cages...you should have seen the feathers...feathers everywhere; and their poor beaks clipped so that they can't peck. I wonder how many hens they've managed to catch ?"

Paul saw a look of admiration cross Sandy's face, but Annabel, remembering the role that she had adopted, relapsed into her usual scowl. "They won't want us to publish those photographs though. They hate that sort of publicity."

"And you couldn't have chosen a better time to threaten them with publicity," remarked Paul.

Chapter 15

At Paul's request a meeting with the County Land and Buildings sub Committee had been set up for following Thursday afternoon and Jim Blakemore, Leader of the Council, agreed to host the discussion. Dennis arrived early, before the meeting of the Planning Committee had finished. He was annoyed to discover that the car park in front of County Hall was jammed with cars decorated with stickers bearing the message "Scrap the Plan." An attendant found him a confined space in a far corner. It had an awkward access and would be even more difficult to reverse out.

On the steps, milling around the pillars, under the Bath stone portico of County Hall a crowd blocked the entrance waving placards and handing out leaflets. Babies yelled, tearful infants in pushchairs wailed and whenever anyone approached they all began to scream in unison " Scrap the Plan. Scrap the Plan."

Dennis brushed them aside. "I'm not a Councillor," he barked.

As he pushed his way through the revolving door someone pressed a leaflet into his hand.

Once inside, the foyer was a haven of peace, green rubberised flooring, and a smell of cleaning fluid. Checked and directed by Security, he made for the wide staircase that lead up to the first floor committee rooms and council chamber.

Committee room three was empty. On a side table coffee waited. He poured himself a cup and sat down to read the leaflet he had been given. It urged councillors to vote against plans to approve Areas of Search for Waste Disposal Sites in the open countryside. He supposed that fellow Sandy Stott was behind this too.

The room was long and narrow with three windows overlooking the car-park to the river beyond. Heavy mahogany tables, blotters set out on their tooled leather surfaces, and a thick green carpet, provided an atmosphere of business-like comfort. Photographs of Mercia's heritage, castles, museums and stately houses were displayed with civic pride on the walls.

The door opened and after a brief interval the face of Paul Rugglestone appeared, hesitant and inquiring. "Right room ?"

Dennis grunted agreement.

"Frightful problem with car-parking. Had to park at the back, by the race-course. Glad we've got a few moments alone before the others turn up."

Dennis did not share his gladness. Paul Rugglestone was the last person he wanted to be alone with.

"It'll be bad publicity for the party if our members agree to spend sixty-seven thousand pounds improving their dining facilities. That money would put an end to those dreadful conditions at The Heath."

Dennis sat stony-faced, wishing there was someone else to talk to.

Paul extracted the photographs from his briefcase. "Have you seen these? They must have sent you copies...Animal Rights will publish them you know..."

Dennis gave a brief nod.

Paul turned to look out of the window and stared down into the car-park, at the crowd on the steps below. "This crowd will be nothing compared to the angry mob that will lay siege to this building if these are published." He waved the photographs at Dennis.

"It will be like the storming of Versailles all over again...I wouldn't be surprised if the college got closed down."

Dennis was relieved that he was spared the need to reply as the door opened again. The presence of Sandy Stott, who he had not expected, made him both angry and embarrassed. He should have been warned. Harold should have told him. He would never have come to the meeting had he known that Sandy Stott would be there. He turned his back on Stott and joined Paul Rugglestone at the window. The disorderly crowd still milled around on the steps. He hoped to God that Annabel was not mixed up with that lot, although in her present mood she might be crazy enough to have joined them.

Paul Rugglestone glanced at Dennis and wondered whether he should have introduced the Constituency Chairman to Sandy Stott, but decided that discretion was the better part of valour. It was a relief to all three when Harold Tuck appeared with Jim Blakemore, the Leader of the Council.

Harold made a point of dealing with the introductions, although everyone except Sandy knew one another. Harold waved a hand at Sandy, "You are Mr Stott, I presume?"

Dennis and Jim Blakemore regarded Sandy with distaste mixed with curiosity. It was an embarrassment for both of them to pass the time of day in the same room as a member of Animal Rights - especially the Chairman - of whom they had heard such frightful tales. If they had been told that Sandy was a serial murderer they could not have shown more revulsion. They acknowledged his presence by the merest nod of their heads, and then turned away. Although the committee room was well heated Sandy felt sure that the temperature had fallen by several degrees.

"Well we're all busy people - no time to waste - we've had to leave an important meeting, and we've got another after lunch." Blakemore gulped down his coffee. "So what's all this about?"

Sandy approached the table and spread out the photographs. "These are copies - I won't waste your time - I'm sure you know all about it...The Animal Rights movement demands that you find the necessary resources to bring all the animal units at the Heath College up to modern humane standards and put an end to overcrowding. We are aware that you have allocated sixty-seven thousand pounds to improve your own facilities..." He paused and looked around the committee room. "From what I've seen this morning you don't appear to suffer from overcrowding, and I haven't heard that the Health and Safety Inspectorate have shown any concern about your welfare."

Dennis, glad to be excluded from such an attack, was amused to see that Harold's face flushed bright puce; his eyes had widened and become pop-eyed behind his thick glasses.

"Scrap the plan...Scrap the plan." The chanting rose from the courtyard

"You appear to be remarkably uninformed on your subject." Blakemore spoke coldly, "and to have a striking lack of knowledge on the subject of animal welfare."

To Dennis's surprise, Paul, who had been standing beside Sandy, leaned forward and pointed to the veterinary report. "On the contrary, if you read this report you will learn that this pig's death..." he stabbed with his forefinger at the photograph of the dead pig, "was caused by overcrowding. I know there is little profit in rearing pigs, but I am surprised that you should be so complacent over the death of an animal, which would, when it was fully grown, have helped to reduce the unit's budget deficit. Are you satisfied that young farmers are being taught, by this kind of example in the County's own college, to keep animals in such conditions? Is that good teaching?"

Harold Tuck cleared his throat. "The new unit is actually programmed."

"When for ?" Paul pressed home his argument, beginning to enjoy himself. He stared at Harold. "Why didn't you send me a copy of the vet's report as you promised? You were sent a copy. Were you worried by the findings?"

"I...I was going to bring it with me...I put it in my pocket...in an envelope...to give you..." he looked around wildly, searching for words. They watched him in silence, waiting for his excuse, "...but my wife took my suit to the cleaners."

The coffee machine gurgled in response. For a moment all four gazed dumbfounded at Harold, astonished at such an abject and desperate attempt to excuse himself.

"Nevertheless, this gets us nowhere." Blakemore spoke hurriedly. "As Harold has said, the pig unit is already listed in the building programme, and the money for the refurbishment of County Hall has been allocated. I give you my word that the new unit will be built."

"When ?" asked Sandy.

Blakemore pursed his lips. "Two - " he shrugged his shoulders. "Maybe three years."

"Three years? Maybe four before it's ready for

136

use." Sandy looked angry. "Unless you re-allocate that money for this year, these..." he waved his hand at the photographs, "will appear in the press next week."

Blakemore turned on his heel. "That's enough...I don't give in to threats. This is blackmail..." He turned to Dennis and Harold. "We're leaving."

As they followed the Council Leader down the corridor, Paul overheard Dennis's rumbled warning. "Don't under-estimate them...they're dangerous."

The Gazette was the first to publish the story and carried it as exclusive. The photograph of Paul, taken for his election leaflet, smiled re-assuringly from the front page, beside heavy black headlines that announced, "M.P. accuses greedy councillors as animals die." Extracts from the veterinary report were included in the text and two photographs showed in grim detail the conditions inside the pig unit.

That same evening Dennis watched as Mercia T.V. interviewed both Paul and Jim Blakemore. In the studio, Jeremy Flaxman, sitting in front of a wall-sized photograph of the dead pig, opened the programme by telling viewers that both Harold Tuck, Chairman of the Governors at The Heath, and George Barnett, Principal, had declined to take part.

"Which is a pity," he said, as he would have liked to have opened up the discussion on the role of the Animal Rights movement. However he promised viewers that they would be able to see a special programme devoted to the activities of protest groups which was to be screened the following month.

From his arm chair in front of the television set Dennis groaned out loud and reached for the whisky bottle.

Flaxman, his dark hair shining beneath the intense lights, turned to the Leader of the Council. "Mr.Blakemore, why are you spending sixty-seven thousand pounds of taxpayers' money on improving the councillor's dining facilities at County Hall?"

Blakemore was an experienced performer in front of the cameras. He flashed a conspiratorial smile at Flaxman and adopted a comradely tone. "Well now Jeremy, you and I both know that County Hall is a public building and as such is subject to stringent Health and Safety regulations. We have Environmental Health inspections and have to comply with Food Hygiene controls - not to mention observing all the latest EU directives. Keeping up with all these rules and regulations causes us continual problems..." Blakeman sounded very reasonable, "...and continual expense. So now we've decided to change over to a whole new system of food storage and preparation."

Flaxman cut him short, "Which reduces the number of staff in the kitchen?"

"Yes, but - "

"And the number of waitresses ?"

"Well, yes – but - "

"Self service cuts down staffing costs ?"

"The long-term saving - "

"How many redundancies?" Flaxman's questioning became relentless, and his voice hardened.

"We hope that natural wastage - "

"So it's all being done to cut down on staff ?"

"There's food costs - "

"Ah yes, food costs. How much is the subsidy on councillor's meals?"

"I haven't got the actual figures."

"Well I have." Flaxman's index finger pointed to

138

the paper on the table in front of him. "Would you dispute the figure of a 60% subsidy on meals and the bar ?"

Blakemore shrugged. "As I have just said I don't have the actual figures with me so it would be wrong for me to even try to guess."

Flaxman raised his eyebrows. "Viewers will no doubt be surprised to hear that you came to take part in a television broadcast without doing your homework, or even bringing the figures with you." He paused for a moment, leaned forward and stared at the Leader of the Council. "You really do yourselves all right, don't you?"

Flaxman turned to Paul, "Paul Rugglestone, isn't it extraordinary for an MP., especially a Tory MP., to get himself mixed up with a bunch of trouble-makers like Animal Rights?"

Paul felt confident. He was prepared for Flaxman's line of questioning. He turned away from his inquisitor and faced the camera. "I'd hope that any MP. no matter what party he belonged to, would demand change whenever he discovered cruelty."

"But these people have broken into laboratories, and released mink into the countryside -"

"Are you content to know that animals suffer in laboratories, that beagles, rabbits, monkeys and other animals are experimented on, forced to inhale cigarette smoke and undergo appalling cruelty?" Paul countered.

"But you've become an embarrassment to your own party members, and your colleagues -" Flaxman got no further.

Paul turned away from the cameras to face him, leaning across the table. The heat from the studio lights brought beads of sweat on his forehead. "If you've

139

ever studied history, which I believe you may have done; otherwise you wouldn't have got as far as you have at the BBC, you will know that civilisation has progressed only through reforms - brought about by people who did not kow-tow to their rulers, their political leaders, or their colleagues. Rightly or wrongly they fought for the things they believed in, and I happen to think my constituents sent me to Westminster to fight for the things that I and they believe in..."

"But don't most MP.s think that to start with?" Jeremy Flaxman cut in. "After all you've only been at Westminster a short time - you're hardly likely to endear yourself to the Whip's office, or be considered as a suitable candidate for a job as a Junior Minister?"

Paul smiled, ignoring the obvious trap. "I have to face myself in the bathroom mirror every morning." He hesitated and laughed. "I've learned that if you're persistent, years later people usually get around to agreeing with you - but by that time they think that they thought of the idea in the first place, and have forgotten about you completely." He paused. "However – to answer your question. If I did get offered a job in the Government I would accept it – always provided that I was free to act."

"Unconstrained by party politics?" persisted Flaxman.

"I just said, able to act freely – as my conscience dictates."

As the credits faded from television screens in homes across the country the phones at the BBC started ringing and jammed the switchboard.

Amongst those who tried to phone Paul that evening was Erica. She was lucky to get through, for at 10-o-clock, exhausted by the stream of congratulations, he switched over to his answer phone.

"My God, you were absolutely brilliant! At last we have one M.P. who fights for what he believes in...Of course Dennis will hate it...You know about Annabel I suppose...he tries to cover it up, but everyone knows. Tomorrow you'll be a national hero...it'll be in all the papers."

It was good to hear from Erica once again. From time to time he had found himself thinking of her and wondering whether he could arrange to meet her, but his work in the House and this business with the College had taken up all his spare time.

"But it wasn't what I really wanted to tell you. I've got good news...Sam has managed to track down your Boy Scout..."

For a moment Paul felt his heart sink - the boy - young man now, would never contradict his own parents and tell the truth about what really happened that night.

"- through the Scout Master who lived in the village...he remembered the hoo-ha at the time - said how sorry he felt for you. Anyway, this fellow - the Boy Scout - he's now the Vicar at St. Boniface, where you used to live, will give evidence - for you. Sam spoke to him on the phone...and he's meeting him next week to get a statement. Sam says there's a good chance that the Gazette will make an out-of-court settlement...pretty quick...a hefty sum I should think!"

Paul sat down heavily on the nearest chair. Suddenly, although it was late in the evening, the sun shone.

"Paul...Are you there?"

"Umm."

141

"God, I thought you'd fainted."

"Can we meet for dinner to celebrate? We'll go somewhere expensive. I'm coming up on Friday. How about Saturday?"

"Stay with me and avoid the Press - you'll be fed up with them by the weekend."

Only three days to go to Friday - and Erica. She was right. The rest of the week passed in a blur of interviews for radio, TV. and the press. Margery Ann, the secretary he shared with two others, dealt methodically with the bulging postbags - she was used to it. When he apologised to her for all the extra work she just smiled and warned him, as she had done in the past to so many other new MP.s that in two weeks time people would be scratching their heads, trying to remember his name.

Chapter 16

Barbara Millar sat beside the coffee table in Tom Anstey's office listening to the discussion that flowed around her. The March sun filtering through the slatted blinds high-lighted the green and gold pattern on the carpet. The room was airless. The combination of central heating, spring sunshine and a heavy lunch following the mornings regional meeting made it difficult to concentrate on the afternoon business.

"O.K., so we've got three-hundred and twenty-five thousand from the Queenswood sale." Tom Anstey leaned back in his chair. "I reckon we could find two-hundred and fifty. Of course it won't satisfy Region; Tony Bradshaw says that the Chairman is expecting at least three-hundred K from us."

Rick Sedley frowned and put down his tea-cup. "And where does he think we're going to get it from? My advice as Treasurer is two-hundred, at the most. We still have a cash flow problem. You remember that coach crash on the motorway last summer? Twenty injured, and five cases needed major surgery. All the passengers came from Lancashire and we haven't been paid a penny. The Authority up there is still arguing over our costs. Our other debtors from neighbouring trusts are always slow to pay up. Some are outstanding more than two years. I'm going to have to go to committee for permission to write off two, at least. It's not worth it. It costs more to chase them."

"Surely, there's no risk is there?" Barbara asked. "After all it's only over one night?"

"Oh no. We'll get paid. Region says we'll be paid next day." The Chief Executive shrugged his shoulders. "I hope they're right."

"Don't forget that we are committed to funding seventy-five percent of the costs of the new nursing home."

"All the more reason to go for it, we need the money." said Tom

"Then there are the auditors..." Rick Sedley broke off and pursed his lips. "We can't risk going into deficit...even for one day. Have you really thought it through?"

Tom fiddled with a biro on the glass-topped table. It rolled along the surface and fell on to the carpet at his feet. There was silence as he reached down and retrieved it. He cleared his throat and looked at the other two. "Well Chairman, I don't know how you feel, but Region will not be best pleased if our contribution is less than two-hundred and fifty thousand. I happen to know that Tony Bradshaw can pick up the odd fifty thousand here and there to reach the Chairman's target. As for the auditors, I understand that the Department will clear the arrangement with them."

Barbara sighed. "Well, in that case..."

"After all it's only an overnight paper transaction. The money won't even leave the bank..." he paused and looked thoughtful. "Maybe we could pass on all the debts we are owed...a notional sum?"

Rick shook his head. "We'd never get that past the auditors."

Bryson and Rouse, accountants, spent six weeks every year in the offices of Marton Health Authority. Once the books were closed at the end of the financial year, they moved in and took over three rooms in the

Finance Department, where they examined every account, receipt, letter and committee report and every scrap of paper provided for them by the Treasurer and his Deputy. Like starved vultures they roamed the corridors of the department demanding more files, print-outs, copies of faxes, and searching for folders that had never even existed, in an attempt to satisfy their insatiable craving.

Peter Vail led the team. A small thin man, with piercing eyes, a sharp pointed nose, and a look on his face that one usually expects to see on someone who has stepped in dog dirt. Every year for three years, the staff in the Finance department had pandered to his every need, keeping up a constant supply of tea and biscuits, typing paper, ink cartridges, paper-clips, and refilling his stapler. Every morning on his arrival he found his computer booted-up, his waste-paper basket emptied of the previous days contents, his pencils sharpened, a fresh sheet of blotting paper in the pad on his desk, and a new pad of 'post it' notelets to hand. Despite the best efforts of the departmental staff and cleaners they had never managed to win a glimmer of a smile or a word of thanks, not even when they took him his coffee and pink wafer biscuits that he demanded.

On the first of June Peter Vail allowed himself the merest suggestion of a look of satisfaction on his face as he stapled together the thirty-six pages of his report. Tonight he would take it home to read, and tomorrow he would present it to the Chief Executive. In his usual meticulous manner, on the first day of his visit, he had carefully written the date of the meeting in his Filo-fax and instructed the Chief Executive's secretary, Cathy, to do the same in Tom Anstey's Data-Day Desk Diary.

By a quarter-to-ten next morning the photocopier

145

had produced two copies of the report, still warm from the machine. Peter Vail personally stapled them together and with some satisfaction of a job well done, slid them inside manila envelopes. At ten-o-clock exactly, as he had arranged, he handed over the copies to the Chief Executive and Treasurer of the Marton Health Authority, then sat down to sip his coffee. which he did as a matter of habit - rather than enjoyment, for NHS coffee was never enjoyable.

"I found your procedures on the whole, fairly satisfactory. You will see that on the penultimate page I have made eleven recommendations to accommodate the latest Treasury regulations...You will need to study these, and let me know - in writing - how you intend to implement them...Next year a new format is to be introduced and it will be necessary for you to purchase up-to-date software and implement a new training programme..." He paused and licked his lips. "However on the final page..." he broke off and sniffed and extracted a white handkerchief from his pocket. As Tom Anstey and Rick Sedley turned over the pages, he dabbed at his nose, "You will observe that I have qualified the accounts."

The Chief Executive thought he detected a note of satisfaction in the Auditor's voice. "Qualified the accounts?" His face was pale. "You had no reason."

"A twelve thousand pound deficit."

"But next day, the first of April-" Anstey leaned forward in his chair.

"We have no interest at all in the first of April. That was the following year. It was not the subject of the audit. The financial year ends on the thirty-first of March as you know -"

"It was a loan, re-paid the next day." Rick

146

interrupted Peter Vail. He raised his voice and emphasised each word "There was a credit of two-hundred and seventy-five thousand pounds owing to us for that year...the year that was subject to audit."

"I know nothing about a loan. All the information I have is that you had a deficit of twelve thousand pounds on the thirty-first of March." insisted Peter Vail with grim satisfaction.

"But the Department of Health - didn't they advise you?" Tom Anstey tried to stay calm but the muscles in his face were taut.

"My instructions come from the Audit Commission, and I work under Treasury regulations." the Auditor reminded them.

"This is ridiculous!" exploded the Chief Executive. "You're being deliberately unreasonable. You know that NHS organisations, dealing with large budgets, cannot be expected to end the year hitting the target on the button. It's absurd to expect it. Four years ago we were so worried that we would end the year with too much in credit that we had to ask debtors to defer paying us until after the year end. Now you want to qualify the accounts because we are going to end up twelve thousand pounds short."

"I don't want to qualify the accounts - I am qualifying the accounts." Vail reminded them. There was a note of hostility in his voice. "We don't expect authorities to end the year hitting the target on the button, as you say. It would be a different matter if you were five, or even six thousand pounds adrift - but this is over ten thousand."

Tom Anstey slammed the report down onto his desk. "I shall do nothing until I have consulted the Chairman, Mercia Region and the Department."

147

"Naturally." Peter Vail got to his feet.

"Then you will hear from us further." The Chief Executive hesitated, and smiled at the Auditor. "I seem to remember that your contract with us is for three years. It comes to an end this year. The Health Authority will as a matter of course, consider whether to renew the contract...and in the light of this..." he shrugged his shoulders.

"You must do as you think best." Peter Vail slotted his papers carefully into his briefcase. "I shall make a full report of this conversation to my superiors."

The five members of the Audit Committee met in the Board Room two days later to consider the Auditor's report.

"I phoned Tony Bradshaw immediately." The Chief Executive looked pale and angry. "He's checking with the Department to find out what instructions, if any, were sent out to the Auditors. Obviously the Department had to clear it with the Treasury first."

"So what are you saying ?" The Vice-chairman, Steve Bartlam, looked worried. He sipped his coffee thoughtfully. "We only did as we were told by Region. Don't they accept any responsibility? They must have known that if anything went wrong we would all be held responsible, especially you and Mick – and the Chairman."

Tom Anstey shook his head in bewilderment. "I'm just surprised that Tony Bradshaw didn't get it in writing."

"Then how did you get to hear that the Department would, as you put it, clear the arrangement with the auditors ?"

148

"At a meeting at Region, with Bradshaw - apparently the Regional Chairman came back with the tale after a meeting with the Secretary of State."

Barbara nodded. "We were told about the meeting, but no details – just advised to discuss those with Bradshaw."

"D'you want me to write officially to both the Department and the Regional Treasurer seeking clarification?" asked Mick Sedley. "Then when this hits the fan we can at least claim that we acted in good faith."

"We did act in good faith, but we had nothing in writing. We'll need the information for the Board meeting in two weeks," Tom Anstey reminded him. "I've asked Peter Vail to attend for this item."

"Can we take it in part two and exclude press and public?" Steve asked.

"Hardly wise," advised Barbara. "The press would wonder what we were trying to hush up. In any case they never turn up. I don't think they even read the agendas we send them. With a bit of luck they won't realise that we have a problem."

"In any case the report won't be made public until after the meeting," the Chief Executive reminded the members. Each member of the Audit Committee voted to accept the procedure, knowing that if the qualified accounts were accepted, and confirmed by Region their futures would all be in doubt.

The Prime Minister's announcement of a September election caught everyone by surprise, even MP.s and Constituency officers who had planned their summer holidays with the intention of returning refreshed for an autumn campaign and an election in late October.

149

Paul had been looking forward to two weeks in Amalfi, now it would have to be a weekend city break in Florence. He also had the added problem of finding a replacement for his research assistant, as James had been selected to fight a Lib. Dem. seat in Cornwall, and was at present on honeymoon in Fowey - "combining business with pleasure." he told Paul with evident delight at the prospect.

At the Mercia Constituency office John Brown's election machine moved smoothly into gear. He was well prepared. He had run parliamentary and local government elections for almost forty years. Now it was just a matter of ticks in boxes, keeping calm, encouraging party workers and shoring up the falling confidence of the candidate who always became more and more agitated as election day approached. Central Office had already phoned to tell him that they were sending a trainee agent to assist him in the office. He smiled, poured his coffee down the cloakroom wash-basin, and set off across the square for his mid-morning break.

Chapter 17

On Thursday morning before Paul left for the constituency Sam Magrudada phoned. "Thought you'd like to know that I've had a useful meeting with Tim Parrish."

"Tim Parrish ?"

"The Reverend. Your boy scout. He gave me a full statement - fits in with everything you said."

Paul breathed a noisy sigh of relief.

"Funny - he remembers everything quite clearly. Mind you he did have time to think about it - read all about it in the Gazette. He'd actually thought of contacting you, but was worried that it might affect his position in the Church. Anyway after talking to him he said that he'd do everything he could to clear your name, especially after seeing you on television. Said he admired you enormously for speaking up against animal cruelty."

"So what now ?"

"I'll contact the Gazette's solicitors and tell them that we have a statement. I've no doubt that they'll want to settle. Soon as I hear from them I'll be in touch. Have a good weekend with Erica !"

"How did you know - ?"

"Phoned her - asked her down for the weekend and dinner on Saturday at Quatre Saisons, but she turned me down - for you. I'm not used to being stood up!"

Paul stared at the phone.

"You there ?" Sam asked. "By the way, Tim Parrish asked if he could meet you. I can't see any harm in it. I told him to write to you at the House, so you may be hearing from him."

In the internal post that same morning there was a letter from the Department of the Environment. It was short and to the point.

Dear Paul,

The Secretary of State has asked me to write and inform you that as a result of his recent meeting with Mercia County Council, the County Council have withdrawn their proposals to carry out refurbishment at County Hall. The savings will be allocated to improving the housing of animals at The Heath Agricultural College.

Yours faithfully,

Nicholas Moore.

Permanent Under Secretary, Department of the Environment.

Paul punched the air, then scribbled a note, 'Fax copy to Sandy Stott, Chairman of Animal Rights,' and stapled it to the letter.

Towards the end of the week the motorway traffic built up, until by Friday the whole network neared gridlock, which was why MPs preferred to travel to their constituencies on Thursdays. For many years the M25 had justified its description as the biggest car park in Europe.

A perpetual programme of roadworks, with signs apologising for delays and announcing that the work was scheduled to finish in two years time caused vehicles to crawl sloth-like, yard by yard. Clutches burned out, radiators over-heated and tempers boiled under the late afternoon sun. Hopes that the turn-off onto the M40 would bring an end to the roadworks were dashed as more directions for contra-flows appeared and drivers were once again commanded to 'stay in lane.' At last, three hours after leaving Westminster, the cones disappeared, the motorway opened out, and three clear lanes stretched ahead. The speedometer needle climbed and the Lancia, free of all constraints, ate up the miles, until south of Birmingham it slowed to a crawl and joined the bottle-neck near the junction with the M5. It was particularly frustrating, when so near to home, and almost in sight of The Wrekin, he sat trapped in the middle lane between lorries, breathing in fumes. For nearly an hour he compared the variety of tyres on the lorries on either side of his car and admired the handiwork of the coachbuilders and the sign writers. Whilst crawling forward inch by inch he called Erica on his mobile.

She answered immediately "Let me guess where you are - no, don't tell me. Rush hour goes on for ever. Don't worry about supper, it won't spoil. I've made a daube - it improves with keeping." Her laughter was like music. It made him smile and feel happy. The bottle of House of Commons Claret , wrapped inside his jacket on the back seat would certainly be chambre by now.

They sat side by side at a table on the patio in the Garden of The Old Rectory. The heat of the afternoon had faded and given way to the cushioned warmth of the late summer evening when scents were headier and colours deeper. A cobalt blue clematis entwined itself around the rustic pergola. On the brick wall behind the herbaceous border gold tea-roses were in full bloom. The aroma of the daube mingled with scented Charentais melon, Camembert and Forme d'Ambert drifted through the open window from the kitchen. On

153

the table the uncorked claret breathed and settled.

Erica picked up her glass of gin and tonic, "Well, here's to the weekend."

He raised his glass in response. "I gather we have to lunch at the Show on Saturday ?"

In the distance a train rumbled on its way towards New Street Station, and as the light began to fade the scent of stocks drifted across the garden.

"You'll enjoy it," she reassured him. "Last year Della got so tiddly that she joined another party. Be warned, she always hangs around the bar expecting everyone to buy her a drink!"

"Why am I invited ?"

Erica laughed. "Because you're a pillar of the establishment. The President always invites the M.P. to join his party, along with the Mayor and the Chairman of the Council."

"And you ?"

'Cause I'm a Sponsor. The family has always sponsored the Championship cup for the Heavy Horse section since the show first started." She got up and Paul followed her into the kitchen, walking behind her, watching her move. He fought against the impulse to put his arms around her waist and kiss the back of her neck.

"By the way, Dennis will be there. He sponsors a cup in the cattle section. He's never been known to miss the President's lunch." She handed him the plates.

"And Harold Tuck ?"

"You bet."

Paul groaned. "Should I wear a bowler ? I don't have one."

"No - just be yourself - I don't think one would suit you anyway."

154

He re-filled her glass. She watched him, the fading light silhouetted her face, and when he placed the glass beside her she put her hand over his, holding it firmly, preventing him from pulling away. Her touch was warm and strong. He leaned across, paused and firmly kissed her on the cheek. For a brief second they were silent, waiting for each other to speak.

Erica gave a soft laugh. "It's years since I last felt like this..." she hesitated, "When I was first married...I never thought I'd ever feel like it again."

"You must have guessed by now how I feel about you...but we've not known each other long...I don't want to rush you."

She put out her arms, pulling him closer to her, kissing him. "You're right of course...but...."

That night Paul moved out of the spare-bedroom.

By mid-morning on Saturday the Vice-President's marquee had begun to fill with pre-lunch drinkers. One hundred Vice-Presidents, their blue and gold embossed badges proclaiming their status and the fact that they had paid their annual subscription and availed themselves of the special facilities not accessible to the hoi-polloi who crowded the public refreshment tent. The bright sunshine turned the July morning into a picture-postcard scene where the tents were white, the sky was blue and the grass was green. Farmers and landowners encircled the bar, took possession of the tables inside the marquee and gathered on the lawn that overlooked the main ring. On the other side of the chestnut palings the band of the Royal Scots Regiment paraded, tartan kilts swinging, marching and counter-marching to the pipes and drums and the inspiring strains of 'Daughter of the Regiment.'

In Ring two the heavy horses paraded, giant Percherons and gentle Suffolk Punch, their brasses gleaming, plaited manes and tails, coloured ribbons and bold eyes causing excited comments of admiration from spectators pressed around the fence. Red and white jumps, a gate and a five foot wall awaited the Show Jumpers in the next event, the Foxhunter Trophy. In the Collecting Ring the competitors circled the ground, calmed their horses, tightened their girths and lined up for the practice fence.

Hacking jackets, twills and trilbys; the uniform of well-dressed farmers, were de-rigueur. Their wives and daughters in cool suits and sensible shoes clustered in groups under sun-shades, and around white metal tables - the leads of their spaniels and labradors hitched to chairs, whose legs, bearing the substantial weight of so many generously proportioned country women sunk backwards into the soft grass, threatening to unseat their occupants.

At the entrance to the enclosure, a uniformed commissionaire admitted only those who displayed badges - smart suited sponsors, bowler-hatted judges, officials, and country-clad Vice-Presidents.

On the other side of the gate, anoraks, jeans and trainers crowded the public areas. The smell of bruised grass mingled with vinegar and chips. Women in high-heeled shoes sank into the soft ground and struggled to manoeuvre push-chairs carrying fretful infants. Flags and banners festooned the Agricultural machinery stands where farmers crowded the bars and, under no pressure from salesmen, downed pints of Boddingtons as they argued over the attributes of John Deere or David Brown tractors. Mowers and Flymos roared into life as assistants demonstrated the simplicity of their operation. Red and silver Quad Bikes, gleaming in the sunshine, waited patiently to be released from their security chains and ridden away.

From the cattle lines and horse boxes came the noise of uneasy animals, whilst the voice of the announcer in the main control-van overpowered all other sounds as competitors were ordered to attend their respective events, or mothers were sought to be re-united with lost children.

Across the show-ground pennants fluttered from the pinnacle of the great cheese tent, and banners proclaimed the fact that the enormous marquee housed an international event sponsored by Cathedral City Cheeses. On trestle tables inside two-thousand British and foreign cheeses of all shapes and sizes were displayed. Creamy Blue Cheshire, tasty Coloured Cheshire, traditional White Cheshire, mature Cheddar, aged Stilton, appetising Double Gloucester, and sharp Lancashire, Goat's cheese and Ewes cheese. Smoked Austrian, Port Salut, Brie, Camembert, Forme d'Ambert and Bleu d'Auvergne as well as Gorgonzola and Edam added colour and interest.

Stalls manned by commercial cheese-makers, supermarkets and equipment manufacturers were ranged around the sides of the marquee encircling the exhibits. Those stalls offering free samples drew the biggest crowds who blocked the aisles and then moved on, munching greedily, only to halt again, tempted by other savoury offerings.

Outside at the rear of the marquee lines of large refrigerated vans hummed noisily to themselves as they waited to reload the dairy products that had been on show. Local Cheese Factors who had already negotiated deals for the winning cheeses lunched in surrounding tents offering wine and cheese tasting to established customers. At the same time, Charlie Bastow, whose van bore the sign 'Marton Cheese Factors,' kept watch from the driving seat through dark aviator glasses at the comings and goings.

In the Vice-President's marquee, at the President's table, Dennis found himself seated between Erica and Harold Tuck, which annoyed him. Last year he was placed in the centre of the table only two places away from the President. Now he was seated further away, down the table. He turned his head to count, eight places, and saw Paul Rugglestone sitting right next to the President. Dennis stared. The fellow wasn't even dressed properly - looked like a bookie's runner, totally out of place in a broad check suit.

"Bloody MP's got no dress sense..." he grumbled at Harold, then paused when he saw that Harold too was wearing what Edith always described as 'a loud check.' He turned to Erica, "Bloody young fool..."

Erica eyed him coldly, raised her eyebrows and sniffed. Dennis had the feeling that he was not going to enjoy his plate of gravadlax in dill sauce.

Paul was surprised to find that he was sitting next to the President of the Show Committee, Robert Phillips. On his other side was the Mayor, a tall, tough, battle-hardened martinet of a woman known to all as Ethel. He frowned, trying to remember her other name. He'd met her once before at the Mayor's ball where she made an impressive entrance into the Civic Hall, reminding him of a ship in full sail, her Mayoral chain lying on her ample bosom, glittering under the spot-lights. Ethel was a forthright member of the Labour party. His host, on the other hand an equally outspoken right-wing Tory. The situation made him

158

smile. Obviously non-political small-talk might be the diplomatic solution - if he could get away with it. .

Luckily lunch was a short-lived affair. It began late as two important sponsors who were driving up from Birmingham had been delayed on the motorway, and it ended early as the Mayor had to attend a Civic engagement and the President was due to introduce the sponsors who would be presenting the cups following the Grand Parade. Paul was surprised to discover that both his neighbours were in agreement as they congratulated him over his television performance, but warned him of the dangers of becoming too closely involved with Animal Rights.

Dennis limped as he followed the President into the main ring. He had forgotten to take his lunchtime tablet. He put his hand into his jacket pocket to reassure himself that the small bottle was still there, and thought of stopping to take a tablet, but was afraid that the group would continue without him and he might lose his place on the dais. The ground was uneven which worsened the pain in his back and his arthritic hip, so that he limped and hobbled as fast as he could to keep up with the rest. He reached the dais breathless as loud-speakers announced that the South Marton Hunt would lead the Grand Parade.

In the collecting ring stewards marshalled the animals and their handlers, led by the prize winners of each class. For a while there was chaos until eventually the Master of Foxhounds accompanied by his two Whippers-in cantered into the arena, hounds streaming ahead in full cry as the Master sounded 'Gone Away.' Dennis took the bottle from his pocket and swallowed two pain-killers. The muscles of his jaw tightened as he watched Geoff Wilkinson, the Whip, lead the

159

hounds around the arena. Twenty years ago Wilkinson was his herdsman, until he came into money, bought himself a farm and took up hunting. Jumped-up bugger, took up with the hunting set, now he's Whipper-In.

The noise increased. Spectators pressed against the fence surrounding the ring, and the Show Champion Hereford bull Salopian Crown Dynasty, curly brown coat and be-decked with rosettes, lumbered forward. His heavy square body, sharp stubby horns on a massive head, and mean rolling eyes warned all around of the dangers of obstructing his path. Close behind plodded Friesian, Charolais and Limousin bulls, led by white-coated herdsmen and owners, controlling their prize-winners by ropes attached to their nose-rings. Guernsey, Jersey and Friesian cows and calves followed, their polished coats gleaming in the sunshine.

In the control-van the announcer who had begun his commentary broke off and demanded the immediate attention of an electrician at the cheese tent. Heads turned as stewards hurried from the main ring.

The show secretary standing beside the President listened intently to his walkie-talkie. "Generator failure - ten minutes and it should be fixed - we always have a back-up. Some of the soft foreign cheeses melt in the heat. We've more than two thousand cheeses." he informed Paul. "It's the biggest show in Europe." He looked worried as he waited for more information.

The Grand Parade came to a halt. The sponsors waited to be called forward for the presentation. A siren wailed as a police Range-Rover negotiated its way through the crowds. The hubbub from the crowds in the grandstand, or seated on straw bales behind the chestnut paling, continued.

The loud-speaker system clicked. The spectators nearby fell silent, listening, anticipating trouble. Distant voices from within the control box, barely audible, spoke hurriedly, drowned by a crackle of static radio activity. The system clicked again, paper rustled, the announcer cleared his throat...hesitated. Inside the van angry voices raised in argument were suddenly relayed across the showground as the sound system remained on. Someone switched it off. Seconds later it clicked back into life.

The announcer coughed and began to speak, slowly, clearly, and very firmly. "Your attention please. This is an urgent announcement. The police have received a warning that a bomb has been placed somewhere on the showground. Please leave the showground and the car parks. I repeat - Do not go to the car parks. Leave the showground immediately...Once again I repeat - "

The announcement was cut short as simultaneously three loud explosions echoed across the ground. A plume of smoke started to drift upwards from the rear of the public bar, followed by a crackle of fire from the lorry park. Fear and panic spread swiftly as spectators began to race towards the exits. The crowds split up, running in all directions, shrieking and shouting, and colliding with one another. Parents grabbed children as pushchairs were trampled underfoot. Pandemonium reached a crescendo. The uproar, drifting smoke and acrid smell of burning, galvanized every animal on the showground. The Grand Parade broke up in disorder. Frightened cattle took off, bellowing and dragging their herdsmen behind them. Heavy bulls, who until then could only shamble, pushed aside their handlers and raced across the ring smashing into show jumps and breaking down fences, overturning hot dog stands and

161

disappearing into tents.

On the Vice-President's lawn spectators scattered as Crown Dynasty charged the wicket fence, trampling it underfoot, and headed for the marquee. Bartenders and waitresses dived for safety beneath the canvas sides of the tent. Glasses and bottles crashed to the ground as the massive animal lowered his head. Two tons of muscle, bone and sinew charged the bar. Crown Dynasty then turned his attention to the trestle tables set out for afternoon tea, scattering cups and saucers and plates of cakes and sandwiches across the matting. Pausing from his activity, and looking around for more pleasurable activities he spotted the main tent pole to use as a scratching post.

For half a minute the marquee trembled, then finally collapsed, overwhelming him in a sea of sailcloth. Exhausted by his exertions he sank to his knees, still fighting and tearing at the canvas with his horns, then swaddled like a new-born infant Crown Dynasty fell fast asleep.

In the produce tent the stampede reached its climax as fruit, flowers and vegetables were trampled underfoot. Goats toured the tables pausing to graze on prize winning floral exhibits, pigs gorged themselves on home-made fruit tarts and cakes, and horses risked colic as they hoovered up every crumb of oven-fresh bread.

Distressed cattle, blinded by fear, raced through the ground, kicking out at everything that stood in their way. Heavy horses, caught up in the mad stampede, joined in, damaging cars and farm machinery on the dealer's stands. As the panic began to die down the sounds of sirens from ambulances and fire-engines re-ignited the tumult, and the exhausted animals once

162

again took flight and careered through the showground towards the car parks and surrounding fields in search of peace.

In the kitchen of the Old Rectory Erica and Paul sat at the table, glasses in hand, watching the early evening news from the Midlands on the television set that stood on top of the fridge.

Nathalie Berand, an attractive, blonde BBC reporter stood amongst the debris of the main show-ring waving a hand at the scenes of chaos. "For the first time ever in this country an agricultural show that gives pleasure to thousands of people has suffered a vicious attack by vandals." She turned to Ken Patten, the Show Secretary. "Did you get any warning?"

He shook his head. "Not enough to clear the ground." Shaken and distressed he read out a hurriedly prepared statement to the film crew that were gathered around. In the background stewards, owners and herdsmen could be seen collecting and calming their panic-stricken animals. Security men and police searched cars and horse-boxes, and ambulances collected injured spectators from the Red Cross tent.

"Did you suspect that this might happen ?"

"Who do you think did it?"

"Why do you think it happened?" The questions were swift and relentless.

The Show Secretary could only shake his head. "Ask the police. I've told you as much as I know. I can only repeat that the police received a bomb warning. The generator that powered the air-conditioning unit in the cheese tent has been vandalised and every cheese in the tent has been stolen. The thieves were seen, loading the cheeses into two big

163

vans. They emptied the marquee." He shook his head. "No one thought to question them – in fact the stewards actually helped them."

"And the explosions?"

"Fireworks - taken from the locked shed where we stored them.." Ken sounded exhausted.

"Who had the key?"

"The lock was picked."

"Why were you storing fireworks?"

"For the display, when the show had ended."

"Do you now consider that your security was adequate?"

"Ask the police. We took their advice. That's all gentlemen." The Secretary turned abruptly and broke off the interview, close to tears.

Paul turned down the volume. "D'you think it was Annabel and her Animal Rights gang?"

Erica shook her head. "She might have phoned the hoax bomb warning, but she wouldn't have set off the fireworks or frightened the animals, beside she's hardly likely to steal cheese." She hesitated, then gave a little laugh.. "Poor Dennis - he's lost his Championship Cheshire cheese and it was Best in Show – I'm almost beginning to feel sorry for him!"

"I saw him taking tablets. His back is bothering him and makes his temper even worse than usual." Paul shook his head, "and I'm not looking forward to the adoption meeting next week if he's in bad shape. Adoption meetings are nerve-racking affairs at the best of times, especially if the Chairman can't keep control.

As the local news came to an end Erica turned off the television. "Don't worry John Brown usually keeps Dennis under control."

164

Chapter 18

Sitting at the long trestle table covered with green baize Paul watched from the platform as the hall began to fill with party members. All of them expecting news of his libel action and re-assurance about the party's chances in the forthcoming election. Most were middle-aged, business-men, senior executives and middle management. Some were elderly, proud to tell everyone that they had voted Tory all their lives. Paul remembered farmers who had lost their entire stock because of Foot and Mouth disease and could even now be faced with the threat of bankruptcy as a result of BSE. Others had suffered financially from regulations brought in as a result of the EU quota system.

The chairs in the two front rows were filled by members of the Woman's Advisory Committee, the 'blue-rinse brigade', who talked non-stop at the top of their voices. Amongst them he recognized Della's hard high-pitched voice competing with the rising level of conversation throughout the room.

Paul watched as members moved around the hall, chatting to each other and taking their seats, then was suddenly startled to catch sight of a young woman on the far side of the room who looked like Annabel. When he spotted the bright emerald green sweat-shirt carrying the message 'Animals have Rights' in large black letters he knew that it was most definitely Annabel - her glasses were round d big and rather owlish. How on earth did she manage to enter the hall he wondered? She would have had to produce a party membership card to get in. Then he recognised Sandy Stott talking to the parson with dark curly hair who sat beside Annabel. Paul turned to watch Dennis' reaction, but the Chairman was busily engaged, talking earnestly to Sir Robert Grant and doing his best to look important. The President turned out regularly every year to preside at the AGM, or at a candidate's adoption meeting when the agenda demanded serious public credibility. So far Dennis showed no sign of recognition that his daughter was in the hall. Erica took her place at the table next to Dennis and behind his back she winked at Paul. The wink, and her soft fragrance of Chanel No.5 reduced the size of the cloud that always weighed him down whenever Dennis was around.

By half-past seven the room was full, with members standing. Every chair in the building had been brought into the hall. Dennis Deane banged his gavel imperiously and conversation paused and died.

"This meeting has been called to adopt our MP, Paul Vere-Rugglestone, as parliamentary candidate for the forthcoming general election on October the twelfth. I cannot stress too strongly the importance of this particular election. Our party has been in power for more than twelve years and the opposition is doing its best to persuade voters that twelve years is too long for any party to be in power. Well, they would say that, wouldn't they?"

A chorus of approval resonated through the room. Dennis smiled. Allowing time for the sound to die away he surveyed the packed hall.

"You know what -" His words faltered. His confident smile momentarily abandoned him and he stared down the length of the hall in disbelief at the sight of his daughter sitting, arms crossed, glaring in defiance. Dennis carefully poured himself a glass of water, removed his spectacles, polished them and replaced them. Paul held his breath, awaiting the reaction.

Years of training hurried to Dennis' rescue. Eyes blazing, face white with anger, he looked down at his notes. Then after only a brief instant he raised his head. Although his eyes were hard as steel, he had in that short interval, disguised his fury with a mask of bonhomie. No one could have guessed that there was a problem. "You know what…" he repeated. "You know… what we're called? We're known as the mop and bucket brigade – because we always have to spend our first years in office clearing up the mess that the Labour party have left behind…"

A ripple of laughter rewarded him. Paul let out an audible sigh of relief as Dennis continued, "so we've got to make sure that the Labour party never do get back and leave us once again with a horrific mess to clear up."

High on the faded blue walls that needed painting, the faces of past party leaders and Prime Ministers stared down from dusty brass frames, waiting to judge Paul's own performance. Addressing party members was just as nerve-racking as making his maiden speech in the House. He waited uneasily and unsure of his reception whilst Dennis completed his Chairman's introduction, then pushed back his chair. Its legs squealed on the worn boards.

As Paul adjusted the height of the microphone Dennis picked up a pen, scribbled a message on his agenda paper and slid it along the table towards John Brown. In thick black capital letters Paul read 'HOW DID MY DAUGHTER GET IN?'

Paul grinned, relaxed, and launched into his speech. "I'm not going to waste your time or mine attempting

167

to explain the motives of The Gazette for the attack on myself and my colleagues in the House except to bring you the good news that I have been completely cleared of the allegation made against me by that newspaper..." He paused as a suddden thunder of applause exploded throughout the hall. "We are negotiating a settlement with the solicitors for the Gazette – a settlement that I will donate to charity." Once again a ripple of applause broke out and Paul held up his hand. "I need to reassure you that I have not allowed this matter to distract me from my work on your behalf. I'm sure you would like me to give you an account of my first years as an MP."

He outlined his battles with bureaucracy and his regular attempts to obtain information that were constantly frustrated by Civil Servants at every level.

"It's not just a matter of asking questions. It's knowing the right questions to ask. In Whitehall and in Council offices throughout the country "Sir Humphreys" do still exist. "Sir Humphreys" never answer questions directly, nor offer information gratuitously." Paul nodded his head. "And yes – "Yes Minister" really is true."

He listed his many campaigns on behalf of his constituents.

"In particular the Inland Revenue. Those brown envelopes labelled OHMS usually contain inexplicable computations of your tax liability. If you should feel like arguing your case with the inspector -then beware, because the interest that the Inland Revenue add on to the amount that you owe them increases day by day; and the many complaints that you send me grow month by month despite the efforts that the Government makes to cut red tape and bureaucracy."

Heads nodded in agreement.

As he related his handful of successes to correct the many unfair decisions by petty officialdom murmurs of appreciation and understanding from the audience increased his confidence. He knew that his speech was going down well. When he reached the end, expressing loyalty and support for the Prime Minister, he sat down to enthusiastic applause.

Dennis got to his feet and cleared his throat. "Are there any questions?" he barked, looking around the room, waiting, allowing time for the critics to compose their thoughts.

A hand waved from the back of the hall. Dennis pointed towards the questioner. "Yes...Ah, Jack Corfield..."

Corfield stood up. A tall thin man, one of a clique of lieutenants who surrounded Dennis Deane and benefited from his patronage. Paul recognised him. Erica had pointed him out several times on other occasions as he stood beside Dennis hanging on to his every word. The Chairman of a small country branch, with the lined thin face of an ascetic, he wore rimless dark glasses, even indoors, which had the effect of reminding everyone who met him of hackneyed war films that depicted sinister Gestapo men.

Corfield surveyed the packed hall and waited for attention. He smiled ingratiatingly.

"Chairman, The MP has given us an interesting account of his first years in the House. However it does seem to me that he has quite deliberately glossed over his affair with the young scout and his libel action against The Gazette. I think he owes us an explanation - if he wants our support." The smile disappeared from Jack Corfield's face, and his voice hardened. "This type of

169

seedy publicity could lose us the seat. Chairman, there is after all still time to re-consider his candidature...This meeting is not a formality. It has not been called just to rubber stamp his re-adoption as parliamentary candidate. We have been summoned here to consider Paul Rugglestone's suitability as our MP."

Chairs scraped as party members turned in their seats to stare at the speaker. A wave of sound welled up from his audience, obliging Corfield to raise his voice.

"There are other candidates who have not been selected for seats. Some of them have appeared before us, and in my opinion would have been perfectly suitable. They didn't appear to be concealing any skeletons in their cupboards..."

Tension spread swiftly through the hall electrifying the four hundred party members, then suddenly peaked and exploded into a volcanic upheaval of exasperation and anger. The clamour of voices rose to a crescendo and hands waved frantically to catch the attention of the Chairman.

As if responding to a signal, Annabel erupted. Springing to her feet and waving a placard bearing the words 'Vote for Paul Rugglestone,' she left her seat and headed towards the platform. At the back of the hall a group of students from the agricultural college unfurled a large banner and led by the curly headed parson began to chant "Rugglestone for MP" as they advanced two by two down the centre aisle to support Annabel.

Distracted by the sudden interruption the party members turned to watch.

Taken by surprise, Dennis lunged forward and attempted to remove the microphone from its stand, but Annabel got there before him. She stared down at the noisy confused audience. "Listen to the truth - " she begged, but was interrupted as Dennis snatched the microphone from her hand. She let it go, turning towards him, her eyes hard with anger. In that brief moment father and daughter faced each other, recognising each other for the very first time, staring into each others eyes. Suddenly Dennis felt overwhelmed by the wave of unbridled contempt unleashed by his daughter, the daughter who he had never really known, let alone understood. In his confusion the microphone fell from his grasp on to the floor. Speechless with embarrassment Annabel bent down, picked it up and handed it to her father. Then Erica was beside Annabel, arms around her shoulders, leading her away to a seat at the side of the platform, away from the mounting confusion.

Dennis' held up his hands, forgetful of the microphone, but his repeated cries of "Ladies and Gentlemen, please..." were drowned in the uproar. Sir Robert Grant joined the fray, fighting for possession of the microphone with the Agent from Regional Office. John Brown, in an attempt to salvage something from the disaster, leaped down from the platform and confronted the students, urging them to return to their seats.

Paul stood at the front of the stage and also held up his hands in a plea for silence, but the confusion continued. Whilst party members argued with each other and called for an explanation he ran down the steps from the platform and came face to face with the parson who was pushing his way resolutely through the group of students. Grabbing Paul's arm the clergyman propelled him back up the steps towards Dennis who had, by then, successfully gained possession of the microphone and was holding it in front of his mouth as if it were an ice cream cornet. However seeing a man of the cloth approach, hand outstretched, Dennis surrendered it readily and with surprising docility, out of respect, and in the hope that the chaos might die down. At a table at the side of the room the press scribbled furiously.

Tim Parrish took the microphone, tapped it and blew into it for good effect. The noise momentarily subsided. He took advantage of that moment and turned to face the audience. "If I could have your attention. Please..."

The party members and students waited, whilst Jack Corfield and his colleagues whispered together, unsure as to what might happen next, but readying themselves to add further doubts about the character of Paul Vere-Rugglestone.

"No one here will know me, except perhaps your MP, and even he may not

at you recognise me." The microphone echoed around the hall, and the young man's breath reverberated through the sound system. "I don't even live in the constituency."

"Then go home and don't interfere," shouted a man sitting near to Jack Corfield.

"Shhh..." the members protested.

"My name is Tim Parrish. I was the scout that Paul Rugglestone, your MP. was accused of abusing." He turned to face Paul..

The audience fell silent, staring at him, waiting to hear more. Paul glanced at Erica. She smiled at him reassuringly. Beside him Dennis's face was stony. He appeared to be glaring uncomprehendingly at the far wall.

Tim's strong, firm voice demanded attention. "That

172

was twenty years ago." He fixed his gaze on Jack Corfield. "You asked for an explanation – and I'll give it to you. Paul Rugglestone no more abused me than any of you would have done if you had found a small boy homesick and miserable - bullied by older boys. He came to my rescue and took me into his own tent. Although I had a sleeping bag I was cold and he covered me with blankets." He paused and glared at his audience, then spoke slowly, emphasising each word. "That is all that happened...There was nothing else."

"But a charge was made - " interrupted Corfield who had regained his composure.

Tim stared gravely at the assembled party members. "I'm sorry to say that the charge was made by my mother. What she alleged was not true...The real truth of the matter is that she and my father bore a grudge against Colonel Rugglestone, Paul's father, because my father was dismissed from his job on the estate." He hesitated. "He was sacked for dishonesty... That is the evidence I shall be giving in support of Paul's libel action." He paused for a moment. "An action which I am sure he will win."

The silence that followed was broken by a burst of clapping. The Reverend Tim Parrish held up his hand for silence. "You have a brave and conscientious man as your MP. I'm sure he is as distressed by all this as I am. Like so many others in public life the press have libelled him. Fortunately for Paul, in this particular case, I have been able to make a statement that completely clears him of these dreadful allegations. Now you too must give him your full support."

The parson switched off the microphone and placed it carefully on the table in front of the chairman. Dennis

173

continued to stare down the length of the hall; for the first time in his life he had lost control of a situation. Tim walked across the platform, took Annabel by the hand, and led her down the steps. Together they walked slowly back up the centre aisle. In their emotion they did not feel the hands that reached out to them as they returned to their seats, or heard the wild clapping as the whole audience, with the exception of Jack Corfield and his colleagues, rose to their feet in a standing ovation.

Erica Barrington reached across for the microphone from the table and walked towards Paul.

"Chairman in view of what we have just heard I have great pleasure in proposing that Paul Vere-Rugglestone is adopted as parliamentary candidate for the Mercia constituency and I ask you to put my proposal to the meeting."

The sound of her voice awoke Dennis from his trance.

"Is there a seconder?" he asked.

A forest of hands rose in the air.

"All in favour?"

Again a mass of hands waved in unison.

"Those against?"

Not a hand was raised in opposition. Jack Corfield sat silently, scowling, his arms folded.

"Then I declare Paul Vere-Rugglestone adopted as Parliamentary candidate for the Mercia constituency."

The resounding cheer as the audience pushed forward to congratulate Paul deafened Dennis. He did not hear the voice of the reporter who stood beside him, notebook at the ready. Dennis waved a weary hand. "Go away." he demanded. "There'll be a statement tomorrow."

By the time that the crowd had begun to thin Paul

looked around for Annabel but she and the students had collected their placards, rolled up their banner and stolen away – probably to the pub, he thought. Smiling to himself he made a mental note to contact her next day. On the platform the constituency hierarchy, besieged by reporters, huddled together in hurried discussion, whilst at the other end of the hall Tim Parrish was doing his best to dodge two cameramen.

Erica took Paul by the arm, "Come on, let's go and rescue him."

The pile of newspapers that John Brown brought him next day did nothing to relieve Dennis's anger or his headache. The headache was the result of consuming an almost full bottle of Grouse whisky when he got home from the meeting, as, having taken his receiver from the phone, he slumped in dismal contemplation in front of his sandwiches on the dining-table. Jumbled thoughts, clouded by whisky, tumbled around in his head. He never did get an answer to his question how Annabel got into the meeting...or the students...he should have been warned. How dared she interfere? He needed to make a statement...tomorrow...put the blame on someone else...Corfield...his own daughter? Then he remembered ...the look she had given him. How could she, Annabel, his own daughter, hate him so much?

He sat staring at the pile of newspapers, whilst Edith brought in the post. She reached across the table and poured him a second cup of tea and as she handed it to him she saw, for the first time in her married life, the large tears that coursed silently down the front of his jacket.

The adoption meeting made headlines in all the

175

daily papers, even the FT ran a short leader forecasting a stronger pound due to the likelihood that the Government would be returned with an increased majority. All the tabloids reported calls for the resignation of the editor of The Gazette, whilst the broadsheets ran articles questioning the right of the media to deceive the electorate, and the need for the press to put its own house in order.

As for the Gazette, the paper published a short statement in bold type in the bottom left hand corner of the front-page, reporting that the management were now 'seeking legal advice' and would make a detailed statement in the near future.

The following morning a crowd of reporters obstructed the exit from the farm drive. Infuriated, Dennis blew the horn of his Rover long and loud to blast them out of the way. They ran alongside his car, flash bulbs popping. He cursed them, knowing that his enraged face would be sure to feature on the front page of the evening paper. He'd need to prepare a statement before his meeting with the Minister next week - something dismissive – to the effect that he was dealing with the trouble-makers. He would need to be seen as strong and very tough; there must never be any sign of weakness when the shit hits the fan.

Chapter 19

The small square at Marchamley was unusually busy for a Wednesday morning. Shoppers leaving the car-park next to the hotel were surprised to see their local policeman on duty on the pavement, mounting guard over a shining red Rover.

"Bookin' 'im then, are you ?" enquired an elderly pensioner who was returning from the newsagents with his copy of The Gazette.

The driver, opening the passenger door laughed. "It's the Minister."

Overhearing the exchange several passers-by paused to find out which 'minister' was visiting Marchamley, and why.

The Mytton Arms, Union Jack above the portico, four star AA, RAC and a substantial polished brass menu holder beside the entrance dominated the Georgian Square with four storey elegance.

When Brendan McKeith got out of the car the small crowd melted away, disappointed, failing to recognise him - except for the pensioner. "Oh him!" he snorted, having seen McKeith on the television news the previous evening endeavouring to explain away the long hospital waiting lists. As the pensioner had himself been waiting for more than two years for a new hip he had not been impressed by the Minister's excuses.

McKeith, shirtsleeves turned back to elbow level, thumb in the loop of his jacket - slung macho-style over one shoulder, brief-case in the other hand, strode into the hotel - action-man in a hurry, with the rictus of a smile on his face.

In the foyer Dennis Deane waited to greet him, whilst in the conference room, indigo-blue ankle-deep carpet and padded gilt chairs, his Vice-Chairman, Alistair Keene briefed the assembled Chairmen of Health Authorities according to his instructions. "No complaints. No criticism of Government policy. Don't forget that we're facing an election. The Secretary of State only wants good news that he can pass on to the media. However, if you can foresee trouble then tell us about it now, so that we can take action...Remember - no surprises in the run-up to the election...or any other time for that matter."

The thirteen chairmen nodded their heads. They knew the form. Coffee cups in slopped saucers, and plates of biscuits were cleared away and crumbs brushed on to the carpet before Dennis Deane and McKeith entered. Deane limping, lumbering forward. Mc Keith still in action-man mode, muscular, hairy arms and early signs of baldness.

The Chairman wasted no time. "There's no need for introductions. You all know the Secretary of State. He's a busy man and his car is waiting outside to take him into the city to open a new cardiac unit in..." he consulted his watch, "forty-five minutes."

Brendan McKeith surveyed the assembled chairmen. They were all there...all thirteen...no one missing.

"We're very pleased that you've found the time to visit us during your busy schedule." Dennis purred.

McKeith leaned forward, palms flat on the table. "Chairman, we're grateful for the generous contribution from Mercia Region. Your loan played a large part in ensuring that the London hospitals were able to meet their commitments. Of course they were obliged to do just that, in accordance with the contracts they entered into when they took on NHS Trust status. However I am sure that you appreciate that London has unique problems...problems that we are currently addressing...I shall of course be making proposals, which will - in the future - resolve the issues that face us." His voice was persuasive, with the hint of an Irish accent.

He hasn't yet thought out what to do, Barbara Millar told herself.

"However - several of you have unfortunately seen fit to compound the problems by your own greed..." He paused, and taking his time glared at each one as he spoke, making them feel uncomfortable. His attitude suddenly changed, and his voice had a hard cutting edge. "Chairman, two of your Health Authorities ended the year in deficit. No NHS organisation, whether it be a Health Authority, a Trust, or any unit for that matter, is allowed to end the year in deficit without prior agreement with me. Any organisation that does so will have their accounts qualified...and it's no use running to us for help or sympathy - it's a permanent black mark on your record. What you have done defeats the object of the exercise."

Dennis Deane cleared his throat. "Of course it's been done without my knowledge - If I'd known I'd never have agreed"

McKeith cut him short. "One more message before I go - I don't want to hear of one cancelled theatre session, one closed ward, or one operation cancelled. I don't want any surprises. The election is only weeks away. That's all. Any questions ?" He gathered up his jacket and briefcase. "Good to meet you again Dennis. I hear you've dealt with your trouble-makers...good for you. They need to learn which side their bread is

179

buttered....we need men like Paul Rugglestone...right sort of chap. By the way I'm hosting a small brain-storming working party next Thursday..." The rumble of words died away as the two men left the room.

The thirteen chairmen turned to look around the table at each other. "Which ?" asked one.

"Mine I'm afraid." James Burton was obviously embarrassed.

Barbara felt sick. "Marton too," she admitted "but the Chairman did tell us, in his own words, that the Department would square things with the auditors."

"And you believed him?" asked another.

It didn't take Barbara long to decide what she should do. She was only a mile out of Marchamley, following the road to the Marton by-pass before she spoke out loud to herself. "You've been made a fool of. Why did you trust any of them?" She listed the things that needed to be done. Talk to Tom Anstey, alert her Vice Chairman, draft out a fax, then sleep on it. But she knew very well that no matter how long she slept on it, the outcome would be the same.

Tomorrow, before the Health Authority met she would resign. By this time tomorrow the fax would have been sent, and she would be out of the job she had held just over six months.

In that short time the excitement of her appointment had turned to annoyance, frustration and finally to anger. The political rough-house of local government that she had been used to had made her first impressions of the work within the Health Authority seem sweetness and light. During her interview for the post of Chairman she was told that she would be her own boss, free to use her own initiative, with her own secretary and a car as well. Very soon she discovered that those promises were worthless, and that her every move was controlled by Region, who carried out the diktats of the Department of Health at Richmond House. The controllers sat in offices in Whitehall, in Westminster and in the Regions. It was they who plotted the moves, rushing out hasty policies one day, amending them the next, and scrapping them the day after, in response to public reaction and press criticism. Health Authority Chairmen, and Trust Chairmen were pawns that were moved around the chessboard by their controllers, the Chess Masters. As for Regional Chairmen, who used the system to further their own ambitions; they drew a good salary and got rewarded with a Knighthood or even a seat in the Lords; and as Knights on a chessboard, they were able to perform surprise leaps in unforseen directions that others failed to anticipate

Barbara quickly learned that NHS Chairmen had short lives. They came and went regularly, unless they were prepared to bootlick. Some did so. They stayed the course longer than the others. But not her. She was no boot licker; on the other hand she had never seen herself as a 'whistle-blower' either. Now she faced that prospect.

Having slept on her decision and awoken in the same mind Barbara walked through the Executive Suite to her office. In her briefcase was a draft of the fax that she intended to hand to Tom Anstey. She saw him, hovering, waiting for her outside his office.

"Chairman, I heard last night - it was too late to phone you - James Burton has been sacked. I suppose you knew...was he at the meeting yesterday ? By the way how did it go?"

James sacked ? It must have been just after the

181

meeting - after the Minister had left. He'd lasted longer than all the others - had a reputation for common-sense. Dennis Deane seemed to respect him, but he too had ended the year in deficit. She bent her head, searching in her bag for her keys. This was the last time she would open up her office.

Anstey followed her into the room. "You didn't know ? I'd heard that Graham Wheeler's job was threatened and that he was to be moved to Region - ostensibly to lead a team investigating drug-related crime in for the Home Office - sidelined - definitely not promotion. He's having to work his way back into favour. Wheeler told me himself that James Burton wouldn't agree to his replacement. He'd already had a row with Dennis Deane."

"And look where that got him..."

Light filtered between the blinds changing the pattern on the wallpaper as the breeze swung the slats from side to side. She reached for the coffee jug. It was heavy, and her hand shook as she filled the cups, slopping coffee into one of the saucers.

Tom clicked open his brief-case and extracted a letter. "This came in the post this morning, from Tony Bradshaw. It's a copy of a letter from the Department, in reply to our enquiry."

She took the letter, knowing very well that it would confirm what Brendan McKeith had told them yesterday.

Dear Tony,

With reference to your query regarding the offer made by the Secretary of State to Health Authorities who expect to end the financial year with surplus funds and wish to invest in other sectors of the service, I can assure you that it was never the Secretary of State's intention that any publicly funded authority should end the year in deficit.. Any NHS organisation that is unable to balance its budget at the year end has acted contrary to its Standing Orders as set out in the relevant section of the Act.

Best wishes

John Francis, Permanent Under Secretary

Barbara nodded. "It's significant that there's no mention of assisting the London Hospitals, nor any details of the offer made to us." The coffee tasted bitter. She looked steadily at Tom. "Nothing has ever been put in writing, has it?"

He shook his head. "There's never been anything in writing, and that letter has been carefully worded."

She placed her coffee cup on the table, and walked across the room. On the wall opposite her desk was a large photograph which she had taken on her last summer holiday of waves breaking on a deserted beach. She reached up and lifted it off its hangar.

"What are you doing?" he asked, puzzled that at a moment like this the Chairman should busy herself re-arranging the pictures in the office.

"Packing up." She carried the photograph back to her desk, and began to search through her papers to find the fax that she had drafted the previous night to Brendan McKeith. She handed it to Tom Anstey. "See this goes off immediately." She spoke matter-of-factly. "Now, if you'll phone the Vice Chairman and ask him to take the meeting I'll clear my desk." She paused and smiled at him. "That's what politicians usually say, when they resign, isn't it ?"

Chapter 20

Henry Pye parked his Saab in the only available space - which was allocated for medical staff - in front of Queenswood Hall. Having spent the night at the Fishpool Inn and enjoyed a satisfying breakfast - the Full Monty - egg, bacon, sausage, tomatoes, mushrooms, baked beans, and black pudding - an especial favourite, which he never got at home. Not that he ever got a cooked breakfast at home, the old girl ruled out anything that smacked of cholesterol. Toast and marmalade with low fat spread started off his day. His wife ate yoghurt. He tried it once, then offered it to the cat who sniffed it and stalked off in disgust.

Henry felt comfortably replete. He enjoyed staying at country inns. It was one of the more pleasurable perks of being a journalist. The Gazette never begrudged its reporters their pleasures so long as they produced results.

The morning was damp and misty. Golden sycamore leaves drifted down onto the gravel and the parked cars. Henry reached for his tweed hat from the back seat, jammed it onto his head and tapped the pockets of his anorak to check for camera and notebook.

He'd learned enough during the convivial evening in the bar the night before to excite his curiosity. The information came quickly. He'd only needed to ask one seemingly innocent question about the large building that he'd spotted from the road before he'd found himself overwhelmed with details about who had built it and everyone who had owned it since then, as well as speculation as to what was likely to happen to it now that it had been sold to Geoffrey Tate, a consultant physician at Marton General, who drove around the district in a coffee coloured Rolls that bore the number plates GT1 RCP. The fact that Tate's wife worked at Regional Headquarters added zest to his inquiries.

This time, now that he was on the job, The Gazette would not have to withdraw any allegations, offer apologies or agree settlements. The gang of youthful journalists who had bitten off more than they could chew in their efforts to finger almost every MP. in the Commons, were now licking their wounds as they tackled the more mundane tasks to which they had subsequently been assigned. Their efforts may have quadrupled the circulation of the paper for six months, but its reputation had been badly damaged when it was forced to withdraw most of its accusations and settle out of court. Share values and circulation dropped, and MPs whose names had been cleared launched official complaints which added strength to those who were still fighting their own libel actions. Now the public were even more of the opinion that 'you can't believe everything you read in the papers.'

The short report in the Health Service Journal of the sacking of James Burton and the resignation of Barbara Millar as Chairman of Marton Health Authority aroused Henry's curiosity. He had driven from London purely on the intuition that the sale of Queenswood Hall was in some way linked to these two events. When he saw the photograph of the hall, offered for sale by Marton Health Authority, in the property section of the Weekend Telegraph he had the hunch that there lay a story that might give him an opportunity to redress the balance and make the name Pye remembered in Fleet Street for many years to come, and Henry Pye's hunches usually paid off All he hungered for was one good story, good enough for the bestseller he wanted to write in his retirement, in between defending his title as Master at the Chess Club. Henry Pye, novelist and Chess Master. He looked forward to his retirement.

The carpet of fallen leaves rustled as he walked around the corner of Queenswood Hall, then paused and looked down over the terraced gardens that fell steeply to the river below. On the opposite bank the gaunt iron skeletons of the chemical industry loomed through the mist, illuminated by a thousand electric lights. The scene reminded him of a giant Panamax freighter he had once seen emerging from a fog-bank. The sun was beginning to break through and he could just make out the high-rise office blocks in the background and the four-square tower of the cathedral, built on a rise so that it dominated the city.

Voices from his left made him change direction to investigate. In a wooden summer-house a plump Care Assistant in a green and white overall and a grey cardigan sat sharing a thermos of coffee with an elderly man. As he came closer Henry could see that the man had close cropped white hair and must have been well into his eighties, but his hearing was good for he looked up at the sound of Henry's footsteps.

"Who is it ? I can't see. My glasses are misted up - it's the coffee."

Henry stepped inside and took a seat beside him on the wooden Bench.

"He always has his coffee out here when the weather's fit. I bring him out most days if I have the time." The Care Assistant stopped and pointed towards the river. "Down there to the left of the church there's a row of houses. The end one on the right - that was his. He lived there for fifty-six years with his wife - ever since they were married. She died three years ago - cancer. He couldn't look after himself. His children, son and daughter, visit every week - and grandchildren." She looked at the old man fondly. "Sarah and Mark You look forward to Sundays, don't you ?"

The old man turned his head and gazed at Henry with questioning rheumy eyes. Like an old dog, thought Henry. Just like an old dog, unable to understand why he had been put in kennels. Henry felt strangely sad.

"Can you see your house, John ?" asked the Care Assistant. "I doubt if he can." she said, turning to Henry.

"When it's clear I can - but next year they're moving us. Then I'll never see it again." John whispered.

"Oh, you'll see it again." the Care Assistant re-assured him. "We take them shopping every week in the van - it takes wheel-chairs. We go past his house to the supermarket." She paused. "We're moving to a new home - Parker's Paddock. It's nearer to Marton."

Henry remembered that someone in the bar at the Fishpool had mentioned Parker's Paddock.

"You'll like it there." said the Care Assistant. "You'll have your own room."

The old man shook his head. "I've never slept by myself."

She pursed her lips. "That's what they all say. They don't want to move. They're used to it here." She stood up. "We must get back. They'll be wondering what's happened to us." She helped him to his feet. "I'll be in trouble for sitting in the summer-house with you." She smiled at Henry and laughed as she put her arm around the old man's waist. "He's always trying to get us girls to go into the summer-house with him. He's really wicked."

Henry handed him his stick. He walked with them as far as the side entrance, then moved away, intending to circle the building.

On the opposite side of the hall lay outbuildings that had once been part of the school. Crumbling cement and decaying brickwork told the tale of years of neglect. Broken tiles, from the roof above the laundry, littered the concrete yard. Fractured guttering and peeling paintwork added to the scene of dereliction. Henry peered through the cobweb festooned windows into the kitchen and surveyed the stained Belfast sink with its wooden draining board. Mildew traced the cracks between discoloured tiles, and he was puzzled by the stained yellowing circles on the rotting linoleum that partly covered the floor.

A stone flagged path lead from the back door to the overgrown kitchen garden. The way was blocked by brambles and the remains of a recent bonfire. Charred pieces of blue and yellow cardboard bearing gold lettering lay amongst the damp debris. He stooped and picked one up and turned it around in his hand, examining it. He rubbed it with his thumb and made out the letters LD and STER. Henry gathered up several more pieces and out of habit slipped them into his anorak pocket. Walking around the end of the building he pulled his camera from his pocket and took two photographs of the ornamental front entrance, then made his way back to the car.

Henry Pye followed the ring-road around Marton.

He drove carefully, looking out for the sign to Parker's Road. He prided himself on his choice of car, an F Reg. maroon Saab 900s with only 15,000 miles on the clock and one elderly owner. He bought it four years ago from a local garage for three-hundred and fifty pounds. It was one of the last of the old classic design, much favoured by publicans because of the ease of lifting a keg into the boot which had no lip. Heavily built, it lacked the acceleration of recent models but was in perfect condition, reliable and safe. The same could be said of everything he owned. He still had his old typewriter, although now he used an electric model, as for gizmos - he was just not interested. Too old a dog to learn new tricks, besides he would be retiring next year, he refused to be instructed on the technicalities of e-mail and computers, although he had once attempted to send off a fax. His effort had jammed the system for days as the machine stubbornly insisted on phoning a wrong number every two minutes.

A muddy lane, its rutted surface imprinted by caterpillar and tyre tracks, lead to the building site where a large sign informed those who had successfully negotiated their way along the track that the land had been acquired by Marton Health Authority for a seventy bed nursing home. Henry parked his Saab on the cleanest stretch of tarmac he could find, extracted his wellingtons from the boot and set off in the direction of the site office.

The comfortable fug of coffee and cigarettes, and the sight of the foreman sitting in front of an electric fire made him feel at home. During his time at The Gazette he had spent many congenial hours in site offices, enjoying coffee and biscuits and picking up information. He knocked the mud from his boots and

189

hauled himself up into the pre-fab.

"Henry Pye - putting together publicity for the Health Authority," he explained, holding out his hand. "They told me to come down and see you."

The foreman, a large man wearing a luminous yellow waterproof, smiled happily, removed his hand from a box of biscuits and proffered it to Henry. He got to his feet, kicked a stool out from under the table and searched for the coffee jar. Pushing aside a bright yellow hard hat, and a jumbled heap of architect's plans that cascaded onto the floor, he placed a chipped mug of Nescafe onto the table beside Henry.

A builder's lorry, loaded with bricks, its engine revving noisily, negotiated the rutted ground and stopped outside the office, its exhaust rattling. Henry made a note of the name that was on the door 'Lewis Gilbert.' The shaven-headed driver, sporting a gold earring in his left ear, and chewing gum, jumped out and swaggered to the door with a printed sheet of yellow paper.

"Where'd 'ju want this lot then ?"

The foreman took the paper, "Usual place - I'll be some time - I've got someone from the Health Authority with me." He turned back to the biscuit box. The dark brown paper crackled as he scrabbled around inside and withdrew two chocolate digestives. He grinned at Henry, "Okay - fire away."

"Be easier really if you were to tell me," Henry suggested, selecting the last pink wafer. "I mean - well, something about the history of the site - had a bit of a chequered history, didn't it? Good spot though - convenient for the town."

"Oh, the site - well the owners were really hoping to sell it for a supermarket..."

190

"Owners? You mean the Health Authority?"

"No, before them...VS&T. They sold it to the Health Authority."

Henry put down his mug of coffee. "Mind if I make notes?" The foreman waved his hand. "Go ahead."

"So who's VS&T ?"

Oh, just a small business - used to be scrap dealers. You know the sort of thing. They cannibalised cars and sold retreads. Then they thought up a smart name - Vehicle Spares and Transplants. When they'd made a bit of money they began to buy up bits of land here and there, and a cottage or two which they did up and re-sold. Gareth Gilbert, brother to Lewis Gilbert is one of the directors - don't know who the other chap is - but they seem to have done all right for themselves."

"Lewis Gilbert ? Wasn't his name on that lorry ?"

"That's right. He runs the building firm."

Henry paused from his note taking. "Isn't that a bit odd, that one of the brothers sells the land and the other builds the nursing home? Or was it part of the deal?"

The foreman shook his head. "Oh no - all open and above board. We tendered for the work - usual procedure. Ours was the lowest tender. Won it fair and square."

In the next ten minutes Henry learned that the hand-over from the builders to the Health Authority was scheduled for the first of March and that the residents would be transferred before April the fifth, on which day the official opening ceremony had been planned. Lady Edith Deane, wife of the Regional Chairman, had been invited to perform the official ceremony as no minor Royals would be available that day.

191

Chapter 21

The Press statement announcing the resignation of the Chairman of Marton Health Authority lay unnoticed amongst the papers that spewed out of the Regional fax machine until Beryl, the Chief Executive's secretary, returned from her coffee break.

Malcolm Yates was not giving his full attention to the Region's business. The latest copy of the Health Service Journal lay open on the desk in front of him displaying, in the Appointments section, a half page advertisement for a Chief Executive to lead the new London Metropolitan Health Authority whose creation the Secretary of State had recently announced in the House. In the run-up to the election the Chancellor, in an Autumn mini-budget, had allocated an exra £5 million a year over the next five years to fund new projects in the Health Service. Malcolm drew a large box around the whole advertisement with his red biro.

'The Authority will work closely with Government to provide London with the newest technology to enable the NHS to offer top quality medical, surgical and Primary Care services for the City in the Millenium."

In the Commons a week earlier Brendon McKeith had announced to those M.Ps who remained in the Chamber after P.M's Question Time, "When this project is up and running the world will beat a path to our door. No other country could possibly compete with the medical and surgical facilities that London will be able to offer." The Secretary of State leaned forward to pick up his file from the Dispatch Box. "We will be the international centre of excellence for medicine and surgery." he declared triumphantly.

Working closely with Government...The leading man, heading up the project - a job like that, not to mention the salary, would most definitely secure his future. He reached for his tea cup, leaned back in his chair and rested his feet on the edge of an open desk drawer - the Government's Chief Medical Officer; Malcolm Yates CBE ? He smiled, MBE - my bloody effort ? OBE - other bugger's efforts ? Sir Malcolm Yates sounded much better - that could lead to KCMG - it was always the joke when Ken Clarke was at Health - Ken calls me God.

Beryl, pencil-line skirt with a side slit displaying an elegant leg, tapped briefly and entered, breaking into his dreams. He watched her walk towards him. Should he take her with him to London ? He'd enjoyed the nights they'd spent together in conference hotels. Now he relied on her always being there.

I thought you ought to see this before I take it into the Chairman." She handed him the fax.

The heading hit him between the eyes. "Resignation of the Chairman of Marton Health Authority. It was announced this morning that Barbara Millar, Chairman of the Marton Health Authority has sent her resignation to the Secretary of State, Brendan McKeith. In her letter Mrs. Millar complained that the Marton Health Authority, when asked to find cash to help the London hospitals balance their budgets, had been given misleading advice by Dennis Deane, the Chairman of Mercia Region..."

The London dream was put on hold. The sound of a door banging against its stop made him jump.

"Have you seen the Daily Express ? The Chairman's having a fit. I'm not sure whether I ought

193

to get the Medical Officer down to see him." The Chairman's secretary dumped a pile of newspapers on Malcolm's desk. "I've marked all the references." Lisa sighed and raised her eyes to Heaven. She was getting used to Dennis Deane's tantrums.

The phone on his desk rang. "We've got The Gazette and The HSJ on the lines. Will you speak to them ?" twittered Mandy from the typing pool.

Beryl began to sort out the newspapers. "Shall I see if the Chairman's free ?"

"Give me half-an-hour to go through the papers," he needed time to think "and tell the Press that we don't wish to comment at present."

In the Chairman's office Dennis Deane studied the fax in disbelief. The bitch...the stupid bitch. He remembered the first time he had interviewed her for the job of Chairman. She sat opposite him, cool and calm, in a Tory blue suit and navy blouse with a floppy bow beneath her chin. Neat coiffeured hair style. She must have been to the hairdresser that morning. He approved of that - she obviously wanted the job. Six weeks later he discovered that, just like all other women, not only had she got a mind of her own, but - worse still - was determined to win every argument. Dennis did not like people who argued with him, especially if they were right - and she was right about John Taylor. She should never have renewed the lease.

He turned back to the fax, misleading advice ? A sick feeling in his stomach nagged him. Tony Bradshaw had told him that she was angry about the accounts being qualified. He'd encouraged Chairmen... not deliberately misled them. He'd never thought for one moment that the auditors would...but strictly speaking they were right. Brendan McKeith

194

knew...Dennis remembered what had been said at the meeting - two health authorities - well he'd already sacked James Burton.

He knew what this would mean - an interview with the Secretary of State - having to explain himself. With an election in the offing Brendan McKeith would blow his top. He could be sacked. No, not before the election - that would create more problems for the Government. But after the election ? When the next batch of appointments were announced. He crumpled up the fax and threw it across the desk. It skidded along the polished surface and rolled onto the carpet. In a fit of fury he slammed his fist down onto the blotter in front of him. It made him feel no better. He swept aside his empty coffee cup and saucer, they too landed on the carpet, unbroken, which gave him no satisfaction. Looking for someone to vent his wrath upon he bellowed for his secretary. Lisa, waiting outside the door ready to retrieve the crockery and anything else that the Chairman hurled on to the floor, when he got into one of his rages, hesitated for a moment, then carrying a dustpan in front of her calmly greeted her enraged boss.

"There's been a call from the Secretary of State's office asking for a meeting tomorrow morning Chairman. Do you want me to book you a seat on the seven-forty morning train?"

Malcolm Yates, with an armful of national newspapers, pushed open the door of the Chairman's office. "You'll need to read these before the meeting tomorrow." He selected a newspaper from the top of the pile. "Demand for a Dirty Tricks Enquiry." shouted the headlines in the Daily Mail. Malcolm began to read out loud. "After accusations levelled at the Tory party by 'Whistle-Blower' Barbara Millar that the party had attempted to mislead both Government Auditors and the electorate about their financial management of the Health Service, the Leader of the Opposition Neil Kinnock demanded a thorough investigation into the whole affair..." Malcolm paused and placed his hand on the pile of papers. "They're all pretty much the same except for the Gazette that carries a leader article and an editorial attacking the Government."

Dennis slumped back in his chair and stared at his Chief Executive. "So what's your advice?"

How many times had he been expected to pull the chestnuts out of the fire ?   This time the Chairman expected too much. "I rather think you'll have to follow the party line on this one."

"The party line?"

"The Department will have already decided on its response - you'll just have to go along with it."

"But surely we could - between us..." Dennis blustered.

"Chairman - they won't want excuses. You're wasting your time. They'll tell you what to say. Their tale will be good - acceptable to those who don't read between the lines - like for instance newspapers who'll put their own interpretation on any story which ever way it's told..." He paused. The Chairman's expression was blank as he stared out through the window at the roofscape of the city, and the ringers of Our Lady and St. Nicholas rang "The Bells of Saint Mary" on the carillon.

How could he expect to get the London job now?

The interview with Brendan McKeith at the Department in Richmond House was held in a cramped meeting room. Usually Dennis was welcomed into the Secretary of State's private room, offered tea and biscuits and addressed by his Christian name. Now, for the first time in his adult life he felt like a small boy hauled up in front of a Headmaster. He fiddled anxiously with the corner of dry leather that had curled away from the tabletop in front of him.

Brendan McKeith was flanked by two members of the NHS Executive who called him Mr. Deane. He recognised one of them from photographs in the HSJ. He was the burly round-faced right-hand man to the Secretary of State, Alan Greenbank.

Brendan McKeith wasted no time. "As Regional Chairman you are expected to keep your own Chairmen under control. I told you - no surprises. You've handled this one badly." He turned to Greenbank. "Alan and his team spent valuable hours last night drafting a press release."

Greenbank peered over steel-rimmed half-frames, adjusted them carefully on the bridge of his nose, and pushed a sheet of A4 across the table towards Dennis. "I'll go through it slowly Mr. Deane. Stop me if you have any questions. We need your agreement to every word. It's important that we all sing from the same hymn sheet, if you get my meaning ?"

Dennis nodded.

"The Secretary of State has received the resignation of the Chairman of Marton Health Authority and regrets that she took this decision without consulting the Chairman of Mercia Regional Health Authority. Had she done so she would have learned the reason why the Secretary of State had decided to redistribute surplus NHS money from the Regions to the Capital.

As a result of the sale of land and buildings in

197

Marton, which were surplus to requirements, the Health Authority received funds which it did not require for immediate use during that financial year. Consequently the Secretary of State allocated that money to the London Hospitals, where it was most needed, having agreed with Mercia Region that the needs of the Marton Health Authority would be considered sympathetically when the Authority had drawn up an agreed programme of priorities for future years."

Dennis nodded, relieved. They appeared to have got him out of a tight corner. "They've been agitating for a dialysis unit. There's a Kidney Patient's Association in the Regional that raised fifty thousand pounds and asked us to match it pound for pound.."

For the first time that morning McKeith smiled, a thin tight-lipped grimace. "Well that's the answer, isn't it ?   We can turn the whole problem around. Get out another press release Alan, something on the lines of..." Dennis watched as McKeith rubbed his carefully manicured hands over his face as he chose his words. "New hope for kidney patients...not only have Mercia Region agreed to match pound for pound...but offered to fund the additional nursing costs for the next...five years ?"

Dennis scowled. "Three years," he protested.

"Then there is the question of accommodation."

"We can't afford a new building - "

"Do you want us to win this election ?"

"All right, I'll order a review of accommodation. Maybe you'd like me to close a Geriatric ward ?"

McKeith's eyes glittered at the sarcasm.

"Obviously you've not picked up on the news that Age Concern are lobbying us to treat the over-fifties as medical and surgical cases rather than classing them as

198

Geriatrics? You must be over sixty yourself. Do you class yourself as Geriatric?" He turned towards Greenbank. "That's it then...Alan...The Department announces the provision of a new Renal Unit for Marton General..."

Dennis frowned. "Well as long as the Department is funding it - "

"You're funding it. Out of your allocation - it's your responsibility. You can phase it in...a five year programme - doesn't have to be done tomorrow. Anyway now that you've lost two Chairman you can save your self some money - "

Dennis frowned.

"Amalgamate the two authorities." McKeith sighed impatiently. "Join them together - they're next door to each other." He looked along the table and snapped his fingers at a clerk seated at the far end. "Pass me that file." The blue leather file was passed down the table. He flipped it open and stared at the notes he had made. "Oh yes, Harry Furnell. We'll send you details of his address and phone number. Chap lives in your Region - big donor to party funds - seems he expects some sort of recognition."

Dennis momentarily closed his eyes in horror at the thought of Harry Furnell being in control of anything that was answerable to the public, let alone handling public money.

"Know him do you?" asked McKeith.

How could he tell McKeith of the constant speculation in the community about how Harry made his money. Everyone knew how he spent it. Even Edie who had lived with him for three years refused to marry him.

"What, marry Harry?" she had reportedly said

during a wild party after the races. "Harry wouldn't spend money on me if I married him. He'd be off spending it on another blonde. Look - " She held out her hands, displaying her rocks. "What Edie wants, Edie gets – as things stand."

"Yes," said Dennis. "I know Harry."

"Good." McKeith rubbed his hands together. "A good morning's work - probably turn out better than we expected - I'll drop a line to your M.P. It's Paul Rugglestone isn't it? You'll need to brief him."

Chapter 22

The news that Harry Furnell had been appointed Chairman of the new Health Authority warranted only a small photograph in the Gazette. It had been taken five years ago and showed Harry leading his horse into the unsaddling enclosure at Haydock. It was the only winner he had ever had, and that was in a small field. He sold the horse next day and it never won another race. It was a good photograph, and showed off his fair curly hair, Armani suit and triumphant grin. He had it enlarged and framed and it took pride of place on the Bechstein Grand in the drawing-room of his mock tudor house eight miles from the city centre.

On his first day as Chairman Harry informed Tom Anstey that he expected his monthly salary to be paid in cash.

"But that's not the way we do things," the Chief Executive had protested. "There's a procedure in the NHS for the payment of salaries. Your salary will be paid into your bank account - "

"It may not be the way you have done things in the past, but I'm telling you - now that I'm Chairman, that's how I want it. You people will have to get used to the idea that there's going to be changes around here."

"I'll need to clear it with Region." said Tom, anxious to place the responsibility firmly in the lap of Tony Bradshaw.

At the end of Harry's first week in office Gerard Stephenson, Head of the Surgical directorate at Marton General took time off from his lunch break to meet privately with Francis Barclay, Head of the Medical

201

directorate, in order to discuss the new Chairmans' internal memo demanding a meeting with all medical staff 'in order to examine the cost of drugs and the economic effectiveness of their use.'

It had been a long morning. The cholesystectomy that had appeared simple from the ultrasound scan had proved tricky, the gall bladder was diseased and it took longer than Gerard had anticipated. He was running behind schedule and would in all probability have to cancel at least one procedure if he was to start his private list later that afternoon at the Nuffield hospital next door. Still in his pale blue theatre gown he carried his plate of sandwiches and a mug of black coffee into the office of the Medical Directorate. "Who the hell does that little twit think he is?" He sank down gratefully into an easy chair and balanced his plate on large bony knees. "What on earth makes the chap think that we would agree to discuss the use and cost of drugs with him?"

Francis pushed a pile of papers aside and cleared a corner of his desk to make room for the lunchtime snack. "I should be careful - remember he's a government appointment - "

"So what? All Chairmen are government appointments."

"On regional recommendation - but from what I hear this one has been imposed on Region."

Gerard carefully selected the crumbs from his plate with slim, well manicured fingers. "In that case I wouldn't think that Dennis was best pleased at having that wide-boy inflicted on him. He's always been scared of being associated with types like Harry Furnell."

"So, what's wrong with him ? He must be well

202

thought of by the party. Surely they wouldn't appoint him as chairman if he was at all dodgy."

The surgeon laughed. "Politicians have never been known to inquire too closely into the source of large contributions to the party."

"How come you know so much about Harry ?"

"From Geoffrey Tate." Gerard put down his coffee mug, stretched out his arms and yawned, he's married to Harry's sister Kathy. Mind you she can't stand him. Mention Harry to her and she goes ballistic. Harry talks big. Never can resist trying to make an impression. Everyone knows that he expects a reward for all he's contributed to the party. Not only that, most people have a good idea where his money comes from..."

Francis leaned forward in his chair. "Tell me."

Gerard shrugged his shoulders. "Re-packaging." he said. "A simple case of re-packaging."

"Re-packaging?"

"Yes, you know. Some of the smaller supermarkets, and mini-markets in city centres sell stock to him, at knock-down prices, stock that's past its sell-buy date. Reputable supermarkets destroy out of date stock."

Francis frowned. "So what happens to the stock?"

"Simple." Gerard grinned. "It's re-packaged and re-dated and sold to third world countries - who, incidentally have been given foreign aid by our Government and the EU so that they can buy the re-packaged stock from Harry."

Francis blinked and opened his mouth to speak.

"Dented cans a speciality," Gerard continued. "Oh and I understand that he collects unsold confectionary - you know - cakes and biscuits from big bakery firms that's past their 'sell by' date. That waste is usually sold on to pig farmers. Well Harry has a contract to deliver it - but some of the better packaged stuff often goes missing on its way through the city centre."

"My God," exclaimed Francis. "My wife's very keen on those sort of cakes - but how do you know all this?"

"Brother-in-law's in the trade." replied Gerard tersely, "but I wouldn't worry if I were you - we get a constant supply of cakes, and packets of tea from the local tea factory through him."

"Good God." Francis sounded shocked. "So you think that Harry might - "

Obvious," said Gerard. "Can't have a chap like that playing the market with medical supplies. You don't know where it would end - interfering in clinical matters." He leaned back in his chair, rocking with laughter. "Just imagine, re-packaging sterile dressings and out of date tablets - the opportunities for cheap offers - buy one get one free - to third world countries would be endless. We could all make our fortunes." He stood up and brushed the crumbs from his gown. "We have to keep the Chairman out of this hospital and never ever become involved in any discussion with him on cost or use of drugs. The less he knows the better. Tell him nothing Francis - nothing at all. I'll reply to him. I'll inform him that we cannot discuss clinical matters."

As he opened the door, he hesitated. "By the way. My neighbour who's on the council tells me that Harry has a new venture going - waste disposal. He's applied for planning permission to dump chemical and toxic waste into a land-fill site. Doesn't miss a trick does he? Sharp to the bottom of the glass! Watch out for his next bright idea - a more effective method of disposing of soiled dressings and medical and surgical waste."

He paused and looked thoughtful. "I wonder whether he'd want to broker a deal on an incinerator for us?" he asked, "instead of paying to have surgical waste taken away. Then he'd have the environmental lobby to battle with – that might keep him happy."

"Then of course there's always the contracts for the kitchens. He might offer us a nice line in tea and cakes," said Francis grinning.

Chapter 23

Henry Pye gingerly explored the jagged cavity in his molar with the edge of his tongue and hoped that he wouldn't need an injection. Well into his generous helping of Beef Bourguignon at dinner the previous evening he felt his teeth grate on something brittle. As he had feared, he'd lost a filling. He took it from his mouth and put it on the side of his plate where it glinted at him under the spotlights.

The waiting room was small and smelled strongly of air freshener. Next to him on the sofa a dark-haired young woman hid behind a tattered copy of Woman's Own, her children squabbling over out-of-date magazines that cascaded from the low table on to the carpet. Henry leaned forward to pick one up and examined the front cover of Mercia Life, Show Edition, with interest.

A crisp voice from the loud-speaker above his head called "Mrs.Ford." The woman put down her magazine and led the children from the room. Henry opened his mouth and carefully felt the pitted surface of the tooth. His finger still held the faint flavour of garlic and he sucked it thoughtfully, remembering the garlic bread he had enjoyed at lunchtime. He turned his attention back to Mercia Life, riffling through the glossy pages of advertisements for country estates, women's fashions, Lancias and Mercedes until photographs of the County Show caught his attention.

Major Greville Dewhurst, Master of the Mercia Foxhounds sat in pink-coated splendour astride his showy chestnut mare, surrounded by a happy pack of hounds who were enjoying the attention of an admiring crowd. But the photograph that attracted Henry's attention was not that of Greville Dewhurst. On the opposite page beneath the heading 'County Champions' he spotted the round self-satisfied face of Harold Tuck beaming like a full moon standing beside a Double Gloucester Cheese and clutching the blue and gold card awarded to the winner of the gold medal champion Double Gloucester cheese. Henry stared at the photograph and frowned. He remembered the two pieces of card that he had rescued from the bonfire, and felt sure that in the envelope that lay beneath his socks in a drawer in his room at the Fishpool was the singed corner of that particular championship card that Harold Tuck grasped in his fat fingers.

Next to that photograph was another that interested Henry almost as much. He turned his attention to the Champion Hereford Bull 'Crown Dynasty' who stood four square, firmly held by a triumphant owner, beside a large silver cup. Henry read the words beneath the photograph with excitement "Mark Clapton, breeder of the Show Champion Hereford Bull Crown Dynasty receives his award from Sponsor Gareth Gilbert, Director of VS&T."

Henry glanced at his watch. They'd kept him waiting twenty-five minutes. He carefully reached into his inner macintosh pocket. He supposed he could have asked permission to take the magazine, it was well thumbed and out-of-date, but he had to have it, right now. It fitted flat inside his wide pocket. He got to his feet and walked out of the waiting room to reception.

"Can't afford to wait any longer. I've a business engagement the other side of town, and I can't be late. You'll have to make another appointment - when you can guarantee to see me on time." He tried to sound angry, but his impatience was genuine as was his urgency to get back to the Fishpool and take a careful look at the charred remains he had collected from the bonfire at Queenswood Hall. The dental surgery lay behind the Civic Centre car park at the back of the Civic Hall. Henry hurried back to the Saab. Across the car park he saw a shaven-headed lad with one gold earring climb into a lorry and drive away. The vehicle looked like the Lewis Gilbert builder's lorry, but bore no identification, except for the noise of a rattling exhaust.

Henry turned on the ignition, reversed out of the parking space and drove around the car park, following the white arrows towards the exit. By the time he reached the bypass a red light on the Saab dashboard winked at him. It was odd; he could never remember seeing it before or noticing that there was even a light there. The light continued to flash regularly. He drove on until he reached a lay by, then pulled in, stopped, and searched in the glove pocket to find the Owner's Manual. He flicked through the pages, examining the illustrations and reading the text. As he might have expected, no mention was made of that particular light. Henry sighed, then remembered that there was a garage and work shop about a mile away along the dual carriageway by the lorry drivers' cafe.

Oily blue overalls, black curly hair and a grin as wide as his face the mechanic placed protective paper over the driver's seat, sat down and switched on the ignition. The red light winked. The engineer switched off the engine and walked around the car, leaned down and inspected the right hand hub cap. "Leave the car here. I'll drive you back, in my car, not this one. Phone me later this afternoon."

Half an hour later the mechanic phoned him back. "Mr Pye? Who's got it in for you? You'll be getting a visit from the police very soon. Someone's released the brake fluid nut. They knew what they were doing. Needed a special spanner for that – could only be someone with the right tools."

He'd hardly replaced the receiver before the bedroom phone rang again. "Police Inspector Hodgkin on his way up. Says you're expecting him"

The Inspector sat down on the only chair in the room, by the window and placed his cap on the dressing table beside him. "Hodgkin. Police Inspector. The FishPool garage called us. I brought a mechanic out with me. It seems that someone released your brake fluid nut. It's lucky for you it was only half a turn. Where were you parked?"

Henry swallowed and felt the sweat running down his brow. He took off his jacket and burrowed in a pocket for his handkerchief and wiped his face. He'd read in the Gazette of things like this happening to others.

"It's an expert job. Do you know anyone who works with cars? Someone who would have the right type of spanner? Another Saab owner perhaps? Not just anyone. Around here, if someone had it in for you, he'd walk past your car with a fifty pence piece and leave a lovely deep scratch, all along the side."

Henry tried to think. "The Civic Centre Car Park?" He shook his head doubtfully."

"A clever job," continued the Inspector. "Just a turn. That's all that was needed. Every time you braked it would release oil. It would take time before it was completely empty, so you would never know where and how it happened. Now – if he'd wanted to

209

kill you there and then, all he had to do was to open the nut fully, so that when you braked you'd have driven straight into the nearest wall or gatepost – or collided with another car. No this was clever – whoever did that knew what he was doing."

"Can't think of anyone." said Henry. "I'll need time to think."

"You newspaper chaps don't go through life without upsetting someone, surely." The Inspector got to his feet. "Try to think who it could be. In any case keep your eyes open and inspect your front hub caps every day. A slick of oil on a hub cap will tell you if anyone tries it again. But think hard. This is serious. Someone has tried to kill you. I'll phone you again tomorrow."

The welcoming atmosphere of the saloon bar enveloped Henry in a comfortable blanket of ale and tobacco. He stared thoughtfully into his glass of Boddingtons. Behind the bar counter Nick Reddy, landlord of the Fishpool paused from polishing the glasses and draped his towel neatly across the handles of the pumps.

"They've been calling you all morning," he said reaching behind him for his memo pad.

Henry read the message. "Phone Rick Keel at the Gazette urgently."

He was surprised that the Deputy Editor should phone him. He had very little to do with Keel who never usually interfered when Henry was on a job.

"I'll take it in my room," he tore the notelet from the pad, then paused on the stairs. "Steak and Kidney Pie and another Boddingtons in quarter-of-an-hour ?" he asked.

The landlord smiled and wrote down the order.

Henry's room at the back of the Fishpool faced the garden. The first yellow leaves of late summer drifted down adding to the dust on the tops of the plastic tables and chairs that had been left out in the hope of a few more warm days. He switched on the bedside light, and a standard lamp in the corner by the dressing table, then turned his attention to the sock drawer.

The manilla envelope, hidden beneath the socks, was grubby with ash and charcoal finger-marks. In the drawer beside it was a small leather games case containing his travelling chess set. It accompanied him everywhere and in spare moments he took the opportunity to practice, moving the chess men in accordance with the game that always featured, every day on the back page of the Gazette. Henry took the envelope and the chess set from the drawer then spread out the centre page of that days' edition of the Gazette on the glass top of the dressing table.

Tipping the blackened pieces of card from the envelope on to the newspaper he began to sort through the charred remains. The blue and gold corner shone beneath the glow of the standard lamp. Henry picked it up and rubbed it with his thumb, then reached for his mackintosh and pulled the copy of the Mercia Life from its inside pocket where he had hidden it when he left the dentist's surgery. Impatiently he pressed down the pages of the magazine with his fist and compared the photograph with the piece of card he held between his finger and thumb. There was no doubt. The gold figures '99' showed the year of the award. Henry felt a surge of excitement. He needed another pint of Boddingtons and time to think. Then he remembered the message and felt in his pocket for the note.

The Deputy Editor spoke excitedly "There's been a

211

new development. Barbara Millar - you know - the woman who resigned as Chairman of Marton Health Authority, the 'whistle-blower,' has agreed to spill the beans - for a sum of course - and we've bought her story."

Henry sucked on his pipe and digested the information. "I thought we had the full story?"

"There's more. This'll kill off any hope for the Government. It's lucky that you're in the area. Get round there - fast."

Before he replaced the chess set into the sock drawer he opened the leather case to check how he had left the state of play. He noted with some satisfaction that the Black King was in check from his White Knight.

Edith Deane sank thankfully on to the deep cushions of the chintz-covered sofa and kicked off her shoes. She had been knocking on doors since mid-morning, with disappointing results, and her feet ached. Nevertheless, she reminded herself, she had chosen to canvas the housing estates on the northern edge of town and had done her best to inspire her team despite having doors slammed in her face, and threatened by vicious dogs and wrathful socialist voters.

"Vote for the Tories? No way luv! It'll take us years to recover from Thatcher –she's done more harm to this country than Adolf Hitler."

In the rural areas the story was different. Blue posters displayed the name of Paul Rugglestone on every tree in gardens and lanes and unless the Labour party were able to spring a last-minute surprise Paul should be returned to Westminster with a comfortable majority.

Edith reached out for the remote control and looked at her watch. Just time for the last episode of Martin Chuzzlewit. The credits for the earlier program scrolled down the screen and Edith felt the need to relax with a whisky. Of course Dennis would grumble. He always grumbled, even when she suggested a night-cap.

"You'll end up an alcoholic." It was his stock phrase, but he always poured himself a stiff one as well. Tonight he was, as usual in his study, on the phone, which prevented her from phoning Annabel. She crossed the room to the cocktail cabinet and had her hand on the key with its multicoloured silk tassel when she heard the study door bang and his footsteps in the hall. She jumped nervously, feeling guilty as she hurried back to the sofa.

Dennis lumbered into the lounge and made for the side-table and the remote control. "Party Political Broadcast - almost missed it."

Martin Chuzzlewit was despatched to oblivion and the face of Brendan McKeith replaced him. Edith sighed. Dennis ignored her demonstration of annoyance and sank heavily into his chair.

"Not only have we met our waiting list targets and reduced waiting times, but every Hospital and every Trust in the country ended the year balancing their budgets. The staff in the NHS - surgical, medical and administrative - across the board, in every unit, have united to support the Government's reforms. The NHS is not only safe in our hands but is a major success story which brings enormous benefits to patients throughout the length and breadth of the British Isles."

Dennis rubbed his hands together in pleasure. "...And they couldn't have done it without help from

213

Mercia Region."

As the tight-lipped smile on the Minister's face faded, reminding Edith of Alice's Cheshire Cat, Dennis pressed the 'stand-by' button.

"But I thought..." Edith began uncertainly.

"Bit of a misunderstanding...all sorted out...got the right result...worked out for the best." Dennis got up and crossed to the drinks cabinet. "We'll win the election now, you'll see - and I'll get to the Lords."

Edith looked at him doubtfully. "But you said..." She stopped when she saw him scowling at her. "Well... I hope it works out."

"Of course it will work out. When the election's over it'll be congratulations all round, and that wretched woman and her trouble-making will be forgotten."

Edith stretched her hand out for the remote control. "Are you going to watch Panorama?"

Dennis nodded. He always watched it, which meant that Edith would be free to disappear upstairs and phone Annabel from the bedroom extension.

The room was cold. Edith sighed. She supposed that Dennis had turned off the master heating switch in the hall. As usual whenever she turned it on, he always turned it off. As she listened to the dialling tone she pulled the green duvet around her shoulders.

Sandy's voice sounded terse, unlike his usual self. "I'm afraid Annabel's not here..."

The silence that followed caused her concern. "I see - I suppose she'll be back later?"

"When you rang I hoped it might have been her – I don't know when she's coming back..."

"Where is she?" Edith tried to stay calm. She always feared for Annabel, the only person in her life that really mattered, the only person she could talk to, and the only person who understood what Dennis was really like. There was no one else she could talk to, it would be too disloyal. "She's not in hospital is she?"

"Mrs. Deane, Annabel is at the police station - we were both taken there for questioning. They're keeping Annabel overnight. I've come back to collect her overnight things. I can't say too much - there's a police officer with me - here - in the kitchen."

"But…"

"It's about the show."

"But you weren't at the show - " A wave of anger flooded over her. How dare they? They'd got the wrong person. They didn't know Annabel - she was the only one that really knew Annabel. Despite her outward bravado Annabel would be frightened.

"I know. But they think she planned it." Sandy sounded desperate. "They'll have to let her out tomorrow - unless they intend to charge her."

Edith heard the catch in his voice. He sounded close to tears. The thought of Annabel locked in a cell made her feel close to tears too.

"You know she'd never do anything that would frighten the animals. It would be the first thing she would think of."

"Shall I go to her – to the Police Station. Maybe I could do something – explain to them. I'm sure I could help."

"No Mrs Deane - I did suggest it, but she was adamant. I'll tell her you wanted to."

"Shall I phone our solicitor?"

"Well perhaps in the morning if they don't let her out. You know I've got a feeling that they've kept her in just to frighten her." Sandy did his best to speak

215

calmly.

How's she coping?"

"Well you know Annabel..." he gave a little laugh. "Demanding her rights, legal aid, a solicitor and anything else she can think of. It's just another challenge - another fight against the establishment. It's almost as if she were enjoying herself."

"Isn't there really anything I can do?" Edith asked desperately.

"Not a thing - not unless you can find out who was behind the bomb scare."

Edith heard Sandy sigh deeply before he replaced the receiver. Wrapped in her duvet she sat on the bed thinking of Annabel. Dennis would have to be told... he would soon find out that Annabel had been arrested...it was best that she should tell him before he heard it on the local news, or read it in the paper. Annabel needed help...but could he really do anything...he had contacts...surely he would want to try? Edith made her way slowly downstairs desperately thinking what on earth she might do for the best.

In the lounge Dennis, tumbler of whisky in his hand, was still watching Panorama. Edith walked across the room and switched off the television.

"For Christ's sake woman." Denis shouted. "I was watching that."

"Annabel's been arrested." Edith raised her voice to drown his grumbling.

"Stupid girl. I knew she'd get herself into trouble. Turn the telly back on."

" That's all you can say, is it?" Edith stood in front of him, arms crossed, blocking his view of the television set. "Turn the telly back on?" she mimicked him. "Turn the telly back on? When your daughter's in prison?"

"I told you – switch it on.. What do you expect me to do about it. It's her own fault, isn't it?

"No it's not her fault." Edith shouted. "It has nothing to do with her. Don't you want to help her? Don't you want to know what she's supposed to have done?"

"She's wrecked the show I suppose . That girl's crazy. There's nothing I can do. She'll have to get that boyfriend of hers to help her. He's got a law degree or something hasn't he?" He looked at his watch. "You've made me miss the end of the programme. He reached for the remote control, restored the programme and pressed the volume button to drown out further conversation.

Edith stared at him in disbelief. "All right, just wait until you're in some difficulty..." She heard her own voice rise even further, "You could help her if you really wanted, but if you won't help your own daughter I will – and I'll pay whatever it costs too." She crossed the room to the door and stood with her hand on the handle. "You'll regret this Dennis." Her voice was bitter as her anger grew. Despite all their past rows she had never felt like this. She longed to hit him, longed to pick up the vase from the table and break it over his thick head, longed to change the stubborn look from his face. "You've gone too far. Don't count on me for help and support. From now on you're on your own."

Edith closed the door and walked back up the stairs. She moved as if sleep walking towards the airing cupboard, hauling out the bed linen and carrying it into the spare room, making up the bed, blinded by tears of fury and desperation. Then she returned to her own bedroom and turned the key in the lock.

It was a quarter past midnight when Dennis lumbered up the stairs. Edith heard his heavy footsteps and noisy breathing. She put down her book on the side table and turned off the bedside light. The door handle turned as he tried to push open the door, then grunted as he slammed his shoulder against the panelling.

"Edith, Open the door."

"Your bed is made up in the spare room," she called out firmly, and as loudly as she dared, thankful that the house was isolated and that there were no near neighbours to overhear the row that would surely follow.

"This is my bedroom. Open the door." Dennis thundered.

Edith turned on her side and gathered her pillow around her head to cover her ears.

Once more he threw himself against the panelling, but the heavy doors of the Edwardian country mansion were made from solid mahogany with brass locks, and Dennis' shoulder was already beginning to feel sore.

"Edith, I shall force the door," he roared in desperation. "I can blow the lock off you know. There's a gun downstairs - in the gun cupboard – so you'd better keep out of the way."

Through the pillow around her head Dennis' roars were muffled, but Edith could detect a note of desperation. She pulled the pillow even more tightly around her ears and closed her eyes.

"Edith. You'll regret doing this. This is grounds for divorce Let me in – I'll give you one last chance."

The hammering on the door went on for some time and as the noise gradually abated, Edith, warm and comfy, and past caring, fell asleep."

When Dennis awoke next day and went to look for his wife he found their bedroom deserted and the bed already made. Nor was there any breakfast on the table. The post lay on the hall floor, uncollected, and Edith was not in the kitchen. The back door that led out to the garage was unlocked and he made his way across the yard. He heard the 'shup-shup-shup' of the milking machine and the sound of his pedigree herd of Jersey cattle as they moved in a patient queue through the milking parlour. In the sunshine swallows skimmed and dived high above as they fed their young in the nests ledged in the rafters of the shippon. The main doors to the garage were open and Edith's car was missing.

Dennis returned to the house. The phone in the kitchen was ringing and he hurried to answer it, banging his hip against the corner of the island unit.

"Yes. Who is it?"

"The Gazette. Sir Dennis, the police are holding your daughter for questioning – will you make a statement?"

Dennis replaced the receiver, then sat down at the kitchen table, trembling, unsure of what to do next. Things were happening and were once again out of his control.

The phone rang again.

"Dennis, it's Edith."

It surprised him that he felt so glad to hear the sound of her voice.

"I'm at the police station. They're releasing Annabel. I gave them a statement – told them that I had lunch with Annabel on the day of the show."

"And did you?"

"Well I wouldn't say so if I didn't." Edith sounded

indignant.

"You didn't tell me." It was Dennis' turn to sound indignant.

"Well I don't tell you everything. I shall spend today with Annabel and Sandy, so you'll have to get yourself something."

Meekly Dennis replaced the receiver then crossed the kitchen and began to examine the contents of the fridge.

Chapter 24

The drive to The Lawns was rutted. It wound around rhododendron bushes until it opened out onto a gravelled parking area in front of wrought iron gates. Henry had begun to wish that he had one of those gadgets that directed you to the very place you were looking for. All his colleagues at Head Office had one - always talking about Gloria, that wonderful woman who guided them to their destinations on their Sat Nav. But he'd always managed with Ordnance Survey maps and got there in the end without too much trouble. This time it took longer to find The Lawns than he had expected and now he was late, twenty minutes late, after stopping to ask at the local garage and a sub-post-office.

He tapped out his pipe on the top of the stone gatepost and pushed the still warm briar into his pocket. Nowadays the smell of pipe tobacco was even less acceptable than cigarette smoke. The house was set back behind tall close-clipped yew hedges, and as he walked up the flagged path he noticed a rose arch and several greenhouses beside manicured lawns. Despite his late arrival Barbara Millar welcomed him warmly and the smell of freshly made coffee wafted through the doorway as he stepped into the hall. Years of experience had programmed Henry to wipe his feet thoroughly and remove his battered hat and hang it on the newel-post of the stairs. He tiptoed carefully across the polished hall floor behind the ex-Chairman of Marton Health Authority and followed her into her study. She was small and slim. Grey hair mingled with nondescript brown. Henry estimated ,that she was in her mid-fifties.   She waved her hand at a pile of documents on her desk. "I've got all the minutes, letters and my notes of meetings if you want to go through them."

Barbara Millar appeared well organized. He shook his head. "Just tell me, more to the point, why you've decided to blow the whistle."

She smiled at him and nodded her head. "In a funny way it's a relief...I suppose that everyone at some time in their lives arrives at a crossroads where they have to decide whether to go on or get out. Twenty three years of local politics, starting when I was young and dewy-eyed intending to put the world to rights - not quite the knight in shining armour – more of Joan of Arc – and look where she ended up! Well I soon had my eyes opened." She gave a deep sigh and paused.

"It wasn't too long before I discovered that most councillors had vested interests.   On the Planning Committee they approved planning applications for friends and relations. Less than a month, as a member of that committee, when discussing an application for a change of use from a farm to a golf club I was told 'Put your hand up and vote – you want to see old Alan make a bob or two don't you?' Of course I didn't put my hand up. Before too long my Tory colleagues classified me as 'a delicate shade of pink.' Things got even more tricky when the Chairman of the Council, Herbert Reade, tried to add me to his collection ..."

Henry frowned and looked puzzled.

Barbara laughed. "First of all you get a little note from his secretary inviting you to lunch at his table. If you don't know the form you take it as an honour; after that you get invited for drinks in his private room to meet the Chief Executive and senior staff - so you acquire a touch of kudos as a friend of the Chairman. Within days you find him sitting next to you in Committee and the next thing you know he's groping you beneath the table."

Henry put down his biro on his note pad. "And then...?"

"I didn't wait to find out. I made sure he never had the opportunity to sit next to me again. I kept right out of his way. After a while he gave up. People soon got the message...word got around, and I gained respect from the officials – but not from most of my own party – it amused them and provided more gossip."

"So...?"

"I got hardened to it. County Hall was rife with nepotism and patronage. My husband once asked me whether I had half a mind to go into politics – he said that was all you needed – half a mind."

"But you stayed for nineteen years?"

"And the Chairmen changed...In the end I came to my senses and retired. Michael, my husband, had decided to take early retirement – so we both thought it would be nice to do things together – perhaps do some travelling."

"Did you?"

"Not for long. Within weeks I was approached to take on the job at Marton..."

"And you did."

He paused and stared at her, and heard himself ask the next question. "Why?" He knew that the question was irrelevant, but something about Barbara Millar intrigued him. "You obviously didn't need the money."

She smiled at him. "I'm sure you've seen retired couples pushing trolleys along the aisles in Tesco.

When you're over fifty you start getting junk mail from Saga, and Insurance companies trying to persuade you to invest your pension to benefit your children and grandchildren, or set aside something for nursing home fees and funeral expenses." She shuddered. "At that age I had no intention of joining the Wrinklies. I still have years ahead of me before I retire."

Henry nodded in sympathy. He knew just how she felt. Mentally he began to draft out the headline for his article in The Gazette. 'Battling Brunett Blows Whistle on NHS Bosses?' No, it didn't sound right. He needed time to think.

Barbara Millar brought him back to earth. "My first interview with Dennis Deane, the Regional Chairman went well."

Henry nodded and returned to his notebook. He longed to get his pipe out.

"I was told that I would be my own boss, with my own secretary, and a car as well. As long as I balanced the budget and got to know the medics all would be well. I thought I understood the message. It was quite clear, it sounded good, and I was happy to go along with it."

She spoke quietly, with calm deliberation, and her voice was pleasant and easy to listen to. Henry was tempted to put down his pen and relax. "As soon as I was in post the messages came in thick and fast. There was to be competition for patients between the new hospital trusts and the Health Authorities... new business, gained from neighbouring authorities would receive increased regional funding. Then the messages changed; we were told that there was to be joint working and definitely no cherry picking. Then it was to be amalgamation, working together. Next - we were told that we were all to be completely reorganised. Week by week we never knew what would happen next." She used her hands expressively and listed the points, ticking them off on her fingers, sometimes holding on to a finger for several minutes as she explained a point. "All that in a matter of months."

Henry scribbled furiously.

"In the first year we were delighted by a Government announcement of a 5% increase in funding – then let down because we only received half a percent after Region had kept four and a half percent to fund a special project dear to the Chairman's heart. Whenever we won new business we were accused of cherry-picking -"

"But to come back to your resignation." prompted Henry.

Barbara paused and sighed "We were promised twelve months interest if we lent money overnight to help the London hospitals balance their budget - "

"But you lent more than you had in your account."

"Dennis Deane told us that the Treasury would go along with such arrangements if it could be justified. We were under pressure to do so. He wanted his own Region, Mercia Region, to be top of the league, to provide the most money."

Henry looked up from his notebook. "Why?"

She shrugged her shoulders. "He believes he's in line for an honour. The rumours are that it could be a seat in the Lords. Health Service spokesman perhaps?"

"So did the Treasury O.K. the arrangement?"

She shook her head. "It didn't. We were naïve to think it would. The Treasury is the one Government department that makes its own rules and plays by its own rules. Nevertheless, the Authority lent all the

225

money in our bank account overnight on the fifth of April, plus the money owed us by other Health Authorities. That's normal. We always bill them when their residents are treated in our hospitals – as a matter of course. Usually they are holiday-makers who have strokes, heart attacks or get involved in car accidents." She halted briefly, leaning forward as he took notes, waiting for him to catch up.

"The money we loaned the London hospitals never left our bank account.." She raised her voice and emphasised each word. "O.K. It was debited from our account, but it was only a paper exercise. Next morning on the sixth of April that same amount was credited to us, plus another fifteen thousand pounds interest."

"That sounds like money laundering."

"One week later the Secretary of State appeared on Panorama and told viewers that all Health Authorities and all the newly formed Trusts had balanced their budgets."

"But on that day, the first day of the new financial year, the London hospitals must have started the new year in deficit?"

"That's right. It's known as being economical with the truth – an everyday occurrence in politics - but it gives the Government breathing space. Not only have the London Trusts been in the red for months, but Marton also ended the year in deficit as we were owed money by our debtors, so we've been penalized. Our accounts were qualified, and we have a black mark recorded against us. It's on our records as a result of the diktat from the Regional Chairman. He's the only one who's likely to benefit if the Tories get back. As usual the electorate has been conned - whichever party wins."

Henry could hardly keep pace with her outpourings. Somewhere at the back of his mind headlines formed and re- formed 'Scandal of NHS cover-up,' 'Now the truth comes out,' 'The public has been misled claims ex-NHS boss.' It was a good tale and if handled properly it could alter the outcome of the election. He smiled happily. Now it was the turn of the White Queen to threaten the Black King.

As the story came to an end Henry tucked his notebook into his jacket pocket and as he did so he felt the envelope containing the pieces of burnt cardboard. It reminded him of his other reason for wanting to talk to Barbara Millar. "Can we talk about Queenswood Hall?" he asked.

She seemed surprised.

"Did the Health Authority ever let any accommodation at Queenswood to anyone else other than the school and the old people's home?"

Barbara started to shake her head, then stopped suddenly and frowned. "Oh there was some chap, name of Bastow. I remember the name particularly, it sounds rather like Bastard." she explained. "He rented two rooms at the back of the building, part of the old kitchens, for several months last summer."

"I need to get in touch with him," said Henry.

"Why? Why do you need … I think I may have his card." Barbara clicked open the lock of her briefcase. Henry watched with interest as she methodically flicked through the business cards that she had arranged alphabetically in the leather holder inside the lid. "There you are – Charlie Bastow." She said triumphantly passing the card to him.

Henry took his notebook from his pocket and began

227

to take down the details.

"You won't get very far with the phone number." she said. "Some months ago the Estates Department tried to contact him about the terms of the lease. The number was unobtainable, and he wasn't in the directory."

"Did they make contact?"

She shook her head. "I don't know. They thought he'd moved, but I don't know where."

Henry snapped his notebook shut. "I'll find him." He opened the envelope and held out the charred pieces in the palm of his hand. "These are all that are left of the prize winning cards awarded in the cheese section of the Marton Show."

Barbara frowned and shook her head, puzzled by the questioning. "What have they to do -?"

"Every cheese in the tent was stolen and taken away from the show in a lorry. I think that they were taken to Queenswood. In which case Mr. Charlie Bastow has some explaining to do." That Black Pawn had been advancing up the Chessboard almost un-noticed. It needed to be watched, decided Henry.

"If the Estate Department did trace him it'll be in their records…"

Henry phoned the Health Authority from the phone on his bedside table.

"It is the Health Authority's policy to give information to the Press, either by a Press Release, or personal interview," the secretary's voice said crisply.

Henry cleared his throat and tried again. "Then I would like to arrange an appointment with the Chairman to do an interview - "

She cut him short. "The Chairman does not give

interviews. The Chief Executive is the only one who speaks to the Press."

"Then may I speak to him?" persisted Henry.

"The Chief Executive is in a meeting."

"Then may I speak to the Chairman?"

"The Chairman is also in a meeting."

"I thought he might be." Henry said dryly. "Perhaps you may be good enough to ask them to contact me as soon as the meeting is over?"

"I will give them your message." Her tone was icy.

Henry put down the phone. He did not expect that either of the two men would phone him back, and he wondered why.

He sat on his bed and stared at the phone, then took his pipe from his pocket and chewed the stem thoughtfully as he started to read through the notes he had made. He felt sure that he had sufficient information to set the hare running. He reached for the phone and dialled Rick Keel on his personal line.

"It's Henry Pye. I've got the story from Barbara Millar." He heard the whirr of the tape as Keel switched on the recorder.

"Go ahead."

"Headline – Scandal of NHS Cover-up – Exclusive - The truth comes out. Stop. The past Chairman of Marton Health Authority, Barbara Millar has exposed the real truth about the fraudulent misuse of NHS funds.

"The statement issued by the Department of Health earlier this year was a deliberate attempt to mislead voters, in the run-up to the general election." claimed Mrs. Millar. "Marton Health Authority always planned to use money from the sale of property to fund improvements in the service." Henry adjusted the

229

overhead light.

Peering at his notes he raised his voice and spoke slowly. "However the Regional Health Authority pressurised us to lend money overnight on the last day of the financial year to balance the budget of the London Hospitals - whose debts amounted to more than four million pounds. Our account was debited by two hundred and fifty thousand pounds on the last day of the financial year – but the money never actually left the bank. The following day our account was credited with that same two hundred and fifty thousand pounds plus twelve months interest. As a result our accounts were qualified by the auditors even though, at that time, we were owed thousands of pounds from other Health Authorities for treating their patients in our hospitals, as is normal practice."

Henry cleared his throat as he turned the page.

"The Health Authority's accounts have been examined and show that the Authority did actually benefit by more than fifteen thousand pounds interest on the deal. The Morning Gazette demands an explanation for the Secretary of State's recent statement that all NHS Health Authorities and Trusts had ended the financial year in balance, and has called for a full investigation into the matter.

Added to that, The Morning Gazette has since learned that the Chairman of Mercia Regional Health Authority, Dennis Deane, failed to disclose the fact that he is a Director of a company known as VS&T who owned land that was sold to the Marton Health Authority as a site for an elderly persons home, and that Lewis Gilbert, brother of Deane's co-director of VS&T Gareth Gilbert, was awarded the contract by the Marton Health Authority to build the home. Stop."

Keel punched the stop button. "Phew. Sounds like you've opened a can of worms. You're sure of the facts?"

"Have I ever slipped up?" Henry asked. " And I've another lead I'm following up."

"It'll make the front page tomorrow. Keep it going and I'll prepare an editorial." Rick Keel promised with obvious satisfaction.

The noise from the back room behind the bar was deafening. Henry nodded his head in its direction "What's going on?" he bellowed.

"The staff from Queenswood - having a disco. Some are leaving. They're moving out." Nick Reddy shouted back.

Henry stopped, turned, and made for the back room.

"It's not your scene mate!" yelled the landlord.

As he opened the door a wall of sound of such intensity hit him that he retreated from the gyrating bodies and flashing lights, back into the bar.

"I warned you,"shouted the landlord.

"Do they ever stop?"

Nick nodded. "They'll be out for supper soon."

Henry reached for the bar menu. "I'll have half a bitter whilst I wait." He watched as the head rose to the rim and Nick mopped up the pool on the counter. "The Barnsley chop sounds good, with chips I think."

The landlord continued to polish the counter. "What's so interesting about the nurses then?"

"There's someone I'm looking for."

"Hoping for a scoop are you?" The landlord picked up the menu and studied it. "Barnsley Chop and chips then. " he said as the noise cut off abruptly.

Henry watched as they spilled out from the disco.

231

Jeans, and tops that left the white flesh of their midriffs bare. He wished he were forty years younger, in those days they didn't have bare midriffs.

He saw her talking to a tall thin young man with long dark hair and new Levi jeans. He picked up his glass and manoeuvred his way through the gaggle of noisy youngsters. "Hello."

For a moment she stared at him. Then she smiled. "Oh it's you..." She turned to her partner who looked annoyed at Henry's unwelcome intervention. "This is the old chap I told you about. You know. We got talking the morning I took John out for the last time." She looked sad. "He died the following week. He didn't want to move."

The description 'old chap' demolished Henry's confidence and upset him even more than the other old mans' sudden death. So that was how they all saw him, as the next candidate for a nursing home. He pushed aside his irritation. "Can we talk?"

"Hang about," said the partner. "This is a private party. I don't think you've been invited."

"Look," protested Henry. "This isn't a pick-up. I want some help – There's someone I'm looking for. Let me buy you a drink. Perhaps you could both help."

Henry ordered doubles. It was an old trick that usually worked. They either got angry or after ten minutes they began to talk.

"Don't mention Charlie Bastow," said the young man after Henry had introduced himself. "By the way my name's Kevin. Charlie Bastow should have been christened Charlie the Bastard."

The Care Assistant reached across the table for his hand. "Don't be too hard on Charlie, after all we got together because of him." She turned towards Henry.

232

"I never told you my name. It's Lisa. Charlie stood me up. We'd arranged to meet here, but he never turned up, instead I met Kev."

Kevin drained his drink. "I owned a lock-up garage that Charlie wanted to rent, but as Lisa said, Charlie never showed up. That's how we met – hanging around, waiting for Charlie."

He once gave me his mother's phone number. I've still got it, if that would help." Lisa volunteered.

Henry took a note of the name and number. This time he deliberately chose to use the phone by the bar. The noise from the disco would assist his plan.

Charlie's mother answered the phone. "Yes. Who is it? I'm afraid Charlie's not here."

"He told me to phone him. It's about a job he asked me to fix." Henry slipped easily into the Brummagen accent of his childhood. "I need to get hold of him. We'll miss the job like, if I can't talk to him."

"Just a minute."

He heard a buzz of voices in the background, then footsteps and the sound of a young man's voice.

"Yeh?"

"Charlie?"

"Yeh."

Henry took a chance. "It's me."

"Lewis?"

This time it was Henry's turn. "Yeh."

As the door to the back room opened the noise made conversation almost impossible. Henry began to shout. "There's a delivery coming. They're unloading the pallets now. Where d'you want them?"

He heard a groan at the end of the line. "I've told you. I've no room. What you playing at?"

233

"I thought you'd fixed a lock-up?"

"It's getting too hot in Marton."

"You must have somewhere."

Charlie paused for a moment. "Look. You know the old engineering workshop behind the car park. I can use that for a couple of weeks – no longer. It's too damp. Meet me at six."

Henry rested the Morning Gazette against the steering wheel. Lacking a fresh story line the headlines had reverted to their banal stand-by of gossip about the sex lives of pop stars. He turned the pages idly, hesitating briefly at the centre page where a footballer's girl friend posed in a bikini, and was about to move to the sports pages when he saw a red Porsche speed across the car park and stop beside the disused engineering workshop. A stocky dark haired youth got out and stood by the car looking expectantly around him.

Henry put down his paper, heaved himself out of the driving seat, adjusted his hat and locked the Saab. He leaned against the rear door, filling his pipe from his tobacco pouch, gathering and tidying it and tamping it down into the bowl. Slowly he extracted a box of Swan Vestas from his jacket pocket and applied a lighted match, patiently sucking as he did so, placing the box over the bowl to encourage the pipe to draw and all the time watching Charlie Bastow. From the branch of a cherry tree across the car park a blackbird 'pinked' in alarm.

Charlie, embarrassed by such scrutiny, busied himself opening the doors to the workshop. He began to feel uneasy. The old geezer with the Saab seemed to be watching him. Charlie wondered whether he could

234

be CID, then dismissed the thought. The chap was too old for that – on the other hand…

Henry took the pipe from his mouth., inspected the bowl and satisfied that all was well, began to walk towards Charlie.

"You waiting for Lewis?"

Charlie stared "How do you…"

"The delivery is off."

Charlie looked relieved. "Oh good…"

Henry peered into the gloom of the workshop, its windows curtained with cobwebs. Pieces of rusting machinery lay discarded on the concrete floor. "Not much in then?"

Charlie shook his head "Nah. Too damp. I'm looking…" He stopped and stared at Henry. "Who you then?"

"Mate of Lewis Gilbert." He paused waiting for a reaction, but Charlie accepted the explanation. "Known him for years – I help him out now and again – driving you know."

Charlie nodded. "What happened to the load then?"

"He sold it on. I'm taking it in the morning." Henry smiled. He was beginning to enjoy himself.

"Where to?"

"One of his regulars. Didn't catch the name on the phone."

"Spect it's Harry." said Charlie.

"Harry?"

"Yeh – Harry Furnell – buys most fings from Lewis. Yeh - useful guy Harry. Shifts most fings." He laughed. "Even grapefruit skins."

"Grapefruit skins ?"

"Yeh. Lewis goes down the dock road collecting them from the fruit juice factory – them and other fings,

235

then delivers them to some place wot makes marmalade. Up in Scotland I think."

Henry swallowed hard. He couldn't believe his luck. A sudden shower of rain wet his face and blurred his glasses. He turned up his coat collar. "About time I got back." he said.

Charlie moved away to shut the workshop doors. "I'll tell Lewis we met."

"Yes, do that." Henry waved his hand in farewell. "The name's Henry Pye by the way." Henry plotted the next move. It was time for his White Rook to begin the advance.

Chapter 25

There was always a Farmers Market in Marton on the last Saturday of the month. In the Conservative offices, across the square Dennis Deane screwed up his copy of the Morning Gazette and hurled it across the room in the direction of the waste-paper basket. His bellows echoed through the office and brought John Brown galloping up the stairs from the photocopying machine. Paul and Erica tried to calm him down but time was short. The Agent, desperate to pacify his Chairman before the arrival of Ken Clarke, Chancellor of the Exchequer, offered him a mug of coffee. Ken was a favourite in the Constituencies, and the news that he was to visit Mercia Constituency had created excitement.

Growling like a caged lion the Chairman waved the coffee away, knocking it out of the Agent's hand. It fell softly onto the carpet creating a wet pool around his feet and spattering his shoes. John Brown bent down and picked it up, and placed it on a Labour party election leaflet he had removed from a letterbox of an empty shop in the High Street on his way to work that morning. Later when he had time he would read it and search for inaccuracies to take up with his opposite number in the Labour office across town.

"Well," he said, "I'll leave you to imagine Ken Clarke's reaction. He'll just laugh it off. All part of the job. It's what MPs have to put with every day."

Dennis ignored him. "He'll have read the papers on his way here."

"Of course he will," agreed the agent. "But it's the Gazette. You know their politics. Don't forget what

237

they did a few months ago - they accused every MP in the House of fraud, adultery and everything else you care to mention. No one takes the Gazette seriously. Now you're on the receiving end for a change. You've had a taste of it, and you don't like it."

In the street outside bored reporters leaned idly against radio and television vans. Camera crews hefted their equipment on their shoulders filming the activity around the market stalls, and sound engineers tested the noise levels, holding furry, grey microphones in front of anyone who was prepared to offer them a sound bite. It was rare for a high Tory to be seen in Marton, and the headlines in the Gazette added spice to the occasion.

Yellow-jacketed policemen patrolled the perimeter of the square, keeping a watchful eye on a group of Anti-hunt Protesters who had set up a stall beside the War Memorial and were assembling a display of posters and banners. The Saturday morning shoppers, aware that something unusual was about to happen, divided their attention between the stalls and the activities that were taking place on the other side of the square.

Henry Pye ambled through the alleys between the stalls. Although the food at the Fishpool more than pleased him he was sorry not to be able to take home a rack of lamb, bred on the Welsh Marches, or spicy pork and apple sausages for his supper; however a jar of his favourite pickled walnuts would keep perfectly until he returned home.

He hovered on the edge of the crowd by the cheese stall. Inside the glass display cabinet a variety of cheeses, surrounded by artificial grapes and plastic parsley were tastefully displayed. Behind the counter

Tom Hartley, in a white overall, busied himself with a cheese wire, cutting, wrapping and packing wedges of Shropshire Blue Cheese.

Henry edged forward to taste the samples from the plates on top of the counter. He selected a square of coloured Cheshire and paused to allow the creamy piece to dissolve on his tongue. "That's tasty."

Tom paused from his work and glanced at him. "Yes, bit of good stuff – don't see much of that quality very often."

"Made locally?" inquired Henry.

"Harry Furnell bought it – didn't say where from." He grinned. "They don't always say, in case we cut them out and deal direct... Sometimes his stuff can be dodgy. You have to be careful with factors. I don't usually buy from Furnell - but this time..." He pointed to a thick wedge of Devon Blue. "Like blue cheese?"

Henry nodded. "What other cheeses have you bought from Furnell?"

Tom waved a hand over his wares. "Just about everything. You name it – I've got it. He seems to have found a good source of supply."

Henry inspected the display. "What about some Double Gloucester?" He turned to watch Tom reach across for the cheese. Two yards away from the stall a shaven-headed man lounged against a pillar box, watching. His hands in the pockets of his stained jeans, chewing gum and sporting one gold earring. Henry frowned, somewhere in the back of his memory the gold earring prompted him to take a second glance.

Behind the War Memorial the Minister's car halted in front of the Conservative Headquarters and Ken Clarke bounded up the steps in a cloud of cigar smoke; an amalgam of beaming cheerfulness, scuffed shoes

239

and shapeless suit that had obviously been worn throughout the long campaign. Paul wondered how he managed to stay so fit. He felt sure that the ex-Chancellor had never seen the inside of a gym since he left school. Ken shook his head at Erica's offer of coffee. "Called at The Little Chef on the way – the Full Monty – and two cups of tea. By the way where's the…" Erica grinned and passed him on to Paul.

At the door a policeman nodded affably as the Agent led the party out into the sunshine. Camera and sound crews tossed aside their cigarettes and began backing between the market stalls ahead of the party. In the background the protesters started to chant. Paul glanced at Ken Clarke. He looked eager to take on the world.

Henry stood watching as the camera crew followed the group around the Square, chatting to the shoppers, examining the produce and buying the token contents of a shopping basket which he had no doubt that they would make use of at the Press Conference that was booked to follow the walk-about. Henry crossed the Square to the hotel car-park carrying his Double Gloucester and pickled walnuts..

He placed his shopping in the boot of the car and reached up to shut the lid. Behind him, across the car park an engine started up and he heard the noisy rattle of an exhaust. Henry moved aside to lock the car and looked around. A grey truck, its worn bodywork battered and rusty, bumped over the pot holes and through the puddles left by the early morning rain. Henry set off towards the rear entrance of The Mytton Arms. The lorry followed, moving slowly between the parked cars, its exhaust clattering loudly. It was then that he remembered the lorry on the building site. He stopped and turned to get a look at the driver but the bright sunlight reflected off the windscreen. He thought he might have just seen the glint of an earring. In the gap between the parked cars and the hotel entrance yellow plastic crates containing empty bottles were stacked against the rear wall, awaiting collection, and a pile of metal beer kegs, four high, stood by the door of the outside toilets.

Henry reached the last row of cars and watched as the truck turned away from the archway that led out onto the road. He started to cross the stretch of tarmac behind the hotel when the truck changed direction and, without warning, swerved towards him. It was only yards away. He hesitated, retreated, and watched as it picked up speed and roared past, inches from the front row of parked cars. He paused between the vehicles, grateful for their protection, waiting and watching as the truck turned, reversed and changed direction. Smoke poured from the exhaust as the engine revved. In an attempt to manoeuvre between the lines of cars it scraped the front wing of a red Audi at the end of the front row. The noise of the collision could be heard across the car park and left a deep grey scrape and broken glass from the side light.

There was no doubt that someone was out to get him. Safe for the moment he stood and considered his options. He was on his own. Safety lay inside the hotel. Facing him across the yard the rear door of the hotel was only feet away. The Saab was two rows behind, across a wide aisle.

Henry turned and ducked down beside a silver Honda and faced the Saab. He put out a hand on to the Honda boot lid to steady himself. Gingerly he moved forward towards the Saab, one foot in front of the other.

241

The driver of the lorry let out the clutch. The exhaust rattled and the lorry moved forward into the aisle to block his path. Henry spun around and ran back between the parked cars as fast as his sixty-five year old legs would allow. Puffing from the effort of his sprint he reached the protection of the crates just as the front bumper of the lorry struck the row of metal kegs. They fell, twisting, spinning on their sides, and rolling noisily around the tarmac, crashing into the crates which fell, catapulting empty bottles, smashing against each other across the yard.

Henry kicked aside an empty crate and ran for the rear door of the hotel, leaning against the door post, panting as the lorry swerved to avoid the kegs and plastic crates. He watched as it crunched its way over the broken glass and out of the car park and felt some satisfaction that it wouldn't get far with at least two flat tyres.

In the saloon bar Henry, his legs weak, leaned against the bar and accepted a Whisky from the Duty Manager. No one had ever tried to run down Henry Pye before, and no one would ever dare to try that again. This time they'd gone too far. This time he really had a story, and this time it would hit the headlines more effectively than all the other political shenanigans in Marton..

"He was out to get me, definitely out to get me," he said angrily.

The Duty Manager looked doubtful. "Do you think he was drunk?"

Henry shook his head. "Oh no. He wasn't drunk." Still shaking he placed his empty glass on the bar top. " I know who it was. I saw him earlier, in the square watching me."

"There are police at the front. I'll report it."

"Leave it to me." said Henry. "Just leave it to me."

The conference room was already filling but Henry was pleased to see that his preferred seat, centre-aisle on the front row; right in front of the Chairman, was vacant. A quick glance around the room satisfied him - almost all his fellow journalists carried copies of the Gazette under their arms. Most were young reporters but he recognised a colleague from the Mail who grinned conspiratorially and waved his copy of the Gazette. Trembling, he collapsed with some relief on to the vacant seat, to recover his composure and review the questions that he expected nearly everyone in the room wanted to ask. Hopefully they would enliven the dullest campaign he could ever remember. As the platform party, lead by Dennis, filed in, taking their places behind the green baize covered table, the spotlights focused on the message beamed on to the wall behind them. In bright blue letters on an orange background it proclaimed "Conservatives – leading the way to prosperity."

As far as Dennis was concerned he hoped to God that he didn't look as worried as he felt. He was unnerved to get into a situation that appeared to be running out of control and that had happened several times recently. Last night after the Gazette had phoned him for his response to the allegations he had hardly slept at all. How much the paper had found out about VS&T and the land sale, he could only guess. The prospect of an honour in the New Year's list had already started to fade after his meeting with the Minister and somewhere amongst the ranks of journalists in the room was the man from the Gazette - the cause of all the trouble. The thought angered him.

243

He'd never met the fellow, but he'd be there — somewhere amongst the crowd, waiting to make more trouble. He stared around the room but didn't know who he was looking for.

John Brown leaned towards him. "Shall we make a start?"

Hurriedly Dennis cleared his throat. "I was waiting for them to settle down," he growled.

"You've got the gavel." The Agent reminded him dryly

Dennis heaved himself to his feet. His blue tie bore the party emblem, the burning torch, and in the breast pocket of his navy pinstriped suit he wore a carefully folded blue handkerchief. "Ladies and gentlemen, as the Chairman of the Marton Divisional Conservative Association, which as you know has been suspended for the period of the election campaign, I have great pleasure in welcoming the Chancellor of the Exchequer, Ken Clarke to Marton." He paused and smiled at the Chancellor. "I am sure that, like me, you all want to see him back in the same job, for I cannot remember any previous Chancellor of the Exchequer who has set this country on the path to prosperity as he has done." His words drew an enthusiastic round of applause. "Ken needs no introduction from me, and I am delighted that he is here with us and that he is going to address this Press Conference this morning."

There was a pause whilst the Chancellor of the Exchequer reached for the microphone and adjusted it. Several cameramen hurried to the front of the hall, and knelt on the floor, adjusting and focusing their zoom lenses on the speaker.

"During the campaign my schedule allowed me only a short time in each place I visited, but I told them that

I must have more time in Marton because I wanted to tell you personally how important it is that you return Paul Rugglestone to the House of Commons." He turned to look at Paul. "This man has a great future ahead of him. His ability and his integrity make him invaluable to the good conduct and smooth running of the nation's affairs that we as your members of Parliament carry out in your interests. There are politicians and there are statesmen, and I have no hesitation in forecasting that Paul will be one of tomorrows' statesmen."

As Ken Clarke listed the achievements of his Government during its term of office Henry wrote, re-wrote, and edited the questions he intended to put to the platform party. He was conscious that if he bungled his questions it would enable the glib, experienced men facing the cameras to evade the issues entirely. He knew that they would try to do so, for press conferences like television interviews, were thoroughly rehearsed before hand.

Henry had to admit that Ken Clarke had the ability of understanding the hopes and thoughts of those who listened to him, and almost by telepathy expressed their desires in his own words, much better than they themselves could ever manage to do. He was known as a tough street fighter, and a man who said just what everyone else was thinking, only in a down to earth, commonsense manner. When he sat down at the end of his speech even the representatives of the Press applauded enthusiastically.

A mass of hands brandishing copies of the Morning Gazette waved at the Chairman. Henry had no need to join in just yet. The incident in the car park was another matter and Dennis had to answer for it.

A woman's angry voice behind him made him turn around. The forest of newspapers subsided and the room fell silent.

"Maybe not everyone here realises that the Chairman of this meeting is also the Chairman of the Regional Health Authority, the same man who gave away the money that our hospital here at Marton needed. Three weeks ago my husband had a heart attack – and on that same day Dennis Deane sacked the Chairman of the Marton Health Authority for blowing the whistle and telling us that he had given our money away."

Henry turned in his seat to take a look at the speaker. In her sixties, lined face, no make-up, straight hair and Birmingham accent. She looked as if life had been hard for her.

Dennis pushed back his chair and made an effort to get to his feet but John Brown leaned across to him and, screened by the baize tablecloth, placed a hand on his wrist. "Wait a minute. Don't rush," he whispered.

"My husband was taken by ambulance to Marton General Hospital, but all six beds in the Intensive Care Unit were in use. There was no room for him. Then he was taken to the City General - at rush hour, and the ambulance was delayed for twenty minutes because of road works. Their four beds were all in use because of an accident on the motorway - their phone lines were jammed - and the driver couldn't get through to the switchboard. So they drove to the Royal Infirmary. On the way my husband had another heart attack and died - despite everything that the Para-medics could do. By the way my name is Ivy Huyton." Her voice sounded bitter. "I hope Sir Dennis that you remember that name. I've written to you three times but you've never replied – nor even an acknowledgement."

Dennis struggled out of his chair. Close up, from the front row, Henry could see him trembling. His hands shook as he screwed up his agenda paper, tearing at it with his fingernails. For a moment Henry thought that he might hurl it at the angry woman - then suddenly he appeared to compose himself.

"Madam. This is a Press Conference and I am taking questions for Ken Clarke…"

A murmur of unrest drifted across the room and Ken waved his hand, dismissing the idea. "Take the question," he advised.

Dennis hesitated. "However… this is obviously important." He paused – "Well - I'm sorry that there were problems…"

Hoots of derision shattered the tension.

"You're not sorry. You of all people knew the situation yet you did nothing. When you gave away our money you knew that people might die."

Pawn to King – Check, murmured Henry to himself.

Dennis felt the tight fist of anger rise in his chest and into his throat. He stood for a moment, speechless, waiting for the pain to pass, desperately searching for a solution. Then experience came to his aid and he reacted instinctively, holding up his hands, smiling, calmly reassuring his audience. "There are times, and this is one of them, when we could devote the whole session to one very important matter – this lady's distressing loss. However we are here to discuss other important matters that affect thousands of people…"

A fresh rumble of discontent rolled through the room. Once again he raised his hands "…but I will make you a promise – that the Authority will immediately set up an Inquiry into this matter, and you

247

will be kept fully informed of the time-table."

The sudden relaxation of tension throughout the room as journalists sat back in their seats indicated to him that the moment of crisis had passed and that his words had calmed the situation.

And if the blame falls on you, thought Henry, how will you get out of that? You'll be the fall guy for a Government discredited by an election cock-up.

He looked up at the Chairman and waved his copy of the Gazette. Dennis Deane, dazzled by the overhead spot lights, peered down at the audience and began to lift his hand, unsure who he was pointing at. Henry got to his feet.. "Henry Pye, Morning Gazette."

Dennis stared in astonishment. He always thought that reporters from the Gazette were smart, young pushy types, but here in front of him stood a battered run-down hack who appeared to present no threat. A feeling of relief surged through him.

"Now see here," said Dennis, his confidence growing once more, "We've all had enough smears and threats from the Gazette. I'm glad you turned up today so as I can tell you personally that people have got wise as to what it's all about. Your scare tactics and empty threats don't worry anyone any longer, because we've woken up to the fact that it's done to boost the circulation of the muck raking gutter press of which the Gazette is a member. So go back to your offices and tell your editor that we've got the best lawyers that money can buy and if you are stupid enough to continue to publish libellous accusations it won't take many of us to put the Gazette out of business."

A roar of enthusiastic support came from the ranks of party activists who packed the hall. Henry stood staring at Dennis, waiting patiently for the laughter and the clapping to die down. Stalemate, thought Henry, but it was his turn to make a move.

"Chairman, despite your attack on my newspaper I hope you will allow me to put my question?"

"Chairman, let him speak." urged John Brown.

Henry waited patiently for the noise to die down. He reached out for the roving microphone offered him by a steward. No one was going to miss one word of his question. "Sir Dennis will you explain to me, and to the people in this room, why a truck, owned by Lewis Gilbert, brother of your partner in VS&T - "

"This is a personal affair." roared Dennis. "Nothing to do with this Press conference."

Everyone on the platform nodded their heads in agreement.

"Let him speak." howled the journalists.

"Next business." yelled the party activists.

The clamour swelled, became a roar, and overwhelmed him. Camera lights blazed, and flashed until he was dazzled. Pain surged through his chest and he gulped and momentarily lost control. He put up his hand in acquiescence.

Taking it as a signal the crowd went quiet and Henry, seizing his opportunity, continued. "Less than an hour ago that builder's lorry, owned by one of the Gilbert brothers, who featured in this morning's newspaper story, tried to run me down in the car park outside this hotel. I was lucky to survive."

A gasp of disbelief washed over the room, followed by noisy consternation as people turned to each other "Did you hear…did he say… I don't believe."

Dennis turned to the platform party shaking his head, then turned back white-faced. "I know nothing at all of this and I strongly suspect that this is a story concocted by your newspaper." He began weakly, then summoning up his strength he warmed to his theme, and his voice became louder and stronger as the pain abated and his confidence returned. "The Gazette, as we all know, has told so many lies before that no one believes anything they read, and your paper has been forced to apologise and pay out substantial damages for the wicked allegations it publishes."

The gasps once again turned to cheers from the audience as the contest turned into a personal battle staged for their benefit in their own town, between the national press and local politicians. Even though, earlier in the day, they had grumbled at having to miss the vital stage of the fourth day of the final Test Match against the Australians on television to attend a political meeting. This game that was being played out in front of them was infinitely more lively and likely to last much longer.

Henry turned to the audience. "Just two days ago the brake fluid nut on my car was deliberately released. This morning there was the second attempt on my life. If you should have any doubts then take a look at the damage in the car park at the back of the hotel - especially the driver of a brand new red Audi that was hit by the builder's lorry"

A young man stood up and hurriedly pushed past his companions in the centre seats and left the room.

Distracted by the noise behind him, Henry turned and nodded in satisfaction, then continued. "You may also like to inspect the broken glass in the car park and see how the lorry hit the crates of empties as the driver attempted to run me down. Chairman, I suggest you now adjourn the meeting and allow the press to photograph the chaos in the car park. Perhaps you would then make a statement. "

Camera crews began to gather their equipment together whilst, from the front of the platform Dennis shouted angrily into the microphone "This conference will continue as normal," but the members of the press had already left. As the room cleared the platform party hurriedly departed, escorted by Police, John Brown supporting his Chairman with a hand under his elbow.

"Checkmate." Henry muttered to himself.

Chapter 25

The press pack, chased him home through the town, along the main road and the narrow lanes. They besieged the farm, ringing the doorbell, demanding an interview, knocking on the yard door, asking for a statement, phoning continuously, until he disconnected the phone, poured himself a large whisky and lay down on the sofa. He didn't want to talk to anyone.

Edith had left the clinging scent of Dolce Vita in the drawing room and a plate of ham sandwiches in the kitchen. He ate two then took the half empty bottle of Bells to the bedroom to watch the news on the bedside TV. He relaxed in the chintz covered armchair alone, with only his dogs to comfort him.. A news flash from Midlands T.V. reported the press conference in dramatic detail. He switched it off and helped by the whisky dozed from time to time.

The phone call from the Secretary of State came sooner than he expected. Early next morning the bedside phone rang. Edith answered it and passed it to him.

"Have you seen the papers?"

He recognized the Minister's voice. "I don't take the Gazette."

"Not just the Gazette. Every paper."

"I haven't seen any papers." Dennis peered at the bedside clock – it was only seven-thirty.

"I'll read you the headlines on the front page of the Telegraph." Brendan McKeith cleared his throat. "NHS scandal rocks the Government. Charges of fraud and attempted murder are likely to be made against senior figures in the Mercia Regional Health Authority.

Police have already begun their investigations and a spokesman for Number 10 confirmed that a local inquiry is to be set up." Brendan McKeith paused. "You can read the rest for yourself over breakfast, and when you've finished that turn to the Editorial on page 21."

Dennis stared at the wallpaper on the far wall, beige, biscuit, a safe choice. Edith always made a safe choice.

The Minister's voice entered his right ear and penetrated his consciousness. "You know what this means?"

He closed his eyes. It was even worse than he had expected.

"Are you still there?"

"What do you want me to do?" .

"What do think? I want your resignation right now. You'll make no statement whatsoever to anyone. Is that understood? You've done enough damage already. This'll lose us the election."

"Shall I get on to my solicitor?"

"You can do as you please," snapped McKeith. "You're on your own. I've a meeting with our legal department this morning and we'll put out a statement later in the day. Of course we'll distance ourselves from your activities."

The phone clicked, and he was left holding the receiver. The noise of the dialling tone provided the background to his jumbled thoughts. Slowly he handed the phone back to Edith. The dressing table mirror across the room reflected his look of disbelief and he stared back at himself.

"You heard?" he asked dully, embarrassed that she had overheard the conversation.

She nodded her head. "I don't understand."

Dennis pushed back the bedclothes and stood up unsteadily. He was surprised to discover that he was trembling. "Neither do I."

He heard the crunch of tyres on the gravel in front of the house and crossed the room towards the window. Two police patrol cars had drawn up by the front door. He padded shakily to the wardrobe and took his dressing gown from a hangar. "You'd better get up. The police are paying us a visit."

They sat in the drawing room all day, unable to believe what was happening, prevented from making contact with the police who searched every room in the house with methodical thoroughness. Nothing was overlooked, every shelf, wardrobe, drawer and cupboard were examined. Dennis was obliged to hand over the keys to his office, his desk and his safe. He watched from the window as they removed boxes of papers and all his business files. They took the computer from the office. In response to Dennis' urgent pleas his solicitor drove over to assess the situation. He inspected the search warrant, confirmed that it was all legal, then disappeared telling Dennis to contact him when they issued a warrant for his arrest.

"When," stormed Dennis. "When - not if, they issue a warrant for my arrest. I always said that the chap was a spineless wimp. Damn the expense I'll get myself a good lawyer, someone who's clever, who knows his way around, who's made a name for himself..." he paused.

"What about that barrister who helped Paul, Sam Madrugada?" Edith suggested. He's made a name for himself."

Dennis frowned. "Isn't he a foreigner with a name like that?"

254

"Do you want to win?" asked Edith. She sounded impatient. "You're facing prosecution, and you quibble over a man's name."

Beside him on the settee lay the Telegraph. He reached out to re-read the editorial.

The network of government administration nationally and internationally provides unending scope for fraud. Whatever checks are built into the system temptations and opportunities present themselves as they have done in the case of Mercia Regional Health Authority. This does not mean that fraud exists at all levels of government administration but it does mean that people who wish to serve this country in an administrative capacity should undergo a strict vetting procedure before appointment.

The power of the press to investigate rumours and allegations must be generally accepted even though it may appear intrusive. If it had not been for a reporter, whose life was threatened whilst working for his newspaper, the fraud that took place within Mercia Regional Health Authority would never have been discovered. The press is frequently criticized and rarely praised. On this occasion it is justly entitled to 'blow its own trumpet' and call the Department of Health to account. It is to be hoped that the Government will now have the sense to appoint someone to lead Mercia Regional Health Authority who has already demonstrated unquestionable probity in this shabby affair.

As Dennis Deane re-read the editorial for the fourth time the Party Chairman met Brendan McKeith to discuss the likely effect of the last sentence on the outcome of the election.

McKeith took off his jacket, draped it over the back of his chair and rolled up his sleeves. "Until today I'd considered the matter a local problem, but now that the Telegraph has become involved...we'll have to act."

The Party Chairman rubbed his hands over his face. "Paul Rugglestone spoke to me over breakfast. He thinks his seat is at risk unless we act quickly. With only a week to go before the election, time is not on our side." He reached for the coffee pot and poured himself a fresh cup. "In any case we can't afford to lose Rugglestone – he's one of the best we've got."

McKeith selected a file from a pile at the end of the table. "Ok. Here's what we'll do – if you agree of course." He looked up and saw the hasty nod of agreement from a colleague who hated making and taking decisions; a man who couldn't manage his own affairs. The whispers had developed into spoken facts. Why the P.M had made him Party Chairman he could only guess.

"Replace Dennis Deane as Chairman of Mercia Region with Barbara Miller – that should please the media, locally and nationally. It wouldn't be my ideal solution – but needs must when the devil drives. After all she does lack experience, but if she lasts until the storm blows over it will get us past the election. Agreed?"

Again he saw the hasty nod of agreement.

He turned the page of the file. "At the same time we confirm that there is to be a Government inquiry into the affairs of the Mercia Regional Health Authority." He paused. "Agreed?"

Again the nod of assent.

"We'll need to draft out the terms of reference and

get someone from the Lords to Chair it. As soon as Barbara Miller has agreed to her appointment we issue a short statement to the press." Brendan McKeith stood up and held out his hand. "Good. Least said the better. Storm in a teacup. Quickly forgotten. I'll prepare a press release for the approval of Number 10."

Chapter 26

The Civic Centre car park was surrounded by buildings. The dental surgery at the north end, side by side with the red brick Primary school, was overlooked by the massive cream coloured Civic Hall. On the opposite side of the car park was a bakery which wafted the scent of newly baked bread into the sale rooms of Pilsons, Valuers and Fine Arts.

On this occasion Henry chose a parking space between two tour buses whose drivers, enjoying their coffee break, were waiting for their passengers to return. He parked the Saab carefully, making sure that the wheels were perfectly straight – as advised by Inspector Hodgkin, so that no one could possibly gain access to the brake fluid nut which lay under the chassis behind the near side front wheel. He locked the car and followed the footpath that lead to the Square, past the bank, a building society and estate agents towards the river. Cars queued at the traffic lights to cross the old bridge. He waited until the lights changed and paused to look down into the water that was streaming through the disused mill race. Foaming cream and chocolate brown it flowed swiftly carrying brushwood and debris after the weekend's torrential rain. Upstream on the island where the mill had once stood Canada geese tore greedily at the grass. Henry counted forty then turned away to stare at the houses on the bank opposite. The noise from a body repair shop reached him above the sound of the traffic and rushing water, then, as if in a silent movie, an old man wearing a knitted cardigan and baggy trousers shambled out into a garden and threw bread to a flotilla of ducks that took off with beating wings towards him.

Henry crossed the bridge and turned into Wood Street following the noise from the repair shop. A square of derelict land served as a car park. Opposite, a roughly painted and badly spelled sign bore the words 'BatiKar, Body Repairs, Panal Beating and Welding.' The din from the workshop hammered against his ears, deafening him. He peered inside. Sparks from a welder flew in every direction threatening vehicles that, Henry presumed, might still have fuel in their tanks. He walked past, turned the corner of the building and halted. Parked on the waste ground in front of him was a builder's lorry. He recognized the dented front wing and the rusting bodywork. There was no mistake, it was the lorry that had tried to run him down in the car park. Its picture was still clear in his mind. He circled the vehicle, then bent down and examined the back. The damaged exhaust had been replaced. Retracing his steps he examined the cab doors. The sign on the driver's side was in place, 'Lewis Gilbert & Co. Builders. South Street. Marton.' He ran his hands around the sign. It was held in place by metal strips and rattled as he touched it. He pushed upwards against it and saw the dents and scratches on the paintwork beneath where it had from time to time been slid in and out of its position.

Henry turned and looked across the car park. The telephone directory had informed him that the office of Lewis Gilbert, Builders, could be found at 5 South Street. He crossed the rough ground. On his left a brick building with torn curtains bore the sign 'South Street Snooker Club.'. Next to it was Clancy's Diner. Henry stopped beside a pair of rusting metal doors and could make out a scratched and faded 5 painted in

259

black. He tried the doors, but they were locked. Beside the doors, on the right hand side, a narrow gate, painted green, swung loosely on rusty hinges. He opened it and found himself in an untidy patch of garden at the rear of Lewis Gilbert's house.

Paving stones and bricks lay in jumbled heaps and a broken concrete path led from a rusting corrugated iron shed to the rear door of the house. The door was open and Henry could hear a radio playing. He stood for a moment looking around, anxious not to be seen. But he had already been spotted. A large brown and white dog of unknown parentage trotted towards him, barking a deep throated warning. The open door of the shed offered a safe haven. He turned and stepped inside. Before he could prevent it the dog followed, pushing his way in.

Inside the shed it was dark. The window was curtained with layers of cobwebs. The remains of butterflies and dead wasps, that had fought for freedom as they tried to escape the smothering cobweb blanket, littered the window sills. The dog stood watching him, barking from time to time. Henry was relieved to see that as it barked it wagged its tail. He felt in his pocket for the toffees he always carried and carefully began to unwrap a butterscotch.

A woman's voice shouted "Tess" loudly and insistently. The dog turned to look through the open door.

"Go on," said Henry quietly, but the dog turned back, watching him, waiting for the butterscotch. He held out the toffee in the palm of his hand. Tess sniffed it, then took it gently.

"Tess. Come on. Tess," the woman demanded. It sounded near to. For a moment the dog hesitated, then trotted obediently out into the garden.

Henry peered through the cobwebs, Tess and a stout grey haired woman walked back down the path towards the house together. Henry breathed a sigh of relief.

By now his eyes had become accustomed to the gloom and he saw that he was surrounded by ladders, tools and sheets of broken glass. In the far corner he made out a collection of vehicle signs and number plates leaning against the wall. They were heavy and dusty. He bent down and with growing interest began to examine each one until he found what he was looking for. Recently painted, it bore the words "Marton Cheese Factors. Established 1989." There was no address, nor even a phone number. And that, thought Henry, was decidedly significant. It was the last vital piece of the puzzle that he needed. Extracting his camera from his anorak he knelt down amongst the surrounding debris and photographed the sign, then dusting himself down, he slipped out of the garage and through the rusty gate back to the town centre car park. A cup of tea at the bus station café was all that was necessary before he set off down the M40 for his drive to the Gazette offices.

On his way to the office next morning Henry stopped to pick up his copy of the paper. The outsize headlines on the front page allowed no space for the latest exciting reports and photographs of a pop stars' wedding in a Scottish castle. That news had been relegated to an inside page. Other copy and two photographs of himself and Harry Furnell had replaced it.

261

"THE GAZETTE EXPOSES CRIMINAL SYNDICATE AMONGST NHS BOSSES."

The Gazette has blown apart a gang-land, mafia style syndicate in the Midlands NHS led by Sir Dennis Deane, Chairman of the Mercia Regional Health Authority. The newspaper has uncovered a plot by Dennis Deane, the 'MrBig' of a gang who twice tried unsuccessfully to murder the Gazette's reporter, Henry Pye. Through weeks of determined investigation Henry Pye uncovered a plot by Dennis Deane to make use of a disused wing of Queenswood Hall Nursing Home to store stolen goods. Several months later Sir Dennis persuaded the Regional Health Authority to agree to the sale of Queenswood Hall so that a replacement nursing home could be built on land that he owned and eventually sold to the local Marton Health Authority.(continued on page 4)

Henry turned to page four, topped up his morning tea and allowed himself a deep sigh of satisfaction. Even though he had driven to Fleet Street and spent most of the previous afternoon and best part of the night in the offices of the Gazette writing and revising his copy he felt lively enough to laugh and smile, or even dance and sing if he were asked to do so. In fact he could never remember feeling quite so deliriously happy. The contents of the morning copy of the Gazette, which he propped up against his typewriter on his desk in the office, exceeded his expectations. Apart from an analysis on the back pages of the football Premier League positions following the previous evenings play-off for the League Championship, the Stock Market prices, the letters page and the strip cartoons, the remainder of the newspaper was devoted to what the editorial described as "The exposure of the biggest criminal conspiracy in the history of the NHS."

The delightful prospect of retirement... an offer of publication of his book on how he cracked the case...he'd need to think up a title... his demand as a guest speaker... money in the bank...a country cottage...a genuine one, not something dreamed up in Country Living. He snorted with laughter at the thought. The dream of the London Editor of that magazine bore no resemblance to the real thing...twee, with rag-rolled painted walls... Furniture that looked distressed and a straw hat hung on a six inch nail that appeared photographically artistic.

His cottage would be small, cosy and warm with an all-night wood burning fire, some nice antiques...he might start collecting...modern kitchen for the wife...and of course a dog.

Henry continued reading. It read well and looked well, even though he himself had written it. After consultation with the editorial board he had been given the all-clear to prepare the copy. The inside page two photograph of Dennis Deane was no problem, there were plenty to choose from. It was more difficult to find one of Harry Furnell, but eventually the computer came up with the goods, a photograph of Harry leading in his winning racehorse at Sandowne Park. Henry smoothed down the creased paper. The snap that he had taken of Queenswood Hall was clear, the building looked elegant. His only disappointment was Charlie Bastow, but there'd be time to catch him on film before too long. This story would run and run.

Chapter 27

At the very moment that Henry was enjoying his breakfast and congratulating himself on that morning's copy of the Gazette, Dennis Deane was in the farm office sorting through the mail and the morning newspapers. His post had dwindled down to junk mail, forms from the Ministry of Agriculture, and letters from the NFU, but he went through it to fill in the time when he would have normally been setting off for the office.

The new Regional Chief Executive Colin Harcombe who had replaced Malcolm phoned the previous day, expressing polite sympathy, asking tactfully about his replacement as Chairman and offering to send his secretary down to deliver Dennis' personal belongings. Dennis pictured his office. The photograph on his desk of his two Springer Spaniels was all that he really wanted. There were letters in the filing cabinet of course, filed away under 'personal.' In the wrong hands they could prove embarrassing; letters from Central Office advising him on the presentation of party policy, the best way to handle criticisms, complaints about long waiting lists and claims relating to negligence. They ought to be shredded for his own protection. How many days was it since the press conference and the phone call from McKeith. He counted back. Less than a week. The police still hadn't finished, although they'd returned his computer and some of his files.

The morning newspapers lay piled on the coffee table. He swung around in his chair to reach them but was interrupted as Edith opened the door.

"A parcel has come for you." She placed the package on his desk and left.

He turned back in his chair and reached for the letter opener, cutting and tearing at the stiff white paper and through the bubble wrap as he drew out the photograph that he knew so well. His two liver and white Springer Spaniels, Tess and Floss, sitting alert, on the banks of the Derwent, raring to go as they waited to compete in a scurry at the Game Fair. He remembered the event, the last Game Fair he had attended before his back became too painful. Now the two dogs lay panting and overweight at his feet in the farm office, and his gun locked in the gun cupboard unused for several years.

He swivelled his chair away from the desk and hauled himself to his feet, crossing the office to the metal gun cupboard, taking the keys from his pocket and choosing the correct combination. His Churchill lay in front of him, waiting in its case, and above it on the shelf was a box of cartridges. Gently he removed the gun case from the cupboard, carrying it to the desk, unfastening the leather straps and the metal buckles. He opened the lid, smelling the familiar scent of oil, lifted the walnut stock, stroking it and running his fingers over the patterned engraving. Picking up the barrel, he peered down the chambers, sat back in his chair, feeling for the linseed oil rag to clean the stock. The rag was hard and dry. He looked inside the case and found the empty bottle, its desiccated cork broke up between his fingers. Wrapped inside a strip of flannel he found a small glass container of Newark's Preparation for Guns. Carefully he dampened the cloth and wrapped it around the cleaning rod.

The two dogs got to their feet, picking up the scent of the shot gun, recalling memories of the past. Their

265

excitement grew as they watched him.

Just one last walk with the dogs. Ideas began to form... he could not take the dogs, it would not be fair to them. He would leave them behind. He would take the Land Rover, follow the track that used to be the driveway across the fields to the old hall, down to the hollow, that had been dug out years ago for cock fighting. It would be so easy. It might even look like an accident, except that he had left the dogs behind. They would wonder why.

As for Edith, well she was tough, she would have her freedom at last, and money to enjoy it. He peered down the barrels once again and reached for the cleaning rod. There must be no mistake. After all these years the barrels would need special care.

The sound of a vehicle turning in the yard distracted him. Dennis watched from the window as Harry Furnell locked his silver Merc. and walked towards the house. What on earth had he come for?

He mustn't be found with the gun. He got to his feet and propped it behind the cloakroom door, pushing the case under the desk with his feet, then sat down and reached for the morning papers. News from Washington about the new administration following the Presidential election took up the main headlines in the Telegraph but a side column caught his eye. 'NEW FRAUD CLAIM ROCKS NHS.' Dennis started to read. 'The Gazette newspaper claims that it has uncovered fresh evidence of widespread fraud amongst Health Authority Chairmen.'

He read on quickly, no names were mentioned. That was a relief. He pushed back his chair and dropped the pile of newspapers on the floor as he searched for the Gazette, snatching it up and placing it on the desk, turning the pages and smoothing them with his hand.

On page four his own photograph alongside that of Harry Furnell stared back at him. Underneath the caption read 'The Rogues gallery (courtesy of the NHS).'

When Harry entered the office Dennis experienced a stab of fury. Harry wore his usual grin and appeared unworried by the latest press publicity. It crossed Dennis' mind that perhaps he had not even read it. He strutted around the room in a check suit that would have been more appropriate on a racecourse, complete with canary coloured tie and a leather waistcoat beneath his tweed jacket. It was hardly the outfit for a Health Authority Chairman, thought Dennis.

" Hi Den!"

"Sir Dennis, please."

Harry flashed him a disrespectful grin as, without being asked to do so, he took his seat and leaned back in the leather armchair facing Dennis. "Come off it Den. I've heard you've lost your job. Can't expect all that kow-towing and three bags full now, can you? You'll be lucky if the Queen doesn't ask for your medal back."

"And you can't expect to hang on to your job much longer. Your photo's in all the papers," retorted Dennis.

Harry laughed. "Oh no. No one can pin anything on me. I haven't been stealing cheese or trying to murder a newspaper reporter. I'm in the clear. You're the one they're after. You're the one who arranged for Charlie Bastow to hide his stolen cheeses at Queenswood Hall. You're the one who's up to the neck in trouble with the Gilberts over the land deal, and

267

you're the one in cahoots with them in the attempt to run down that reporter who found out too much." He leaned forward, lifting his hand and waving a finger at Dennis. "Now listen to me. I've come here to try and help - although I don't know why I should – but if you don't want my help then I advise you to pack your bags 'cos you're in for a long spell of porridge at Her Majesty's pleasure."

Dennis listened, reluctantly, and fought back a wave of sickness as he faced up to the charges that could be levelled at him. How could Harry possibly help him and how could anyone trust Harry? His thoughts turned to his gun leaning in a corner behind the cloakroom door – he had his own solution.

"Harry you've thought up a good tale, but it's not good enough. You'll be charged with handling stolen goods, and Charlie Bastow will blow your case apart. He's a sharp lad and he's got to protect himself."

Harry waved a hand in the air, "No problem Den – at least not a problem for me. I've got the job sorted. Your replacement really is a dish, nicest little filly you could meet. We get on well together...now what I suggest...if you and I..."

Harry's words sounded distant, like someone calling through a loud-speaker in a far field. Dennis tried to concentrate on Harry's words. "My replace-ment?" He spoke with difficulty. The words sounded jumbled and reverberated through his skull.

"Your replacement Den? You don't know? They didn't tell you?"

Dennis was about to shake his head, but decided to bluff it out. Of course he should have been told, but he hated to admit his ignorance.

"It's Barbara, Dennis. Little Barbara who you

sacked. They must have told you."

He tried to raise a smile, to nod, to look confident, but his pen fell from his right hand onto the desk. He opened his mouth to speak and his lips twitched in a senseless mumble. He tried to grip the arm of his chair but his right hand would not respond.

"Dennis?" Harry stared at him. "Are you ok? Hey Den don't take on so. We all have bad patches - " He watched with alarm as Dennis slumped forward in his chair, hitting his head against the desk light that crashed sideways onto the floor.

Chapter 28

His room, No. 28, was small, not much bigger than a store cupboard and was hot and stuffy. The door to the en-suite bathroom was ajar and the smell from the toilet and the soiled clothes lying in a pile on the floor invaded the room. There was only one chair. When Edith brought a visitor she usually sat on the bed. Today Samuel Madrugada sat on the bed. The bed was high and his feet swung inches above the plastic floor tiles. His shoes shone at the end of pin stripe trousers and navy socks. Beside him on the pale green coverlet his leather brief case bulged with papers.

Dennis stared at the television morning chat show. The colours were garishly bright and the sound, turned up full, made conversation impossible. Edith leaned forward in her chair and switched off the set. Dennis grunted in annoyance and fumbled for the remote control on the bedside table in front of him. A Get-Well card lay on the window ledge. In an effort to distract him Edith picked it up. "It's your card from Annabel," she said. "She's coming to see you this afternoon."

The card fell from his lap and Dennis leaned forward in his wheelchair to catch it, but his foot slipped from the footrest and lay trapped and helpless in the gap between the two supports. Edith kneeled down, released his foot and picked up the card. He gazed down at the writing. "Anna..." he said.

"He always keeps the card with him. Never lets it out of his sight," said Edith.

Samuel Madrugada glanced at his watch. "They've taken Harry Furnell in for questioning, however I believe that we can keep your husband out of court. I've had a word with his consultant who will give evidence that he's unfit to plead." He turned towards Dennis and raised his voice. "I hear that they've also charged Charlie Bastow with stealing cheese from the show."

Dennis ignored the information and continued to stare at the television, pressing the buttons on the remote control in an effort to restore the picture and the sound.

"You'll not get through to him," Edith raised her voice above the noise. For a brief moment she watched her husband, then stood up, anxious to keep her weekly hair appointment. She was due for a silver rinse. With a hint of backcombing it made her look, and feel, ten years younger. Then she would return to the peace and comfort of her home. Now that he was not there, stomping through the rooms, grumbling when she was on the phone and shouting at the farm manager, she felt able to relax for the first time for years. She planned to take a holiday, do as she pleased...perhaps go on a cruise. The thought of being able to have the freedom to do as she pleased excited her. She realised that it might all eventually pall, but every morning she smiled with satisfaction whilst she dressed and put on her make-up in front of the large mirror in the en-suite bathroom with the twin marble hand-basins and gold plated taps.

In the afternoon Annabel arrived. Dennis was still watching television. The sounds of Emmerdale Farm met her as she walked down the corridor and turned the corner past the nursing station. "It's impossible to get him to turn the noise down. Everyone complains," said the nurse.

271

When she entered his room he turned away from the television and smiled at her. She could never remember her father smiling before, it was as if he had been waiting for her. She bent down to kiss him. His cheek was dry and rough and his hand trembled as he grabbed her arm, squeezing until it hurt. Annabel picked up the remote control from the bedside table and turned down the noise. Dennis grunted impatiently and took it from her, pointing it at the set and switching it off. His hand shook.

"Dress," he said, stroking the material. "Nice...smart frock."

She sat down close to her father, reaching for his hand. "I came to show you this."

She held up her left hand. It trembled unsteadily.

He grabbed her hand roughly, staring down examined the ring. "Sapph...ire," he said. He looked up at her, scowling, "Sandy?"

She shook her head. Her hair fell across her face and she brushed it away between her fingers. "That's been over some time."

He frowned at her in bewilderment.

"I'm engaged to Tim."

He shook his head, unable to understand.

"I thought Mother had told you. You remember Tim? The Vicar who came to that meeting?"

Dennis stared at her and his eyes blurred with tears so that he no longer saw her. He coughed and tried to clear his throat, "The Parson?"

"He's a Rural Dean now." she said. "We're going to live in an old Georgian rectory - next to the church in Artlebury. I don't suppose you've heard of the village but it's quite well known down south."

"A parson's... wife," said Dennis. He nodded his

272

head and tears ran down his cheeks as he spoke. He reached for the tissues from the box on the bedside table and tried to mop the stream of saliva that dribbled down his chin, embarrassed that she would see the spittle that ran on to his jacket. Annabel took a tissue from the box and handed it to him, noticing the long white whiskers on his neck which the razor had missed.

"We're getting married next month… in July," said Annabel. She picked up a leather bag from the floor, searched inside and pulled out an envelope "I've brought you your invitation."

Dennis looked down at his wheelchair and banged the arm with his hand. He scowled and grunted and shook his head.

"No problem," she said.   "We'll get you there…we'll arrange everything. You have to be there."

When she had left Dennis pointed the remote control at the television set and turned up the sound full blast.

Next day no one came to visit. The stout care assistant in a green and white overall wheeled him into the garden. "It's a lovely day. Too nice to spend watching television."

She wheeled him along the path towards the summer-house. "You get a good view from here," she said. "Can you see the Cathedral across the river?"

Dennis shook his head.

"The Queen's going there next month. The cathedral's five hundred years old. They sent us an invitation to take our residents to the service. Would you like to go? We can take wheel chairs in the van."

Dennis glowered.

"All the big-wigs will be there, the Mayor, the

MP's, the Lord Lieutenant...You'll know them all I expect. Shall I put your name on the list?"

Dennis shook his head. "Shops," he said. "Go... to shops."

The Care Assistant looked puzzled. "Shops?"

"Wedding present." said Dennis.

Chapter 29

The lane that led to Queenswood Hall was narrow. At the end of the drive that wound its way through the fields up to the hall an aged oak had for years served as a notice board for local events.

Henry drove carefully avoiding the debris that littered the roadway after the previous night's storm. A stiff breeze ripped and snapped at the torn remnants of a UKIP election poster that had been nailed to the trunk of the tree before last week's general election.

As far as Henry was concerned all political parties were guilty of mismanagement. Few editors, or experienced journalists ever took on face value statements made by politicians, it was simply spin and made cynics of them all. Hidden agendas and unspoken messages lay tucked away in the small print. Nevertheless they were there if you asked the right questions, and if you didn't ask the questions you were never given the answers. Even the readers had long since ceased to believe anything they read in the papers as Fleet Street bosses pursued their own political agendas.

Henry usually avoided political interviews but the events of the past months and his frequent meetings with Paul Rugglestone had changed his views somewhat, but who knows how long it would be before even Paul resorted to spin? However for the present he could only admire his guts and determination. He was genuinely delighted that Paul had held his seat with a greatly increased majority, mainly due to the work of his fiancee Erica who had planned his campaign, and also the extensive canvass carried out by the students at the Heath College led by that odd young woman, Annabel.

The day after the election the Prime Minister appointed Paul as Secretary of State for the Environment. She couldn't have chosen a better man.

As Henry drove past the oak tree he saw the small yellow notice fixed on the other side of the trunk. It bore the logo of the South Mercia Borough Council. Henry slowed down and opened the window on the passenger side door but the print was still too small to read.

He got out of the car and crossed the grass verge. Adjusting his glasses he read the notice, frowning as he took in the message.

QUEENSWOOD HALL

Application has been made for a change of use for the building and grounds of Queenswood Hall to a Championship Golf Course, Hotel and Residential Development.

Details of the application can be inspected at the offices of South Mercia Borough Council.

Henry did not bother to read further. He crossed the lane to his car, reversed into a lay-by and drove directly to the Council offices. He had intended to return to London as soon as the election was over, but now, just as he was about to leave, his nose detected the scent of a new trail.

Henry sat in front of a table in the planning office whilst an earnest young man cleared a space for him to inspect the bulky file.

"I thought it was going to be a nursing home," said Henry.

276

"That was the original idea. But the first purchaser had planned a modern purpose built nursing home - which meant that the old building would have to be demolished, and as Queenswood Hall is a listed building we, of course, advised him that he was unlikely to get permission."

"Hadn't done his homework," observed Henry. He turned the pages, examining the plans and studying the papers. "Who made this application then?"

"The new owner." The planning officer leaned over and picked up the file. "The place was sold very quickly." He began to search through the file until he found the name on the application form. "Here it is."

Henry peered at the name. "Harry Furnell. My God, it's Harry Furnell – That man never misses a trick does he?"

He stared at the young planning officer. "Is it likely to be approved?"

"That all depends... if the Secretary of State decides to call it in. He would have to call it in if an application were to be made to demolish it – but this application for an hotel could save the building and hopefully restore it."

"I wouldn't be too sure of that old son." said Henry. "This lad is as slippery as an eel. He's not applied to demolish any part of the building then?"

The planning officer picked up the file and read out loud from the application form " Demolition of the old kitchen block...that's a nineteen sixties addition. Restoration of the main Queen Anne building; new kitchens and storage areas in the basement. Health and safety matters, re-wiring, plumbing, and general restoration. It's quite a big job."

"Well watch him carefully...very carefully." warned

Henry. "Whereabouts is the residential development?" he asked, looking down at the map.

The planning officer pointed to an area hatched in red. "On the edge of the golf course, behind the club house. The applicant suggests affordable housing - we're very short of affordable housing. We need to increase our stock."

Henry snorted in disbelief. "Affordable? What exactly is affordable in a championship golf course setting? Who will control who buys them?" He began to chuckle, "They'll make nice second homes for golfers"

"We can put conditions " the planning officer began to explain.

Henry snorted. "Harry Furnell will drive a coach and horses through your conditions."

He ran a finger around the proposed site. "There's no natural boundary to the area. It could easily be extended on to the surrounding farmland, and I bet there are farmers out there who already have an understanding with Harry Furnell. Harry always rolls his pitch before he plays on it."

"They wouldn't be allowed to develop on a greenfield site or close to the golf course. In any case we shall insist that the golf course be completed before we agree to any detailed permission for housing."

"Well if you are determined to approve the application, may I suggest that you tie up Mr. Harry Furnell as tightly as possible with all the necessary conditions you can think of, because it won't he too long before he re-applies to change every condition you have placed on your approval." Henry shook his head. "Far be it for me to tell you your business, old son, but this chap is a very dodgy customer."

On the way back to the Fishpool Inn he retraced his route to the lane that led to Queenswood Hall. He turned into the drive and drove slowly up to the hall, swerving to avoid the potholes and leaving his car in the same place as before. He followed the path through the weeds and brambles to the back of the building. The back door hung on rusty hinges. The brickwork was in need of pointing, loose, and stained with rain water from a broken gutter. He put his shoulder to the door and it gave way to the pressure. It had not been locked. The building awaited his inspection.

The smell of damp pervaded the rooms and black mould spread over the kitchen walls. The conditions were much worse than when he last visited the place over eight months ago at the end of the summer; now the ravages of neglect and a cold wet winter had made the place uninhabitable. He shivered, zipped up his fleece-lined anorak and stuck his hands in his pockets.

Henry walked through the stone corridors to the front of the building. In the draughty reception rooms, which had been used as dormitories for the elderly, the marble fireplaces had already been removed. The wind gusted down the chimneys. Nothing of any use or value remained, even the light bulbs had been removed. Wash basins with their brass taps had been ripped from the walls and ornamental cornices and light fittings torn from the ceilings. Mahogany doors no longer graced the entrances to the main reception rooms and the elegant circular salon had lost its window seats and central chandelier.

Was this simply vandalism, wondered Henry. In what antique emporiums and warehouses lay these symbols of past elegance. Were all those fine artefacts no longer needed in a modern hotel? In a matter of

279

minutes Henry reached a decision that a hunt must now be on for the perpetrator of such vandalism. Fleet Street would have to wait a little longer for his return. The newly appointed Secretary of State for the Environment was probably not aware of the problem a mile further along the lane from his constituency home in the Old Rectory.

Henry retraced his steps and walked around the outside of the building, admiring the architecture, the Corinthian columns with their acanthus leaves at the front and the carved decorations; then leaning backwards he gazed upwards. The effort made him feel dizzy and the wind appeared to rock the broken remains of the statues that lined the balustrade around the edge of the roof. He stepped back just as a stone pineapple rocked by the breeze fell and crashed on to the terrace where he had been standing. It was time to go. Might that have been third time lucky for him?

Later that day he tried to contact Paul Rugglestone, but discovered that when a chap has been turned into a Secretary of State he is not all that easy to get hold of. Luckily Erica still made herself available.

She listened and gave him Paul's private number.

"I'll fax Mercia and ask for a full report. Meanwhile I'll ask them to notify the applicant that they need more time to reach a decision." said Paul.

Henry replaced the receiver thoughtfully. For some inexplicable reason he felt a sudden urge to return to Queenswood Hall and climb out onto the roof.

It was mid-morning next day before he returned. He walked through the empty rooms towards the main hall. In the drawing room, gold silk hangings, rotted and torn, trailed from the wall. He took a photograph of the blackened hole in the wall where a marble Adam fireplace had once decorated the room. In the dining room, faded wallpaper contrasted with bright square patches where pictures had once been hung.

Henry had only just begun to climb the main staircase to investigate the sounds of activity from the floors above when the double doors at the other end of the hall were suddenly flung open and a shadow fell across the floor.

Henry leaned over the bannisters. "Well if it isn't Charlie Bastow," He laughed. "And what brings you here to this stately home ? Thinking of moving in, or are you looking for a job running the new hotel?"

Charlie looked puzzled. "Oh yeah, I know – you're the geezer who said you worked for Lewis. I told him we met, but I couldn't remember your name, funny - he didn't seem to remember who you were either. Anyway it looks as though there's been a bit of a mix up somewhere. So what' yer doin' here then?"

"Just checking, " Henry thought quickly. "Checking that there's nothing left. All cleaned out now is it?" he asked.

At that moment a crash on the landing above them interrupted the conversation. Charlie ran across the hall and raced up the stairs. Henry turned to look. Two workmen were struggling with what looked like a large, blue and white, floral pattern china lavatory.

"Never get this down there," said one of the removal men. " Too bloody heavy. Have to slide it. We'll have to go back for more planks." he puffed. He leaned on the bannisters for support. "Any case it'll have to be cleaned. I'm not touchin' that until someone cleans it – and cleans it proper- the pong is summat awful."

The two men walked down the stairs. "Need to go for a pee," said one, "but with all the loos gone we'll

281

have to use the garden. Maybe see you this afternoon if we can get some help. Can't manage it by ourselves. We'll have to see what the boss has to say."

"So who's their boss?" asked Henry.

"Harry, Harry Furnell," said Charlie. "Says he's too busy to check that this place is cleared out properly. Got a meetin' or somefink – so he sends me. Those chaps won't be back today. Harry's busy like – the whole day at the police station I hear."

Henry followed Charlie up the last flight of steps and on to the landing. They stood together inspecting the lavatory.

"Seen one of these before?" asked Charlie.

"Not that size," replied Henry "and not with flowers all over it."

"Edwardian," said Charlie authoritatively. "Cor it don't half pong. Still think what it'll look like in Belfield's window when it's cleaned and polished up. Half a minute - they've forgotten the brass pedal, and the mahogany back, and the seat and it's cover. Blimey it'll look like a throne when Belfield sets it up. Folks'll be fallin' over themselves to buy it – specially the Yanks. It'll cost them the earth."

"All the stuff going to Belfields?" Henry searched in his pockets for his pipe and his pouch of Holland House.

"Gone into store."

"You arrange storage then, do you?" asked Henry casually, tamping down the tobacco and applying a lighted match.

Charlie Bastow winced as the first cloud of smoke stung his eyes.

"Yeh, for the moment – till Belfield collects it."

"I'd like to get some photos of the grounds," said

282

Henry casually. "From high up you know – for publicity. Harry wants a brochure for the hotel. In any case we need a good view of the grounds to plan the golf course. The roof would be a good place to start. How do I get up to the roof?"

"I'll take you up." Charlie volunteered. "I've nothing much else to do until the removal men get back.." He led the way up two flights of stairs into the attics and along passages, peering into rooms where more than a hundred years ago the staff had slept. Iron bedsteads, moth-eaten mattresses, trunks and suitcases told tales of life 'below stairs.'

" 'alf a mo," exclaimed Charlie "take a look at those fireplaces. They're werf a bob or two."

They climbed a narrow staircase and squeezed their way through a small door. A blast of fresh air heralded their arrival on to the eaves.

Henry paused to get his breath then gingerly made his way along the lead lined gully around edge of the roof, keeping his eye on Charlie. He was afraid to touch the balustrade, it was badly cracked and parts were missing. He kept thinking about the pineapple that fell off. Being alone on the roof with Charlie boy made him feel uneasy. He turned the corner but could go no further as the lead had been removed, exposing the joists beneath.

"Hey Charlie. Take a look at this." he shouted.

Charlie edged his way towards him. " No problem mate. They're repairing the roof."

"Who's repairing the roof ?"

"The builders. Lewis and his mates."

"So where are they then?"

"They don't work Wednesdays." Charlie sounded defensive.

283

"If they finished work yesterday, where's the tarpaulin? After last night's storm the rain must have gone through to the rooms below." Henry took his camera from his pocket. "I'll take some photographs before we go down." He took his time in the pretence of photographing the surrounding parkland, but made sure that the damage to the roof was also included.

As they returned to the attics Henry could see that the room immediately below had already been affected by damp. A brown stain had spread across the ceiling. Two large water tanks aroused Henry's curiosity and he lifted the heavy covers and peered into the depths. They were both empty, but had once contained water that had fed the internal plumbing system. It occurred to Henry that if any accident happened to either of the tanks then the ceilings would collapse and that side of the house would be totally flooded.

The room had been used as a storeroom, bedheads and mattresses with rusting springs protruding through their stuffing lay propped against the wall beside the window. The catch was broken but he was able to push up the rotten wooden sash window sufficiently to peer down at the decaying brickwork. He eased his head and shoulders back into the room, but despite his best efforts he was unable to close the window.

On his return to the Fishpool a quick phone call to the planning office soon elicited the information that eased his mind.

"Yes we are checking for vandalism. We've been told that there is a problem."

"Do you know that lead has been stripped from the roof?" asked Henry

There was a sigh at the other end of the line.

"We'll visit Queenswood again later in the week."

284

the Planning Officer assured him.

"You'll probably be too late."

Henry put down the receiver and leaned back in his chair, trying to fit the pieces of the jigsaw together. Where did Charlie Bastow fit in? With the Gilberts? With Dennis Deane? There was a piece missing. He made his way down to the bar and studied the dinner menu.

Nick reached up to the message board and handed him a note. "Came this morning. A young lady wants you to phone her. You should be so lucky. She said it was from Friends of the Earth."

Henry stared at the note. "Are you sure this is for me? I've never had anything to do with Friends of the Earth. A half of Boddingtons please and I'll take this in my room."

"Annabel speaking." The voice sounded business-like.

"Ah... I was trying to get through to Friends of the Earth."

"This is Friends of the Earth. I shut the office at five."

"Well I had a message to phone."

"Is that Henry Pye? This is Annabel Deane. The name may mean something to you, but I don't think we've ever met."

"Dennis Deane's daughter?" Of course he'd heard about her.

"Can we meet tomorrow? It's important. The office at my place if you don't mind. The Vicarage, Marton – right by the church."

Chapter 30

There was coffee waiting when Henry arrived at the Vicarage. The Annabel who welcomed him bore no resemblance to Annabel the rebellious Animal Rights activist, whom he had heard so much about – with the exception of the large round spectacles.

Tim Parrish, the Vicar, waited for him in the study. "My apologies. I'm afraid that I have to dash off as I'm taking a funeral in half an hour."

"My fiancé," explained Annabel. "We're getting married in July," she hesitated, "You've probably heard of me. I used to be with Animal Rights, but when I heard that Friends of the Earth were looking for a secretary I applied for the job."

"Congratulations on both counts," said Henry. "Friends of the Earth sounds a mite more respectable for a prospective Vicar's wife, than Animal Rights."

He watched Annabel as she poured the coffee. Dark brown corduroy trouser suit and spectacles hanging from a gold cord around her neck. Smart and efficient. Quite a transformation from the old Annabel who wore a tee shirt emblazoned with feminist messages, jeans and trainers, and released animals from their pens at the Heath College. What a difference falling in love can make.

"Friends of the Earth check all the planning applications that are published each month by South Mercia Borough Council " explained Annabel. "This month there was an application for change of use of Queenswood Hall for a Golf Course, Hotel and Residential Development. We discussed the application with our colleagues in CPRE who agree with us that an application for housing within the green belt is totally out of the question. We will oppose it for that reason alone. In any case the building itself is listed."

Henry felt for his pipe, took it from his pocket and stared at it. "So why contact me?"

She offered him a plate of biscuits and an ashtray "Publicity," she said sweetly. "But do smoke if you wish – it's one of Tim's vices."

He thought better of it and put his pipe back in his pocket.

Annabel sat on the sofa beside him. "I heard that you were still in the area. In fact everyone knows you at the Fishpool so I thought I'd get in touch, in case you might be interested in what's going on at Queenswood."

"So what is going on there?" asked Henry. "Mind if I make notes?"

"Ok, but keep my father's name out of it. I don't want him involved. He's a sick man and all this publicity's killing him. You haven't helped – caused him a lot of trouble."

Henry almost choked. "Well can you blame me? That's my job – then someone tries to kill me off. How would you feel?"

He swallowed a mouthful of coffee. "I can't promise to keep your father's name out of it. It depends what you have to tell me. It's up to you."

Annabel nodded. "I know I'm taking a risk. Anyway you've come across Harry Furnell I suppose."

Once again Henry almost choked on the coffee. "Who hasn't?"

"Whatever Harry gets involved in is bad news, and we're not too sure what his game is this time."

"I've got a good idea, but before we talk about

287

Harry – where does Charlie Bastow fit into all this?"

"You know all about VS&T I'm sure? Well in order to operate the directors needed a scout who could travel around the country attending used car auctions, buying up old cars, and vans. They cannibalised them for spare parts. Charlie was ideal, he'd taken a course in vehicle maintenance at the local college of F.E. and he was a sharp lad with a gift of the gab when it came to buying and selling. Not only that, but he's got a brother who runs a garage in Marton who could do the work. It all fits in nicely doesn't it?"

Henry scribbled busily. "So Charlie brought in the business."

"And people came for miles around for spares, particularly for vintage cars and obsolete parts and little things like badges, wipers, old gear sticks. It's a big market."

"But a VS&T employee, receiving and storing stolen goods?"

"Nothing to do with VS&T. Charlie's private operations were his own business - although I'm sure that he would know that part of the Queenswood Hall building was empty – he was in and out of the office every day and probably overheard my father and the Gilberts discussing their plans. Of course I knew nothing about all these goings on at the time. It was only when they tried to frighten you off that my mother broke down and told me."

"Frighten me off? You mean the two attempts to kill me ?"

"Yes, well they told father they were trying to frighten you."

"Well whatever they tried to do I'm glad to say that the attempts were bungled. Anyway where does Harry come into this?"

"You probably know that my father once owned a turkey farm – hundreds of turkeys in every shed – poor things. I hated it. That's why I left home and joined Animal Rights. Anyway Harry bought the turkeys from my father and processed the meat, then sold the processed meat to schools. It was easy for the cooks and dinner ladies to cook and slice, and it was cheap. The kids told their parents that they had roast turkey for dinner. Of course it tasted nothing like the real thing but everyone was happy."

"No outbreaks of food poisoning?" asked Henry hopefully.

"Frequent outbreaks, but nothing they could pin on Harry. About that time slimmers began buying turkey meat, it's low in calories, and Harry cashed in big time – made himself a fortune with that and other things."

"But why would he want the hall?"

"Harry's sharp, doesn't miss a trick. That sale was a put up job," said Annabel. "Of course VS&T would have liked to buy and develop the whole of the Queenswood Hall estate, but that was out of the question, father being a director. Anyway Geoffrey Tate also wanted to buy the hall for a nursing home and sell the remainder of the land for development."

Henry stopped writing. "So where does Harry come in to all this?"

"He heard of Tate's plans and offered to buy the remainder of the land," explained Annabel. "Then when the nursing home project fell through Harry offered to buy the whole estate providing he could find a partner and that is how Harry got together with Lewis Gilbert. Of course VS&T couldn't get involved."

"Then of course Harry and Charlie have always

worked closely together," said Henry.

"So who masterminded the cheese theft? " asked Annabel. "They both sail close to the wind but I never thought that either of them were real criminals."

Henry laughed. "Oh I know the answer to that," he said. "No doubt about it. The Gilberts are the real criminals. Why do you think they tried to kill me off?"

"Frighten you off," corrected Annabel.

"But why would they tell your father? He must have been involved too."

"Just boasting. He wasn't involved, I'm sure." Annabel sounded adamant "From what mother told me he was angry - and frightened. After hearing what you said at that meeting he realised what had happened and confronted them."

Annabel got up and walked over to her desk, extracted a leaflet from a pigeon hole and handed it to Henry. "Now it seems that Harry's branched out from food production into property development."

On the top of the front page was the heading 'Weddings R Us' the text entwined with flowers and bells. Beneath were the words "If you are getting married why not leave it all to us? Magnificent family chapel in a superb parkland setting. Top of the range quality marquee. Dress hire, Cars, Choir, Flowers, and a Wedding reception tailored to suit your requirements." In the centre spread was a big photograph entitled "Queenswood Hall eighteenth century family chapel." And on the final page of the leaflet a photograph of a flower bedecked marquee on the main lawn. The advertisement ended with the words "For the happiest day of your life contact Harry Furnell & Co."

Henry read the leaflet carefully.

"So why advertise a marquee when they could make use of the hall?" asked Annabel.

"Because Harry is trashing the hall, stripping it of anything of value, and that includes the lead from the roof."

"But why would he do that?"

"It's obvious - in a year or two the building will deteriorate so badly that it will be classed as unfit for human habitation and will be left to mercy of the elements and become a ruin," explained Henry. "Then he'll apply for a demolition order because it's unsafe - and then he can build more houses on the site."

"Can't we stop him?"

"Not unless we can catch him in the act of stripping the roof. In any case I suspect that he'll claim that the roof is in need of repair and that all the other things are being put into store for protection during the restoration project."

"So what's the plan of action?" asked Annabel suddenly, rubbing her hands together.

Now this is the old Annabel, thought Henry.

"Well you of all people should know how to take action. Friends of the Earth have to act fast. Get on to the Council. – ask them to issue a 'Stop' notice." He looked out of the window. "It's pouring with rain now. Several months of this and the place will be a ruin, too expensive to repair."

"Won't the Council carry out repairs?"

"They couldn't afford to. In any case they'll never get their money back from people like Harry."

"Leave it to me, I'll talk to our Committee - I've also got contacts."

"I'd be surprised if you hadn't," said Henry "but don't tell me what your plans are – and don't forget that before too long you'll be married to a Vicar."

Annabel grinned. "One last mad fling," she said.

Chapter 31

The appetising scent of fried bacon, a hint of blue sky, and the weather forecast on the bedroom television held out the prospect of a good day. The south-westerly gale with torrential rain that was forecast to lash the midlands had delayed its arrival until the following day. All this combined to encourage Henry to take a day off and find somewhere with an extensive luncheon menu. That idea vanished as quickly as it came when Henry went down for breakfast and met Inspector Hodgkin in reception.

"Sorry to delay your breakfast but we'd like you to meet us in the car park at the back of the pub," said the Inspector. "The landlord phoned us late last night to say that he saw a man wandering around the car park examining the vehicles. We took him in for questioning but had to let him go when he said that he was looking for his car keys. Anyway I'd like you to go and check your car."

At that time in the morning there were only a few vehicles in the car park, mostly staff cars. The Saab looked fine, but he saw that he had forgotten to straighten his front wheels when he parked it and he remembered being in a hurry to draft his report for the overnight edition.

A police mechanic stood by the Saab. "I've washed the hub-caps. Now I'd like to take your car for a test drive Mr. Pye. I'll drive it around the car park then head towards those straw bales we've put there." He waved his hand towards a wall of straw bales on the other side of the car park. "Not too fast. Then I'll apply the brakes – hard. That's of course if you agree?"

Henry swallowed hard. "Will you pay for any damage? I'm fond of this old car."

"Don't worry, we're insured. Better to risk a bit of damage to your car than risk your life Sir. If there should be any problem with the brakes I'm sure I can handle it," the mechanic assured him as he got into the Saab and adjusted the driver's seat.

Henry watched in horror as his car roared into life and circled the car park, faster than he'd ever driven it. "Oh my poor car," he moaned.

When it neared the straw bales the brake lights came on and the Saab skidded on the muddy surface, slewed around and turning full circle came to a halt beside Henry.

"A neat piece of driving," observed the Inspector, bending down to examine the hub-caps. "There's fresh oil on the wheels. If he pumps the brakes any more there won't be any brake fluid left. You can't possibly take this car on to the road. I'll send for a low-loader. Sorry Mr. Pye we'll have to have the car in and check it over thoroughly. Do you need a hire car?"

Henry shrugged his shoulders. "Can't manage without one; so much for my idea of having a day off." One thing that was top of his list was to keep an eye on Annabel and her friends.

Whilst Annabel cleared the oak dining table for a battle conference a convoy of cars from the Heath Agricultural college wound their way through the lanes that lead to the Vicarage. She believed that she had persuaded Tim to take the chair for the meeting and he was pleased to let her think that that she had done so. In fact he was secretly relieved to be asked to do so. Someone had to curb their fanatical enthusiasm with practical advice. An uncontrolled alliance between Annabel and students could once again lead to a riot, and he had no intention of taking part in the action. All he could do was to offer advice. In his opinion a fair amount of planning and stealth was required. Their enemy had years of experience and were probably anticipating trouble.

Lewis Gilbert removed the advertising signs from the side of the wagon and helped Mick load the tools. Mick's resemblance to Yul Brynner, with his shaven head and gold earring earned him his nickname of Yul.

"We'll use the rear entrance and go through the gardens. If we park the lorry in the back drive it won't be seen," said Lewis. "That Charlie can't keep his fucking mouth shut. He ought to know better than take that fucking reporter chap up to the roof. We need to take off the rest of the lead today before the council planners pay us another visit."

"Not to worry," laughed Mick. "This time I've really done for him. We won't hear any more of Mr. Henry bloody Pye."

"What do you mean? Done for him? What have you done?"

Mick looked pleased with himself. "Well maybe not exactly killed him. Only scared the pants off him. Released the brake fluid nut good and proper this time."

Lewis stared at him. "You bloody fool. So what do you think will happen when he crashes the car?"

Mick looked uncomfortable. "Well they won't blame me – will they? They let me go when I told them I was lookin' for my car keys."

"Who let you go?"

"The police."

Lewis held his head in his hands and groaned in disbelief. "You flamin' idiot. Get in the wagon and let's finish this job. Then you'll have to lie low."

The rutted track through the woodland gardens was lined with rhododendrons and Lewis found a clearing where he could park. It was well hidden and only a few yards from the back door.

Their footsteps echoed in the empty building as they climbed the back stairs that lead up to the bedrooms and the attics. Lewis took the key from the hook and opened the narrow doorway on to the roof. After the gloom of the corridors lit only from skylights the bright sunshine dazzled them. They eased their way between the balustrade and the hipped roof and crawled along the leads on their hands and knees..

"Can't be seen behind this balustrade," said Mick confidently, rising to peer over the parapet.

"Keep down you fool or someone will see you," ordered Lewis.

"Anyway there's no sign of the Saab, I sorted that out good and proper. And there's a fire escape – goes all the way down. Why don't we use that?"

"Too risky. The brick work's rotten."

Sweating and exhausted, bent double, they prised up the lead, rolling and folding it as they progressed. It was a heavy, tiring job but Lewis was determined to finish that day. At mid- morning they stopped for a can of Lager and relieved themselves down the downspouts, laughingly wondering if anyone happened to be standing below. As they worked they failed to hear the arrival of Annabel and her team who had moved stealthily through the gardens, following the tracks of the wagon and letting down its tyres. One by one they slipped silently through the back door and took up their positions. As Annabel lead the way up to the third floor and along the passage they heard the sound of workmen above, the clatter of tools, and the panting and cursing as the lead was wrenched from wooden joists.

The door to the roof lay wide open with the key still in the lock. Annabel held her breath and reached for the handle. The rusted hinges squeaked as she swung the heavy door slowly towards her. Carefully controlling it she eased it forward, pausing with every squeak until the door settled firmly into its frame. Releasing the handle, which clicked shut, she turned the key and locked it.

On the roof Lewis noticed a change in the sound and direction of the breeze that had blown all morning. There was no echo in its tone and it blew straight across their   line of work. He paused and listened. Easing himself to his feet he hurriedly leapt across the joists as he set off over the roof. In his haste he missed his step. Trying to regain his balance he slipped and fell heavily. His leg twisted beneath him as his foot broke through the plaster-board and crashed through the ceiling. With both legs contorted in agony and groaning horribly he began to fall through the roof into the room below, but came to rest as his capacious belly became wedged between the timbers which dug fiercely into his ribs, bruising his chest until he could hardly breathe.

"Was'up?" called Mick hidden behind a vast chimney stack.

"Come and help." panted Lewis. "Get a bloody move on."

Mick set off, crossing the roof he glanced down over the balustrade. One hundred and fifty feet below

297

in the gardens a crowd of jeering students waved to him. He stared in horror as he noticed a group of policemen gathered on the terrace awaiting the arrival of two police cars that were speeding up the main drive towards the hall.

"What you playin' at?" gasped Lewis. "Get a ruddy move on."

"Trapped," exclaimed Mick, as he saw that the roof door was closed. "Ruddy well trapped – and police outside." He looked around for Lewis and saw what had happened. "Bloody hell – I'll never lift you out of that."

"Well you can try, can't you?" Lewis tried to stretch out an arm to Mick but the weight of his body threatened to drag him even further through the hole and pain speared him across his chest as the joists tightened their grip.

In the room below Henry had been waiting, camera at the ready, hoping to catch the dramatic moment of arrest as the police gathered on the landing by the entrance to the roof. He had just got his pipe nicely alight when a sudden crash from above brought down a large part of the ceiling and Lewis' boots and legs appeared through the hole. Henry's pipe and matches fell from his hands as he grabbed his camera, releasing it from its case and photographing the lower half of the body that dangled above him, distributing a thick shower of dust and plaster over his head and jacket and turning his hair grey. After successfully capturing several close-up shots of Lewis Gilbert's lower half and deciding not to offer assistance, as the wildly kicking boots were too dangerous to be approached, he watched as the body was eventually hauled upwards to safety on the roof whilst more showers of plaster cascaded down.

Eventually the face of a policeman appeared in the hole, stared down at him and disappeared.

The thump of boots as a quartet of police raced into the attic room caused him to move hurriedly out of their way.

The sudden arrival of the local constabulary up the stairs and out on to the roof panicked Mick into action. He raced towards the fire escape, clambering over the balustrade and balancing on the top step of the rusty ladder. As he started to descend the metal frame began to shake and pull away from the wall. Brick dust and rotten cement showered down. He reached across the widening gap to grab the stone base of the balustrade but it was already out of his reach. Glancing down he saw an attic window only feet away; stretching out an arm he looked for a handhold, his fingers scrabbling at the plaster moulding above the window. It was covered in bird droppings and pieces of plaster broke off as he grabbed it. In desperation he lifted one leg from the ladder in an effort to step across on to the cill but only found a precarious toe-hold. Clinging to the remains of the moulding Mick hung against the wall unable to move or save himself. Hearing shouts from above he looked up and saw faces peering down at him over the balustrade.

The attic room was dim and only lit by light from a grimy, cobwebbed, sash window. Henry scrambled about searching for his pipe. By the time that he had found it, and his box of matches, and once again got the pipe nicely alight, a noise outside the window accompanied by the sight of Mick's leg on the cill hurriedly caused him to find a safer place for his pipe.

299

He chose an old mattress, resting the pipe protectively amongst the stuffing, and the protruding springs. Grabbing a handy metal bedpost Henry attacked the window.

The noise of breaking glass almost caused Mick to lose his precarious grip on the plaster moulding. At the same time as a rope let down from the roof of the building hit him in the face, the stone window cill under his boot began to disintegrate beneath his weight. Almost immediately two uniformed arms were thrust through the broken window seizing him in a vice-like grip in the region of his crotch and attaching the rope around his waist. Mick screamed in pain and fright as he lost his grip on the plaster decoration and began to slowly fall sideways.

With one foot trapped between the rungs, the ladder buckled and broke. Cursing and yelling he felt himself hauled bodily through the broken glazing bars and shattered glass of the window into the attic.

Henry Pye dusted himself down, as Mick lay on the floor trembling with shock.

"We'll need a statement." said the sergeant to Henry as he pulled Mick to his feet and bundled him and Lewis, handcuffed together, towards the stairs, too late for Henry to get his photograph..

In the back of the police car Henry patted his pockets. "My pipe," he called out loud, trying to open the rear door of the car and go back into the house to retrieve it.

"Won't take long," replied the sergeant briskly. "I'll bring you back later."

Lacking his pipe left Henry feeling strangely bereft and curiously unable to compose his statement for the police even with the assistance of a WPC. Alone in the Interview Room he searched the pockets of his jacket once again. His matches were also missing – then he remembered filling his pipe and lighting it just before he saw Mick dangling in front of the window.

The WPC returned to the interview room with two cups of tea. "You've not got much further'," she observed gazing over Henry's shoulder at the statement. "It's eight o'clock and I'm off duty in ten minutes. Ah well if they want more they can always call you back."

Outside the open window the sound of a fire engine made them both look up.

"Must be that fire at Queenswood," she said. "That's the third engine in the last five minutes. You didn't see anything of it, I suppose?"

Henry shook his head. "Queenswood Hall? What started that?"

"Who knows? Can't tell until Forensic's been through the building. The local radio reported that the fire started on the top floor. I suppose those chaps on the roof could have been smoking."

Henry frowned, remembering that he put his pipe and matches on the mattress beside the window. They could have been dislodged as the police struggled to rescue Mick; then he remembered the draught from the window. He closed his eyes and groaned as he realized what must have happened – the warmth of the pipe, the box of matches, the tinder dry stuffing of the old mattress. No use asking the police to take him back for his pipe, or even putting in a claim.

It would be Harry who would be putting in his claim and laughing all the way to the bank. Lucky old Harry, he could jump in the Severn and not get his feet wet.

Henry stared down at the statement he had made, reached inside his jacket pocket for his pen and signed the page with a flourish. Least said the better. He could just imagine the headlines in the Morning Gazette. What a story it would make, a police inquiry, Harry Furnell suing the Morning Gazette as their reporter sets fire to his mansion. One day, in his retirement, when he wrote his book, he would tell all and solve them mystery of the fire. In the meanwhile he had another story to tell...

In his office in the city centre Peter Vail collected the pages of his report from the printer, sniffed, and began a final check. The police file recovery investigation on Dennis' computer had filled the gaps in his knowledge and revealed the fact that Dennis was actually a director of VS&T at the time that Parker's Paddock was sold to Marton Health Authority; a fact that the Morning Gazette had uncovered at the time. Privately he criticised himself for missing it. At this early stage he refused to allow himself the ultimate pleasure of anticipating the final outcome, but he had little doubt that his meeting that afternoon with the Crown Prosecution Service would swiftly lead to a prosecution.

Chapter 32

The local paper carried a front page photograph. The building, enveloped in clouds of smoke, was blackened and gutted, but Harry was still his cheerful self.

"Can't say what caused it, but the Police are already carrying out an investigation and the Loss Adjusters will be on site next week.... It's a complete ruin, no question of rebuilding... Good thing I moved out all the fixtures and fittings before we began restoration." For a man who had just seen his most important asset burned to the ground he seemed remarkably happy.

In the interview room of the Marton police station Harry enjoyed a cigarillo with his mid-morning coffee.

"'Elf and safety," he declared. "That's what it's all about. It's all happening these days, don't you know. New legislation, 'ard hats an all that."

"Like removing all those valuable baths and toilets?" asked the Inspector.

"Plumbing," said Harry. "Cor you should'av seen those old drains. Wouldn't be allowed, not nowadays."

"And the fireplaces?" persisted the policeman.

"Blimey," said Harry. "It's a wonder there hasn't been a fire before now – had to renew all the fire bricks and the firebacks – crumbling away, they were."

"But stripping the lead from the roof?"

"Don't suppose you ever took a look at that roof?" asked Harry. "Leaked like a sieve. As a copper you wouldn't know about roofs. Well, over the years all that lead expands in the sun. The joints move – after all, two hundred and fifty years it's been up there – can't go on for ever you know."

"Why didn't you employ a firm of roofers to do the work?"

"I'm not made of money." protested Harry.

"You started work before the Council granted permission." accused the Inspector.

"Time's money," said Harry. "Can't wait for those pen-pushers for ever. They're either on holiday – 'on leave' they call it – or on the sick."

The Inspector put down his pen and wafted away the cigar smoke with his papers. " I've got others to talk to"

"Well go easy on Den – he's a sick man," advised Harry. "Look bad if the police get accused of killing him." He got up from his chair and waved a cheery hand at the policeman. "If you want me, you know where to find me."

The Inspector in charge of the Queenswood Hall case waited on the door step to be allowed entry into the recently completed Queenswood Residential Home. The exterior doors were always securely locked to prevent confused residents from escaping, but if one did successfully make a break for it the local police force were usually called in to assist. It was not a place that he particularly liked to visit. How many years would it be before he too might have to face up to ending his later years in a home? Well, probably thirty at the very least – long enough not to worry about it for the time being, but as his half century passed and the years galloped by at increasing speed his thoughts turned more often to making provision for his old age and so far he had not found anywhere that he could happily live. Although this home had only been in use for a few months the smell of urine soaked carpets had already begun to pervade the atmosphere and the residents were rapidly becoming moronic.

The carer who answered the door recognized him.

"Morning Inspector. Lady Edith is already here with Mr. Madrugada. It's Matron's day off but she's asked me to tell you that you can use her office if that would be of any help."

Sir Denis Deane's room was small but with extra chairs it might be easier to persuade him to talk in his own familiar room rather than use the office.

As the Inspector balanced his notepad on his knees and sipped his coffee he noticed the wedding invitation prominently displayed on the low window ledge beside Dennis' chair.

"You'll be looking forward to your daughter's wedding," he said.

Dennis stared vacantly across the room and made no reply.

"I wouldn't be too optimistic about getting much of a response," said Sam in a low voice.

From his wheelchair Dennis stared at the floor whilst Edith sat beside him, holding his hand and occasionally wiping the spittle from the corner of his mouth.

Sam searched through his papers and passed one to the Inspector.

"Consultant's report." he said.

The policeman began to read 'Sir Dennis Deane needs assistance to communicate. Special effort may be needed to ensure accurate interpretation of his speech. A carer or family member may be able to anticipate his replies due to familiarity with this patient. He is very withdrawn, his speech is hesitant and his vision and short term memory are both severely impaired. Skilled intervention will be needed to elicit any response to questioning.'

The Inspector leaned forward to speak "Sir Dennis. I need to ask you some questions. Can you hear and understand what I say?"

Dennis showed no response and continued to stare at the floor.

"Did you hear what the Inspector said?" asked Edith.

There was not a flicker of recognition from Dennis that anyone had spoken to him.

"No point in wasting your time," said Sam, hurriedly slipping his papers back into his briefcase. "I'll be in touch if there's any sign of change." He got up from his seat on the bed, said good-by to Edith and held open the door for the Inspector

"With a medical report like that I don't think that the CPS are likely to proceed any further," said the Inspector as they walked down the corridor.

As Edith was about to leave Dennis lifted his good hand, grabbing her by the arm.

"Look," he said and pointed down to his bedside locker.

Edith looked surprised. "Do you want something?" she asked.

"Champagne." he whispered.

She bent down and opened the door to the locker, lifting out two bottles.

"Who brought these?" she asked with surprise.

"Annabel," he said quite clearly and pointed to his wardrobe. "Morning suit – in there."

Edith opened the wardrobe door.

He chuckled with pleasure. "Hired - for her wedding. Get glasses- have a glass before you go."

He smiled. It was a crooked smile, on one side of his face; nevertheless it was a smile and Edith tried to remember when she had last seen him smile.

Edith laughed out loud, leaned forward and kissed the top of his head. "I'll get someone to open it for us."

The End